THE ENGLISH ASSASSIN

MICHAEL MOORCOCK

THE ENGLISH ASSASSIN
A Romance of Entropy

Illustrated by Richard Glyn Jones
title page by Mal Dean

Allison & Busby, London

First published in Great Britain 1972 by
Allison & Busby Limited, 6a Noel Street, London, W1V 3RB

Reprinted 1976

© Michael Moorcock 1972

SBN 85031 043 1

Made and printed in Great Britain by
Billing & Sons Limited,
Guildford, London and Worcester

CONTENTS

For Arthur and Max Moorcock

The English Assassin is the third novel in a tetralogy about Jerry Cornelius and his times. The two previous books are *The Final Programme* and *A Cure for Cancer*. The last book will be called *The Condition of Muzak*.

Many of the newspaper quotations used here might cause further distress to parents and relatives of the deceased if they read them. Therefore I have in some cases changed the names. No other part of the quotation has been altered.

MICHAEL MOORCOCK

PROLOGUE [commencement]

As a child I lived in that well-kept back garden of London, the county of Surrey. In this century, at least, Surrey achieved vitality only once. That was during the World War when the incendiaries fell, and the Messerschmidts blew up, and the V-bombs dropped suddenly from the silent sky. Night flames, droning planes, banging ack-ack, shrapnel and bombed buildings are the happiest impressions from my childhood. I long to find them again. The pylon, the hoarding, the ruined street and the factory are images which to this day most satisfy and pacify my psyche. I was very happy then, while the world fought its war and my own parents quarrelled, suppressed quarrels and finally parted. The War was won, the Family lost, and I remained, as far as I knew, content. But now, with great effort, I recall the nightmares, rages, weeping fits and traumas, the schools which came and went, and I know that, after the war, I was only happy when alone and then chiefly when I was able to create a complicated fantasy or, in a book, enter someone else's. I was happy but, I suppose, I was not healthy. Few of my illnesses were not psychosomatic and I became fat. Poor child.

. . . I suspect that many people experience this nostalgia and would dearly love to recreate the horrifying circumstances of their own childhood. But this is not possible. At best they produce reasonable alternatives.

MAURICE LESCOQ, Leavetaking 1961

1

SHOT ONE

SHOT ONE

ADDICT WAS DEAD WITH SYRINGE IN HIS ARM

A young North Kensington addict who had made an attempt to give up drugs was killed by his addiction, the Westminster Coroner decided last week. Anthony William Leroy (sometimes known as Anthony Gray) died at St. Charles's Hospital in the early hours of August 29, after taking two shots of heroin in his arm when he was found, the coroner was told. Leroy was a boutique manager . . . Professor Donald Teare, pathologist, said that there were two recent injection marks on Leroy's right arm. Cause of death was inhalation of vomit due to drug addiction.

KENSINGTON POST, September 26 1969

4

A BUNDLE

*South of Bude and its neighbour, Widemouth Bay, you come to
the quaint little harbour of Boscastle, with its grey stone, slate
roofed cottages and background of sheltering hills, and thence to
Tintagel, home of the legendary King Arthur and the famous
cliff-top ruins of his mediaeval castle. Although other counties
in the West may dispute Cornwall's claim to be the sole possessor
of the original authentic stronghold of the Knights of the Round
Table, Cornishmen stick as closely to their time-honoured con-
tention as the limpets to the rocky, sea-washed walls of Merlin's
mysterious cave at the foot of the great granite cliff. It is the
blood spilt by the magic sword Excalibur, they insist, that keeps
a small lawn of turf within the precincts of the castle for ever
emerald green, as if constantly fed by spring water where none
exists. And what else, they ask, was Camelot if it were not the
old name for Camelford, the little inland town on the River
Camel not half a day's horse-trot away?*

CORNWALL: A TOURIST'S GUIDE

Sometime ago, possibly in the winter of 1975, the following
events took place at Tintagel Bay on the north coast of Cornwall:

5

Tintagel's bay is small and walled by high, bleak cliffs, a natural subject for romantic painters and poets of the past two centuries. Most of the castle ruins stand on the inland cliff, but some are on the west cliff, which is a narrow promontory now crumbling dramatically into the sea and carrying the ruins with it.

Though, in the summer, Tintagel is a great tourist attraction, at other seasons it is virtually deserted, save for a few local inhabitants who remain in the village some distance inland. One dull December morning two of these residents, a butcher and a retired chemist, who had been born and brought up in the area, were taking their regular stroll along the cliffs when they paused, as usual, among the ruins and rested on a wooden bench provided for people like themselves who wished to enjoy the view of the bay in comfort.

The view on this particular day was not really up to much. The water in the bay was flat, sluggish and black. On its surface drifted grey scum and dark green weed. The sea resembled a worn-out blackboard upon which an inspired idiot had scrawled equations and then tried to erase them. The sky was clammy and the air was thick with too much brine. From the small patch of shingle on the beach below there came a strong and unpleasant odour of rotting seaweed. It was as if the whole place — castle, cliffs, sea and beach — were in a process of sudden decay. The butcher and the chemist were both old men, bearded and grey, but the butcher was tall and straight, while the chemist was small and bent. The wind tugged at their beards and hair as they huddled on the bench and massaged their legs and hands. Their skins were cracked, wrinkled, weather-beaten and, in colour and condition, very little different from the leather jerkins they wore to protect themselves against the weather. They chatted for about ten minutes and were ready to continue their walk when the tall butcher narrowed his eyes and pointed at the gap between the cliffs where the sea entered the bay.

" What d'you make of that, then? " he asked. He had one of those unfortunate voices which is naturally aggressive in tone and liable to misinterpretation by those who did not know him well.

The chemist frowned. He reached into his jerkin and found his spectacle case. He put the spectacles on and peered out over the water. A large, shapeless object floated in the bay. It was drifting with the tide towards the shore. It might have been the remains of a shark, covered in rotting algae; a tangle of dead eels, or just a mass of sea-weed.

" It could be anything, really," said the chemist mildly.

They watched as the bundle drifted closer. It came to rest on the shingle below. It was vaguely cylindrical in shape but just a little too small to be any kind of wrecked boat. The weed which wrapped it seemed to have decayed.

" Bloody unsanitary looking, whatever it is," said the chemist. " The council should do something about this beach."

But the beach itself was unwilling to accept the bundle. The next wave that came in was forced to withdraw it. The bundle bobbed about twenty yards offshore: the sea wished to be rid of it, could think of nowhere else to deposit it, but refused to swallow it.

The chemist, a morbid man by nature, suggested that the object might be a corpse. It was the right size.

" What? You mean a drowned man? " The butcher smiled.

The chemist understood that his suggestion had been too sensational. " Or a seal, I thought," he said. " You don't know, do you? I've seen nothing like it before. Have you? "

The tall butcher hadn't any inclination to follow this line of thought. He got up; he rubbed his beard. " Well, she'll probably be gone by tomorrow. It's getting a bit nippy. Shall we ——? "

The chemist took one last, frowning look at the bundle before he nodded agreement. They walked slowly inland, towards the almost deserted village.

After they had vanished, the tide began to turn. It hissed. It whispered. It sighed. As it receded, a lip of a cave was revealed in the west headland, a black gap flaked with foam. The sea pushed the bundle towards the cave; it forced the thing into the mouth which gurgled reluctantly, but swallowed. The tide fled, leaving behind it the weed-smothered beach, the salty stink, the foam-flecked entrance to the cave. The wind blew stronger, whining and moaning about the castle ruins like a dog at its master's grave, pawing a tuft of coarse grass here, sniffing a clump of shrubs there. And then the wind went away, too.

By now completely exposed to the air, the gloomy cavern

contained a comprehensive collection of debris: rusty cans, pieces of drowned wood, glass shards worn smooth by the action of the ocean, plastic bottles, the torso of a child's doll, and the twisted corpses of about twenty deformed, oversized crabs; the creations of an effluent only recently introduced to this coast. On a shelf of rock about half-way up the slimy far wall, well out of the faint light from the entrance, lay the bundle where the sea had lodged it.

A gull flew in from the grey outside and perched on the bundle before fluttering down to peck at the soft shells and the hard flesh of the mutant crabs.

When the texture of the day had grown a little less disgusting, a cumbersome skiff, powered by an outboard motor imperfectly mounted in the stern so that its screw often lifted completely clear of the water and caused it to progress in a series of spluttering jolts, rounded Tintagel Head and made for the small patch of shingle leading up to the cave. There was only one person in the skiff. She wore yellow PVC oilskins, a yellow sou'wester and white plastic trousers tucked into red rubber seaboots. The sou'wester shaded her face. The tiller was tucked firmly under one arm as she directed the skiff at the beach. The engine coughed, screeched and spat. The bottom of the skiff rasped on the pebbles and the motor cut out. Awkwardly, the girl clambered from the stationary boat and pulled it completely clear of the sea; she sniffed the wind, then she reached over the side to remove a big blue Eveready flashlight, an old-fashioned gasmask and a coil of white nylon rope. She sniffed again, by way of confirmation, and seemed satisfied. She looped the rope over her shoulder and trudged in the direction of the cave. When she reached the entrance she hesitated, switching on her electric torch before going in. Her clean, protective clothing gleamed in the reflected glare. Her booted feet crunched on the corpses of the crabs; a beam of light illuminated the awful walls, disturbed the carrion gulls. They squawked and flapped nervously past her head to the open air. She directed the beam over all the filthy flotsam before focussing on the shelf of rock from which came a smell partly of brine and partly like cat's urine. She put the torch in her pocket and used both hands to ease the gasmask

8

under her sou'wester and over her hair and face. Her breathing became a loud, rhythmic hiss. Adjusting the rope on her shoulder she again took out the flashlight and looked the bundle over. The thing was predominantly black and green and had resumed its earlier, roughly cylindrical, shape. There were small grey rocks imbedded in it, some yellow grit, a few supine starfish, seahorses and shrimps, a fair number of mussels and limpets and pieces of what looked like tropical coral. The black and green areas were unidentifiable; they were possibly organic; they might have been made of mud which had started to solidify. It was as if the bundle had been rolled along the bottoms of the deepest oceans, gathering to it a detritus which was completely alien to the surface.

The girl bent down and wedged the flashlight between two large stones so that the beam stayed on the shelf. Then she crossed to the wall and began to climb skilfully and rapidly until she stood with her legs spread wide, balancing carefully on the ledge beside the bundle while she pulled on a pair of rubber gloves. Steadying herself with her left hand against an outcrop of granite, she bent and felt over the bundle with her right hand. At last she found what she was looking for and withdrew it with a squelch from a tangle of weed.

It was a transparent polythene bag dripping with green algae. She wiped the plastic against her thigh until it was as clean as she could get it, then she held it in the torch's beam so that she could see the contents. There was a single sheet of white paper inside, covered with doodles in black ink:

9

She was satisfied. She stuffed the message into an inside pocket and unslung the rope from her shoulder, winding it round and round the slippery bundle until it was thoroughly tied up. With considerable difficulty she managed to brace her back against the wall and with her booted feet shove the bundle to the edge of the shelf. Taking a coil or two of rope around her right arm she was able to lower the bundle to the cavern floor. Then she let the end of the rope drop and climbed down after it. She rested for a moment, retrieved her torch, switched it off and put it away. Working in the faint light from the entrance, she picked up the rope and wound it twice on each hand. She turned so that the rope was now braced on her shoulder. She strained forward, hauling the bundle after her. Broken corpses of crabs scattered in its path as the girl slowly pulled it from the cave and dragged it bumping down the beach to the waiting skiff. Panting painfully into her gasmask she heaved with the last of her strength and got the thing into the boat, putting her whole weight against the bow so that the skiff slid back into the sea. Standing knee-deep in the seedy water she pulled the painter until the bow was pointing away from the beach, then she carefully got in and resumed her place at the tiller, lowering the screw into the sea and tugging at the motor's cord.

After a number of false starts she brought the outboard to life and the screw began to turn. The boat moved into deeper water, going back the way it had come. It still made jerky progress, so that at times the girl in the yellow sou'wester, gasmask and oilskins was lifted completely from her seat. At last she disappeared round Tintagel Head, bouncing out to sea.

As if commissioned to wash away from the bay all traces of these events, the sky let loose its rain.

MAJOR NYE

"Another age will see all this in quite a different perspective."

It was not certain what he meant as he stared about him at the little white laboratory, at the formica-topped benches, the racks of test-tubes, the specimen jars and the aquarium which occupied one whole wall.

" So you say, general." The young Japanese marine biologist sounded sceptical as he held a bottle of sea-water up to the light from the plate glass window which offered a view of the Atlantic.

" M . . ." Major Nye put his hands in the pockets of his thread-bare blazer and drew out a crushed wooden matchbox. He held it with the tips of his fingers, in both hands, as if afraid to damage it further. Part of the tray was still inside the box, but all the matches were gone. The label was predominantly blue, white and brown and the picture showed three dark skinned men in blue loincloths and red caps trying to launch a sampan into the sea. Along the right edge the label was torn a little but most of the trademark was visible: a diamond with the word *WIMCO* printed inside it. In the top left quarter of the box was the slogan: **SEA-FISHER.** At the bottom centre: " SAFETY MATCHES Made in India." On the reverse side of the box it said: *These matches are made in India by the celebrated WIMCO works at Bombay. They are specially imported by* THE CORNISH MATCH COMPANY *Av. contents 45.*

11

Major Nye was a stringy man in his late sixties with a scrubby grey moustache and pale, introspective blue eyes. He was just above average height. The veins in his hands and wrists were prominent and purple and matched the ink-stains on his finger-tips. The badge of his old regiment was stitched onto the breast pocket of his blazer and the badge was as faded and frayed as the blazer itself. He put the matchbox carefully back in his pocket. He cleared his throat and went to his seat behind the green steel desk which had been erected for him at the far end of the lab. There was nothing on the desk. He opened a drawer and took out a Rizla tin. He began to roll himself a thin cigarette.

"I only agreed to do all this because my daughter was keen on it." He seemed to be trying to explain his embarrassment and apologise for it. Not so long ago he had loved India and sworn loyalty to the Empire. Now he had only his children to love and only his wife demanded his loyalty. This was something of a come-down after a sub-continent.

He lit his cigarette with a Swan Vesta, cupping his hand against a non-existent wind. He puffed hard and began to hum a tune — always his unconscious response to small pleasures like smoking. Through the window of the little square marine biology lab Major Nye could see the rocks and the grey, roaring sea. He was puzzled by this coast. Cornwall was alien to him; it depressed him. He could not understand the Celtic point of view. These people seemed to enjoy burrowing into the ground for no particular reason. Why else had they built their fougous? He had noticed, too, how they had turned quite naturally from wrecking to tourism without, apparently, any change of spirit. His right hand went to his thinning grey hair and smoothed it, descended to the grey eyebrows and smoothed them, came finally to the grey moustache and smoothed that. With both hands he tightened the small knot of his regimental tie and tugged at the frayed collar of his shirt, which was white with thin blue and red stripes which had almost faded to invisibility. There was a khaki handkerchief protruding from his left sleeve. The cigarette was now unnoticed and unappreciated in the corner of his grey mouth.

A surly looking laboratory technician, with long, black hair falling over the shoulders of his white coat, came in, hovered over

12

a bench, picked up a rack of test-tubes, nodded moodily at the Japanese and the Englishman. Then he left.

Major Nye got up and went to look at the bound and spread-eagled assassin who lay on the slab just under the window-sill. The wrists and ankles were in steel clamps.

" How are you feeling, old son? "

He had spoken awkwardly and gruffly. He cleared his throat again as if he wished he had been able to use a more natural tone.

Jerry Cornelius snarled. A high-pitched screech broke from his writhing lips. He began, pathetically, to struggle on the slab.

" *Eeeeeeeeee! Eeeeeeeeee!* "

Gently, Major Nye frowned. " Damned shame. Poor old chap." He turned his pale eyes upon the Japanese biologist who had been attracted by the screech and now stood beside him. " How long was he down there? "

The biologist shrugged and scratched behind his left ear with his right hand. "A year? The brain has been flushed. The flesh, however, is surprisingly fresh. Like a baby's, general."

Major Nye plucked at his heavily veined nose and rubbed the under edge of it with his right forefinger. " Poor old chap. Young, too, eh? "

" Who can say? It is a strange physiology. Hard to guess the age without the proper instruments. We should have been warned. Then maybe we could have had some equipment sent down from London. As it was, he was just dumped on us. Like a baby on a doorstep."

Major Nye's ulcer bit suddenly and he straightened his shoulders and firmed his jaw to take the pain. " Sorry about that," he said. He removed the cigarette from his lips and dropped it to the floor. " There really wasn't very much time, as I understand it. It was ' goodbye Dolly I must leave you ' and then ' tramp, tramp, tramp the boys are marching '."

" I realise that. I was not complaining about your organisation, general. I was merely explaining our inability to do more than superficial tests."

" Naturally. You've done jolly well, anyway. Splendid show." The major looked at his watch. It seemed to be losing again. " First class," he muttered absently. " Not my organisation

13

though, you know. Nothing to do with me. Friend of my daughter's . . . Well, we'd better get off before dark. It's a goodish run from here up to Sussex."

" You're taking the truck? "

" The old lorry. Yes, I thought so, unless —? "

" No. No. By all means take it."

" Splendid, Good, well, shall we um? "

Jerry Cornelius was all but insensate. His eyes glowed, his lips curled back from his stained teeth, his fingers curved like claws and he still stank of brine and tar. Even after they had cleaned him up (using for the most part methylated spirits and linseed oil) he had continued to glare at them silently, like a mad gull.

Major Nye and the Japanese biologist wheeled the slab from the lab and out onto the concrete which had replaced the turf. Parked close to the cliff was a run-down 1947 Bedford two-ton military lorry with a khaki canvas canopy. Major Nye untied the canopy flaps, got into the back and let down the tailboard. He pushed two planks from the lorry to the ground so that they made a ramp up which they could roll the slab with Cornelius on it. They wheeled the slab to the far end of the lorry, nearest the cab, and secured it there using chains. Major Nye turned the key in the padlock and put it in his pocket. He straightened up and crossed back towards the tailboard. As he did so his foot struck a rusty spanner on the floor of the lorry. The spanner skidded and clanged against a greasy jack pedestal. Major Nye winced. He jumped down, slid the planks into the lorry, bolted the flap up and fastened the canvas. He shook hands with the Japanese, walked round to the cab, opened the door and climbed onto the tattered bench seat. He rolled himself another smoke in his Rizla machine before giving his attention to the controls. He had some difficulty starting the engine and getting into gear but at last with a wave he drove off down the bumpy mud track towards the tarmac road which led to the A30 and thence to the M5.

The sky changed from cold white to cold, dark grey and a cold rain was falling by the time Major Nye left the lane and headed

14

north between flat, grey fields.

He shivered. Keeping his left hand on the steering wheel, he buttoned up his threadbare blazer.

The lorry rattled and whined. It snarled with every gear shift. The noise did much to drown the occasional screech from the back. The fumes from the engine helped cover the smell of brine.

It was nearly dark when they reached the A30. Major Nye rolled himself another cigarette as he waited to get onto the road. The rain was beating down on the black tarmac. The Bedford's single windscreen wiper clacked erratically. Moving out, Major Nye began to sing to keep himself awake. He sang *Hold Your Hand Out (Naughty Boy), My Old Dutch, I Love a Lassie, It's a Long Way to Tipperary, Pack Up Your Troubles, The Army of Today's All Right, Burlington Bertie from Bow, If It Wasn't For the Houses in Between, Are We to Part Like This, Bill?, The Honeysuckle and the Bee, You're the Cream in My Coffee, Dolly Gray, On the Road to Mandalay, Rio Rita, Maxim's, Only a Rose, Moonlight Becomes You, Jolly Good Luck to the Girl who Loves a Sailor, Am I Blue?, Change Partners, Fanlight Fannie, Auld Lang Syne, White Christmas, The Riff Song, My Little Wooden Hut, We're Here Because We're Here, The Cornish Floral Dance, Maggie's Wedding, Phil the Fluter's Ball, My Old Man, Mammy, The Eton Boating Song, Yesterday* (half), *A Whiter Shade of Pale* (part), *What Shall We Do With the Drunken Sailor?, The Dying Aviator, When This Bloody War is Over, Sonny Boy, Sally, Maybe It's Because I'm a Londoner, I Belong to Glasgow, Molly Malone, Land of My Fathers, Underneath the Arches, Run, Rabbit, Run, Rose O'Day, I'll Be Seeing You, Coming in on a Wing and a Prayer, That Lovely Weekend, Lucky Jim, September Song, The Man Who Broke the Bank at Monte Carlo, Mr Tambourine Man* (part), *The Physician,* until at last he reached Ironmaster House in Sussex croaking the last few bars of *Has Anybody Here Seen Kelly?* and stopped the lorry by the brook.

UNA PERSSON

"The peak was reached in 1808 and civilisation has been in decline ever since, thanks, in particular, to the Saxon race — many of whom happened to share my view. Here's to Beethoven! "

Prinz Lobkowitz saluted with his stein, lowered it to his lips, tilted his leonine head and swallowed a litre of Bil beer. His voice had been drowned almost entirely by the first movement of the " Pastoral " played by the Berlin Philharmonic Orchestra conducted by Eugen Jochum which came from the two great Vox speakers on either side of the bay window. Wiping the foam from his moustache he went to the ornate Victorian mantelpiece on which stood the newish Garrard deck with its Sony amplifier and turned a knob to reduce the volume slightly, adding: " Open the window. It stinks of disinfectant in here." The first movement ended and the second began.

From a gilded chair upholstered in stained red and white Regency stripe, his mistress Eva Knecht efficiently rose and with long strides crossed the wide 18th century room which was full of half-emptied packing cases, a grand piano with roses painted on its light walnut wood, scattered dust-sheets and piles of objets trouvées. Reaching the diamond-paned windows she raised her hands to the catch but paused as the huge bulk of a Zeppelin filled her entire field of vision; it was flying low over

16

the ruins to the South East of the city. It coursed towards the sunset. She smiled quietly and pushed open the double windows. The distant mumble of the Zeppelin's engines reached her. She took a deep breath as if to inhale the sound rather than the stink which blew from the Koenigstrasse gravepit. She looked back enquiringly at the Prinz who waved his hand. " I suppose so. Though I don't know which I prefer — that or the DDT. It's about time something was done for Berlin."

There came a faint vibration and a faraway thump as the Zeppelin began to distribute its first incendiaries of the evening. Prinz Lobkowitz lit a Jamaican corona and burnt his thumbnail with the match when the beginning of the third movement (Merry Gathering of Peasants) struck up. " Fuck," he said, and then: " What's German for fuck? "

" I haven't got that far yet." She started towards the shelf of dictionaries in the far alcove.

" Don't bother, Nobody else does. What's the point of trying to revive a dead language? Who wants a ' national identity ' any longer? Politics has come down to rather more fundamental issues."

" Who wants to *talk* about it? " Eva smoothed her skirt. " That newspaper soon went back to English."

" The bloody language is always at the root of it." He coughed and put the cigar in the Directoire chafing dish he used as an ashtray. " Do you still want to go to the waxworks tonight? "

" Suits me."

" I bet it does! "

He roared with laughter, frowned, and turned off the stereo.

The house, most of which was still intact, had been restored in 1850 and was huge with lavish appointments. It had all the tatty grandeur of a Versailles, with the same fading gilt, fly-specked mirrors and chipped, painted terra cotta.

A gentle knock on the great oaken double door.

" Come," said Lobkowitz.

The doors opened and a small black and white cat walked in, its tail erect. It stopped in the middle of the dusty Persian carpet. It sat down and looked up at them.

It was followed by a beautiful girl in a black military topcoat and patent leather boots with gold buckles (from *Elliotts*). Her

17

brown hair was cut relatively short and her face was heart-shaped, amused, controlled. She held a heavy Smith and Wesson .45 revolver in her right hand and her left hand was still resting on the door knob as she paused and surveyed the room.

Eva Knecht scowled. " Sebastian Auchinek's sidekick," she muttered. " Una Persson. What an actress! "

Eva, only slightly beautiful, with the same kind of b own hair, felt herself fade. She wished that she were wearing something other than the fawn Jaeger twinset and green spikeheels as she hissed: " Proper little heroine of the revolution, isn't she."

Prinz Lobkowitz ignored his mistress. He flattened one palm against his waistcoated diaphragm and made his dignified way towards the door, the other palm extended. He was wearing a black frock coat and pinstripe trousers. In the lapel of his coat was the tiny button of the Legion de Liberté. Under the trousers were the outlines of his brown riding boots. He had forgotten to take off the silver spur attached to his right heel. He smirked (though he thought the expression one of friendly dignity) and as a consequence ruined the handsome lines of his face. He rumbled some pleasantry, of which his smirk made ingratiating nonsense, and introduced himself to the newcomer. " Prinz Lobkowitz."

" Una Persson," she replied contemptuously. "Auchinek said you would take delivery."

" I thought it was tomorrow." Lobkowitz looked vaguely about him. " Tomorrow." Slowly the smirk dissolved.

" I saved time by coming through Czechoslovakia." Una Persson put the gun into her deep pocket. She turned and snapped her fingers. Four unhealthy Slavs stumbled in. There was a pine coffin on their shoulders. The coffin was stamped *VAKUUM REINIGER (ENGLISCHPRODUKT)*. The Slavs put it down on the Persian carpet. They trotted off.

Una Persson reached inside her maxicoat and withdrew a document and a blue ballpoint. " Sign both copies, please," she said. Lobkowitz put the papers on the lid of the walnut grand piano and signed without reading. He handed them back to her. "And how is Auchinek? "

" Very well. Shall I open the box for you? "

" If you would."

18

She slipped out her Smith and Wesson and accurately shot off narrowly missed Eva Knecht. With the barrel of the gun Una the bolts on the coffin's four corners. One of the spent bullets Persson plucked away a blanket, revealing the glaring countenance of Jerry Cornelius, still stinking of the sea.

Lobkowitz backed off and went to put the Mozart Clarinet Quintet in A on the deck.

"Mein Gott!" said Eva Knecht self-consciously. "What caused that?"

Una Persson shrugged. "Some form of hydrophilia, I gather. A disease with symptoms similar to enteritis in cats."

"I mourn the Age of Steam," said Lobkowitz returning with a box of *Rising Sun* matches. They were made by the Western India Match Co. Ltd.

"A peculiar diagnosis." Eva Knecht bent to look more closely at the creature. "Where was it found?"

"On the coast of North Cornwall, eventually, but he'd been seen once or twice earlier. They think he went in somewhere around the Bay of Bengal. I was to take delivery of five cases of M16s?"

"Yes, yes, of course." Lobkowitz indicated the crates laid out under the grand piano. "With ammunition. Shall I get someone to load them for you, or . . .?"

"Thank you very much."

Lobkowitz pulled a frayed velvet bell-rope near the mantelpiece. "This is the old Bismarck mansion," he told her.

"I gathered." With a battered brass Dunhill Una Persson lit a long brown Sherman cigarettello. "I should like to wash my hair before I leave."

As best she could, Eva Knecht flounced from the room. "I'll check if the water's on."

Four ex-POWs with shaven heads and wearing stained blue dungarees, came in and began to take the crates of M16s outside to Una Persson's Sd Kfz 233 armoured truck. The ornate ormolu 'Empire' style telephone commenced to ring. Lobkowitz ignored it. "They all do that. It means nothing."

"Well, I think I'll just . . ." Una Persson strode across and lifted the receiver to her head. "Hello."

She listened for a moment and then replaced the receiver.

19

"A sort of rushing noise."

" That's right." Lobkowitz moved rapidly towards her, his spur jingling. " Jesus Christ, I'd like to . . ."

She placed a small hand against his chest and kissed him on the chin.

Eva Knecht stood in the doorway, one hand clutching her Jaeger cardigan round her shoulders. " I'm afraid there'll be no more water today."

Una Persson stepped away from Prinz Lobkowitz and nodded gravely at Eva. " I'll be off, then."

Lobkowitz coughed behind his hand. His eyes fell on his right boot and for the first time he noticed that he was still wearing one spur. He bent to unstrap it. " Don't leave, yet . . ." He glanced up at Eva and added briskly : " Well, cheerio, my dear."

" Cheerio," said Una Persson. Decisively, she left the room.

Eva Knecht glared at Lobkowitz as he straightened to his feet, holding the spur in his hand. " Mozart! " she said. " I should have . . ."

" Don't be corny, sweet." Lobkowitz put the spur on a pearl inlay table.

" Corny! "

Picking up an Erma 9mm machine pistol from the Jacobean sideboard, she offered him a round in the hip. He pursed his lips as if objecting to the noise rather than the pain, and went down on one knee as the dark stains dilated on his jacket and pin-stripes. He clutched the ruined hip.

She spent the rest of the clip on his face. He fell. Smashed.

Una Persson came back at the sound. She raised her S & W and shot Eva Knecht once below the left shoulder blade. The bullet entered Eva's jealous heart and she toppled forward. Murdered.

Eva Knecht's murderess took a black beret from the pocket of her maxicoat and adjusted it on her head, glancing once into the mirror above the mantel. For a moment she looked thought-fully from the coffin to the corpses. She replaced the S & W in her other pocket. She opened her mouth a quarter of an inch and then closed it. She took off the Mozart and flicked through the pile of albums on the floor until she found a Bach Branden-burg Concerto. She put the record on the deck, glanced down

20

at the contents of the coffin, hovered undecidedly by the door, and then she left as quickly as her coat would let her.

The Brandenburg was an inferior performance, spoiled further by a persistent screeching from the box.

From below there came the noise of an Sd Kfz 233 starting up, backing out and roaring off down the emergency track through the rubble.

The screeching assumed a melancholy note and then ceased. Night fell. From time to time the room was illuminated by incendiary explosions from the East. Later there was darkness relieved by a little moonlight and the sound of the Zeppelin returning to its shed. Then there remained only a rustle of atmospherics from the speakers.

The small black and white cat, forgotten by Una Persson, woke up. It stretched and began to walk towards Lobkowitz. It lapped at the congealed blood on the face, then moved off in disgust. It washed inside beside Eva's corpse and then sprang into the coffin to curl up on Jerry's chest, heedless of the insensate, agonised eyes which, wide open, continued to stare at the terra cotta ceiling, before slowly filling with tears.

SEBASTIAN AUCHINEK

The long, gentle hands came down to reveal a sensitive Jewish face. The large, red lips moved, emitting softly-accented English: " Perhaps you should have brought him back, Una? " He was a thin, pale intellectual. He sat on a camp chair with its back against the far wall of a dry, limestone cave. He was dressed in standard guerilla gear; it hung on his thin body like a wet flag.

The cave was full of crates; it was lit by a tin oil-lamp which cast black shadows. On one of the crates stood a half-eaten Stilton cheese, an almost full bottle of Vichy water and a number of East German and Polish military maps in leather cases.

She was undoing the top button of her black maxicoat. " That would have been theft, Sebastian."

" True. But these are pragmatic times."

"And we agreed we wanted no part of them."

" True." He sucked his upper lip into his mouth, his large lids slowly falling to cover his eyes.

She said defiantly: "The M16s are as good as new. There's plenty of ammunition. He kept his side of it. Many new Germans are very straight in that respect." She shrugged. " But her violence upset me." She lit another Sherman's with a match from a box on the nearby crate. " I've still got a feeling I've forgotten something." She reached into her pocket and pulled out her gun, turning it this way and that. " What else could I do? If saving her would have brought him back to life . . ."

" True."

" Well, I know if I'd thought about it for a moment I might not have done it. But so many people waste time thinking about things and when they act it's too late. I didn't want to hurt anybody."

Sebastian Auchinek got up from the camp chair and walked to the cave entrance, drawing back the camouflage net. Outside, the drizzle fluttered like a tattered curtain in the wind and Auchinek peered through it, hoping to get a sight of the tiny Macedonian village in the rocky valley below. A herd of goats emerged from the thin rain. They bleated their discomfort as they trotted down the mountainside and disappeared. The water swished on the rocks and it smelled faintly of benzine. At least the air was reasonably warm.

" Sebastian."

His inclination was to leave the cave, for he hated any form of homecoming ceremony, but he turned.

She was kneeling by the chair wearing a gold and brown puff-sleeved shirt with a long black waistcoat and matching black trousers. Her coat was folded neatly beside her.

With a sigh he returned to his place and spread his spider legs. She reached forward and undid his fly. He gritted his teeth and his hand stroked her head once or twice before falling back at his side. He squeezed his eyes shut. Her face was grave as she moved it towards his crotch, as if she were considering different and more pleasant things while conscientiously performing a distasteful but necessary task.

Auchinek wondered if she did it because she thought he liked it. She had done it regularly for the past few months; at first he had pretended to be pleased and now he could never tell her the truth.

When she had finished, the fellatrix looked up at him, smiled, wiped her lips, swiftly closed his zip. He gave her a strained, bewildered smile in return, then he began to cough. She offered him one of her cigarettellos but he waved his hand towards the bottle on the upturned crate. She did not notice the gesture as she lit and then drew upon the long, brown Sherman's, staring pensively at her own shifting shadow on the floor. Her eyes

23

were blue and private.

"Perhaps I should go back for Cornelius. We might need him if things get any tougher. On the other hand he might be dead by the time I got there. Is that my fault, I wonder? And the Cossacks are supposed to be moving in, too. Did you say you wanted a cigarette?"

His pale face was puzzled, his gesture nervous as he lifted an exhausted hand to point again at the bottle.

"No," he said. "Water."

MRS C AND COLONEL P

" Yerst." Folding her hands together on her great stomach, the fat old bag got her forearms under her unruly breasts and jostled them in her dress until they were hanging more comfortably. " 'S'im, orl right." Her three sly chins shivered. Her round, red stupid head cocked itself on one side. Her tiny eyes narrowed and her thick mouth opened. " Pore littel bleeder. Wot they dun to 'im? "

"We do not know, Mrs Cornelius." Colonel Pyat stepped away from the coffin which lay where Una Persson's Slavs had left it. The other bodies were no longer visible, though the small black and white cat was still hanging around. " But now that you have positively identified him . . ." He drew off his white kid gauntlets. They were a perfect match to his well-cut, gold-trimmed uniform, to his kid boots, his dashing cap. ". . . we can try to find out. I almost caught up with him in Afghanistan. But the express was delayed as usual. This could have been avoided."

" 'E always wos a bit'v a pansy, I s'pose," Mrs C said reflectively.

Colonel Pyat went to the grand piano where his vodka things had been arranged by an orderly. " May I offer you a drink, madame? "

" Where's all them balloons gorn? I 'eard . . ."

" The Zeppelins have left the city. They belonged to the

25

Nieu Deutchlanders whom we routed yesterday."

"Well, I'll 'ave a small one. Did anyone ever tell yer — yer look jest like Ronal' Colman."

"But I feel just like Jesse James." Colonel Pyat smiled and gestured towards the record player on the mantelpiece. Faintly, from the Vox speakers, came the muffled sounds of a Bob Dylan record. The colonel poured an ounce of Petersburg vodka into a long-stemmed Bohemian glass, poured the same amount for himself, crossed back and handed Mrs C her drink.

She drained it. "Ta." Then, with a fat, knowing chuckle, she flung back her monstrous arm and hurled the glass at the Victorian fireplace. The glass shattered against the edge of the mantelpiece. "Sköl! Eh? Har, har! "

Colonel Pyat took an interest in his white knuckles. Then he straightened his shoulders and quietly sipped his drink.

Mrs C ran a grimy finger round the neck of her cheap, red and white print dress. " 'Ot enough fer yer? "

"Indeed? " Pyat put a finger to his lips and raised his eyebrows intelligently. "Aha."

"Wouldna thort it. Not in bleedin' *Germany* — innit? "
"No? "

She turned, digging at a rotting back tooth with her thumbnail so that her voice was strangled. "Will 'e get better, Kernewl? "

"That's up to the boffins, madame."

"Coorst, 'is *bruvver* — Frankie — was allus th' nicest of 'em. I did me best after 'is dad run orft, but . . ."

"These are unsettled times, Mrs Cornelius."

Mrs C looked at him with mock gravity for a moment, a little smile turning up the corners of her crimson mouth. She opened the lips. She belched. Then she burst into laughter. "Yer not kiddin' — ter-her-ka-ka — ooh — give us anovver, there's a pet . . . nkk-nkk."

"I beg your pardon? "

"Nar — sawright — I'll 'elp meself, won' I? " She waddled to the grand piano. Grunting contentedly, she poured half the remaining contents of the bottle into another long-stemmed glass. She rounded on him, raising her glass with a leer and tossing off the best part of the contents. " 'Ere's ter yer! " The drink

warmed her further and large beads of sweat sprang out on her
happy face. She sidled up to Colonel Pyat, nudging him with
her lumpy elbow. She winked and nodded a streaky orange head
at the vodka. " Not bad." She belched again. " Not 'alf! He, he
he! "

Colonel Pyat clicked his heels and saluted. " I thank —"

A piercing screech came from the coffin. They both turned
their heads. " Gawd," said Mrs C.

Cautiously, Colonel Pyat went to peer in. " I wonder if they've
been feeding him."

" 'E never wos much of an eater." Mrs C's bosoms heaved
as she joined the colonel and stared sentimentally down at her
son. " I never knew where 'e got 'is energy from. Proper little
fucker you wos, woncha, Jer? "

The head rolled. The stink of brine was nauseating. The
screech came again. The hands, thin and knotted, with broken
nails and bruised knuckles, were rubbed raw at the wrists by
the twisted nylon cords holding them in the coffin. The mouth
opened and closed, opened and closed; only the whites of the
eyes were visible.

With a decisive and slightly censorious gesture Mrs C looked
away from her child, finishing her vodka. She glanced almost
thoughtfully at the colonel before putting her glass on the
Jacobean sideboard. She wriggled her massive shoulders, rubbed
her left eye with the index finger of her left hand, gave the
colonel a quick smirk of encouragement and said: " Well . . ."

Colonel Pyat bowed. " Some of my men will escort you back
to London."

"Ah," she said. " That wos it . . ."

" Madame? "

" I wos thinkin'v seein' some o' th' sights whilst I wos 'ere.
Y'know." Another wink.

" I will instruct my men to make a tour of the city. Though
there are very few sights left."

" Oo! All them soljers all to meself! Oo-er! "

"And thank you so much for your help, Mrs Cornelius. We'll
get your boy back to normal. Never fear."

" Normal! That'sa good 'un! " Her entire body quivered
with laughter. " You'll do, Kernewl! Eh? Har, har, har! "

27

She shambled cheerfully from the room. " You'll do! "

The Bohemian glass fell off the Jacobean sideboard and landed unbroken on the Persian carpet.

The sounds from the coffin became pensive. Colonel Pyat was filled with sadness. He picked up the fallen glass and took it to the grand piano where he poured himself the last of his vodka.

REMINISCENCE [A]

Beautiful love.

Beautiful love.

LATE NEWS

Terence Green, 9, and Martin Harper, 8, died last night when overcome by fumes from water heater while having bath in house in Estagon Road, Norwich.

SUNDAY TIMES, April 5 1970

At least 90 Vietnamese men, women and children, held behind barbed wire in a compound at the Cambodian town of Prasot, were killed by machine gun and automatic rifle fire early yesterday, as a Vietcong force launched an attack in the area.

The events surrounding the killings were not clear.

THE TIMES, April 11 1970

A French woman, aged 37, stabbed three of her children, killing one of them, before committing suicide in Luneville yesterday, police said. Mme. Marie-Madeleine Amet stabbed Joanne, aged 14, and Philippe, aged 11, who managed to escape. But Catherine, aged 10, was killed.

GUARDIAN, April 14 1970

The Alternative Apocalypse 1

It's a shame, really, said Major Nye as they stood on the flat roof of the looted dispensary and watched the barbarian migration cross the swaying remains of Tower Bridge. The sky began to lighten and to some degree improve the appearance of the horde's filthy silks, satins and velvets. A few were mounted on horses, motorbikes and bicycles, but the majority trudged along with their bundles on their backs. Some were playing loud, primitive music on stolen Gibsons, Yamahas, Framus twelve-strings, Martins and even Hofners. It's a shame, really. Who can blame them?

Jerry fingered his new gloves.

You and they have more in common than I, major.

Major Nye gave him a sympathetic glance. Aren't you lonely, Mr Cornelius?

For a moment self-pity flooded all Jerry's systems. His eyes gleamed with water. Oh, fuck.

Major Nye knew how to get through.

When half the barbarians were on the South Bank, the bridge, shaken by a hundred different twelve-bar blues and a thousand moccasins and calf-length suede boots, fell slowly over into the grease of the Thames. Large stones broke away from the main towers as they toppled; pieces of asphalt cracked like toffee struck by a hammer. The whole mock-Gothic edifice, every inch of grimy granite, was falling down.

Their long hair fluttering behind them, their babies not in slings and packs falling from their arms, their guitars and bundles scattering around them, their beads and furs and laces flapping, the barbarians sank through the air, struck, and were absorbed by, the river. For a moment a cassette tape recorder could be heard playing *You can't always get what you want* by the Rolling Stones and then that, too, was logged by the water.

Arriving too late, a Panther patrol lowered its .280 EM1s as if in salute to the dying. Standing in single file along the North Bank they watched the children drown.

The Panthers were led by a tall aristocrat in a finely tailored white suit, a neatly trimmed Imperial beard and moustache and short hair cut close to the nape of his black neck. He carried an elegant single-shot Remington XP-100. The bolt-action pistol was borne more for aesthetic effect than anything else. He held it in his right hand and his arms were folded across his chest so that the long barrel rested in the crook of his left elbow. The Panthers in their own well-cut cream uniforms, looked inquiringly at their Head. It was unquestionably a problem of taste. The Panthers lived for taste and beauty, which was why they had been the most virulent force against the barbarians. The war between the two had been a war of styles and the Panthers, under their American leaders, had won all the way down the line.

At last the Panthers on the North Bank reached a decision. Lining the embankment, they turned their tall backs, dropped their chins to their chests and lounged against the balustrade, listening to the fading cries of the dying until there was silence in the river again. Then they climbed back into their open Mercedes and Bentley tourers and rolled away from there.

A few barbarians stood on the far bank, twisting themselves joints, hesitating before rejoining the exodus as it ploughed on towards the Borough High Street, heading for the suburbs of Surrey and Kent and what was left of the pickings.

And those, said the major, indicating the disappearing Panthers, do you identify, perhaps, with them?

32

Jerry shrugged. Maybe a little more. No — no, there's nobody left at all, major, let's face it. I'm on my own in this one and I can't say I like it. My fault, perhaps.

Possibly you lost sight of your targets, Mr Cornelius.

I've hit all the targets, Major Nye. That's the trouble. He took out his needler and turned it this way and that to catch the light on its polished chrome. Is there anything sadder, I wonder, than an assassin with nobody left to kill?

I shouldn't think so. Major Nye's voice was now more than sympathetic. I know exactly what you mean, my dear chap. And I suppose that's why we're both standing here watching. Our sun has set, I'm afraid.

Keep moving towards the sun and it will never set, said Jerry. That's positive thinking, major. It will never happen. It's a matter of finding the right pace. The correct speed for forward momentum.

Major Nye said nothing as he shook his grey head.

It will never fucking happen! Jerry shouted.

The masonry had blocked the flow of the river and was making it flood over the embankment. A few corpses were washed up and there was other, fouler, flotsam, too.

Jerry went back to the skylight and put his feet on the scarred wooden steps. He was going inside. Coming, major?

No, I'll stop here for a while, old son. And keep your chin up, eh?

Thanks, major, Same to you.

Jerry climbed down into the ruined bedroom and stood staring at the dreadful corpse of the girl in the fourposter. The rats ignored him and went on eating. He aimed the gun but, after a minute or two, replaced it in his holster without shooting. Even the rats couldn't last much longer.

The Alternative Apocalypse 2

Smoothly, with mock-apologetic smiles, they nailed him to the lowest yard of the mizzen. They were standing off the Kent coast, near Romney, out of sight of land. The three-masted schooner-rigged yacht rocked in the heavy sea. The sea tugged at the anchors, hurled its weight against the white sides. Waiting for the waters to subside, they paused in their hammering. Almost expectantly they looked up at him. The two women, who had nailed his hands, were Karen von Krupp and Mitzi Beesley. They were dressed in deck pyjamas and chic little sailormen's hats. The man who had nailed his feet was his brother Frank. Frank wore grey flannels, a white open-necked shirt and a fairisle pullover. He was kneeling beside the mizzen, the hammer in both hands.

Jerry spoke with great control. I made no claims.

But many were made *for* you, said Bishop Beesley through a mouthful of biege fudge. He stood by the rail, his bottom wedged against it. You didn't deny them.

I deny nothing. Have I disagreed with your opinion?

No. But, then, I'm not sure . . .

We have that in common, at least.

The sea grew calm. Bishop Beesley made an impatient gesture, withdrawing a Mars Bar from under his surplice. The three resumed their hammering.

Together with the nails in his palms there were ropes support-
ing his wrists so that the weight of his hanging body would not
rip the impaled flesh too quickly, for they wanted him to die
of asphyxiation, not of pain or loss of blood alone. He breathed
hard. The sharp pressure increased in his chest. The last blows
fell. The three stood back to inspect their work. The corpulent
Bishop Beesley licked his lips, sniffed the odour of the stale sea.

Dead fish, said the bishop. Dead fish.

LATE NEWS

Alan Stuart, aged four, who sprayed his mouth with what is believed to have been a pressurised oven cleaner at his home in Benhillwood Road, Sutton, Surrey, has died in hospital.

THE SUN, September 28 1971

A boy aged 14 died after being stabbed in the chest in the playground of Wandsworth School, South London, yesterday. He died in Queen Mary's Hospital, Roehampton, soon after the stabbing, which happened during the morning break at the boys' comprehensive school. Last night another boy, also aged 14, was accused of the murder. He will appear at Southwark North juvenile court today.

GUARDIAN, November 19 1971

Shirley Wilkinson, aged 16, daughter of the train robber Jack Wilkinson, died last night in the South London hospital where she had been detained after being injured in a car crash.

GUARDIAN, November 20 1971

Scores of rush-hour cars flashed by as a 10-year-old girl fled naked and terrified from a sex maniac. But not one driver stopped. And motorists took no notice of the girl's frantic cries for help as the man dragged her into his car. Later the man raped and strangled her. The body of little Jane Hanley was found at the weekend in a field outside Rochester, New York. "At least 100 people must have seen her," said a policeman. " She had apparently been kidnapped but jumped from the man's car and pleaded with passing motorists to help. The kidnapper grabbed her and drove off again." Now rewards totalling £2,500 have been offered by newspapers and citizen's organisations for information leading to the killer. Three drivers have now admitted they saw the drama on Highway 400 — 10 miles from where Jane disappeared while on a shopping errand. One said: " I went by so fast I couldn't believe what I saw."

THE SUN, November 22 1971

REMINISCENCE [B]

Save us.

From the basement in Talbot Road. From mother's breath and mother's saliva. From cold chips. From dirty hand-me-downs. From stained mattresses. From old beer bottles. From the smell of urine. From damp squalor.

From the poverty trance.

MRS C AND FRANKIE C

"So we fetched up 'ere agin 'ave we?" Mrs Cornelius said sullenly as her lean son guided her off the decrepit street and down the foul basement steps. "Yore doin' okay fer yerself, incha? Yer ole mum'd never know it."

"You prefer it here, mother," said Frank patiently. "When we got you that council flat you complained."

"It wasn't the bleedin' flat it was the arrangements. Orl them stairs. I can't get inter a lift it makes me sick. And them neighbours reckonin' theirselves . . ."

"Well. There it is." Frank took the door handle in both hands and lifted it so that the damp wood just cleared the step. "I'll get you some more batteries for your wireless."

They entered the stinking gloom.

"I could do wiv a drink."

Frank took a half-bottle of Gordon's gin from the pocket of his sheepskin coat. She accepted it with dignity and placed it on the warped and littered sideboard, near the primitive television which had stopped working well before the electricity had been cut off. "I'd make yer a cuppa tea," she said, "but . . ."

"I've paid the gas bill. They're coming round to turn you on tomorrow."

She waded through the litter of old newspapers and broken furniture. She lit the two stumps of candles on the rotting drain-

39

ing board. She moved a pile of old, damp Christmas cards.
" Wot yer fink Jerry's chancest are, Frankie? "

"Ask the experts." Frank shrugged and rubbed at his pale
face. " It's probably nothing more than exhaustion. He's been
overdoing it recently."

" Workin'! " said Mrs Cornelius derisively.

" Even Jerry has to graft sometimes, mum."

" Lazy sod. 'Ow's yer antique business doin'? "

Frank became wary. " So so."

" Well, at least yer 'elp out sometimes. I don't see 'im one
year ter the next." She sighed and lowered herself into the dis-
coloured armchair. " Ooooh! Them fuckin' springs. Damp as
Brighton Beach, too." The complaints were uttered in a tone
of comfortable approval. She had been too long out of her
natural environment. She reached up for the gin and began to
unscrew the cap. Frank handed her a dirty glass from the sink.

" I must be off," he said. " Got everything you need? "

" Couldn't lend us a coupla quid couldya, Frankie? "

Frank reached into the right pocket of his cavalry twill
trousers and removed a mixed handful of notes. He hesitated,
then extracted a fiver. He showed it to her and put it on the
sideboard. " You'll have to go down to the assistance on Monday. That should do you for the weekend. I won't be around
for a while."

" Be up in yer flat in 'Olland Park wiv yer nobby mates, eh? "

" No. Out of town."

" Wot abart the shop? "

" Mo's looking after that. I'm off to Scotland to see what's
still going in the big houses there. Everybody's running out of
antiques. There's nothing left in England — even the sixties
have gone dry. We're catching up on ourselves. It's funny." He
smiled as she stared uncomprehendingly at him. " Don't worry,
mum. You enjoy your drink."

Her features flowed back into their normal lines of stupid
complacency. " Thanks, Frankie."

"And give Cathie my love if you see her."

" That slut! Wors'n Jerry if yer ask me! I 'eard she was on
the game. Shacked up wiv a black feller."

" I doubt if she's on the game."

40

" I disown 'er," Mrs Cornelius said grandly, raising the bottle to her lips, " as any daughter o' mine."

Frank buttoned up his suede car coat and pulled the lambs-wool collar around his dark face. He smoothed his Brylcreemed hair with the palm of his hand then slipped the hand into a suede-backed motoring glove. " Mo said he'd come and clean this place out — give you some better furniture."

" Yeah? "

" When shall I tell him to come? "

She looked nervously around her. " Later," she said. " I'll 'ave ter fink abart wot I do and don' wanna keep. We'll discuss it later, eh? " She hadn't thrown a thing out since well before the war.

" You'll have that bloke from the council round again," he warned.

" Don't worry abart *that!* I can deal with the fuckin' council! "

" They might find you alternative accommodation."

Her heavy face was full of apprehension. "Abart time, too," she moaned.

He left, pulling the creaking door shut behind him.

She leaned the gin bottle on the arm of the mephitic chair and looked tenderly around at her home. It had been condemned in 1934, was scheduled for redevelopment by 1990, which meant any time after the turn of the century. It would last her out. The first candle guttered and threw peculiar shadows on the mildewed walls. The gin began to warm her chest and belly. She peered at the cracked mantelpiece on the far side of the room, locating the faded pictures of the fathers of her children. There was Frank's father in his GI uniform. There was Cathy's father in his best suit. There was the father of the dead twins, of the three abortions — the one who had married her. Only Jerry's father was missing. She didn't remember him, for all she'd borrowed his name. Through all her marriages she'd always been known as Mrs Cornelius. She'd only been about sixteen, hadn't she? Or even younger? Or was that something else? Was he the Jewish feller? Her eyelids closed.

Soon she was dreaming her nice dream as opposed to her nasty dream. She was kneeling on a big white woolly carpet. She was completely naked and there was blood dripping from

41

her mangled nipples as she was buggered by a huge, black, shapeless animal. In her sleep her hands fell to her lap and she dug at herself with her nails and stirred and snorted, waking herself up. She smiled and drank down the rest of the gin and was soon fast asleep again.

AUCHINEK

"Poverty," said Auchinek to Lyons, the Israeli colonel, "increased markedly in Europe last year. This, in itself, would not have threatened the status quo had not a group of liberal politicians persistently offered the people hope without, of course, any immediate prospect of improving their lot. Naturally they moved swiftly from apathy to anger. Without their anger I doubt if I should have been anything like as successful." He smiled. "I owe at least some of my success to the human condition."

"You're modest." The colonel stared approvingly at his troops as they joined with their Arab allies and began, systematically, to lay dynamite charges throughout what was left of the city of Athens. "Besides, wasn't the collapse to some extent cultural? "

"It was a culture without flexibility, I agree. I must admit I share the view that Western civilisation — European civilisation, if you like — was out of tempo with the rest of the world. It imposed itself for a short time — largely because of the vitality, stupidity and priggishness of those who supported it. We shall never be entirely cleansed of its influence, I'm afraid."

"You aren't suggesting that the only values worth keeping are those of the Orient? " Lyons' murmur was sardonic.

"Basically — emotionally — I do think that. I know the question's arguable."

"I detect a strong whiff of anti-aryanism. You support the pogroms?"

"Of course not. I am not a racialist. I speak only of education. I would like to see a vast re-education programme started throughout Europe. Within a couple of generations we could completely eradicate their portentous and witless philosophies."

"But haven't our own thoughts been irrevocably influenced by them? I can't echo your idealism, personally, General Auchinek. Moreover, I think our destiny is with Africa . . ."

"The chimera of vitality appears again," Auchinek sighed. "I wish we could stop moving altogether."

"And become like Cornelius? I saw him in Berlin, you know."

"There is a difference between tranquility and exhaustion. I had a guru, colonel, for some time, with whom I would correspond. He lived in Calcutta before the collapse. He convinced me of the need for meditation as the only solution to our ills."

"Is that why you became a guerilla?"

"There is no paradox. One must work in the world according to one's temperament."

The hillside, covered in tents, shook as the white ruins of Athens began to powder under the impact of the dynamite explosions.

Dust clouds rose slowly into the blue air and began to form peculiar configurations: ideograms from an alien alphabet. Auchinek studied them. They were vaguely familiar. If he studied them long enough, they might reveal their message. He changed the angle of his head, he narrowed his eyes. He folded his thin arms across his spare chest.

"How beautiful," said Colonel Lyons and he seemed to be speaking of Auchinek rather than of the explosions. He placed his brawny hand on Auchinek's bony shoulder. His large digital wrist-watch shone beneath the tangle of black hairs, the coat of dust. "We must get . . ." He removed his hand. "How is Una?"

"In excellent health." Auchinek coughed on the dust. "She's leading our mission in Siberia at present."

"So you are serious about your loyalty to the Oriental idea. Have you forgotten the Chinese?"

44

" Far from it."

" Would they agree to an alliance? And what about the Japanese? How deep is their reverence for occidental thought? "

"A few generations deep in both cases. You've seen their comic books. All China wants, in international terms, is her old Empire restored."

" There could be complications."

" True. But not the confusion created artificially by western interference since the fifteenth century."

" *Their* fifteenth century," smiled Colonel Lyons.

Auchinek missed the reference.

PERSSON

Una Persson watched the military ambulance bouncing away over the yellow steppe towards the wooden bridge which spanned the Volga. The sky was large, livid, on the move, but it could not dwarf the Cossack sech with its ten thousand yurts of painted leather and its many corrals full of shaggy ponies. Compared with the sky's swift activity the sech was almost static.

The ambulance reached the bridge and shrieked across it, taking the Cossack wounded back to their special encampment. A dark eddy swept through the sky for a hundred miles. The Volga danced.

In the strange light, Una Persson left her Range Rover and strode towards the sech. Cool and just a trifle prim, with her big coat completely open to show her long, beautiful legs, the short multicoloured kaftan, the holstered S & W pistol on the ammunition belt around her small waist, the knee-length black boots, she paused again on the edge of the camp, allowing her blue-grey eyes to reveal the admiration she felt for the Cossack Host's picturesque style.

These were not the Westernised cossacks who had taken Berlin with their sophisticated artillery and mechanised transport. These were the atavists; they had resorted to the ancient ways of the Cossacks who had followed Stenka Razin in the people's revolt three hundred years before. They wore the topknots and long flowing moustachios copied from the Tatars who had been their ancient enemies but who now rode with them. All who presently dressed in Cossack silk and leather had been recruited east of the Volga and most of them looked Mongolian.

Their leader, wearing a heavy burka, blue silk trousers and yellow leather boots typical of the Zaporozhian cossack, rode to where she stood. A Russian SKS carbine jostled on his back as he dismounted from his pony and wiped a large hand over his huge, hard face.

His voice was deep, humorous and resonant. " I am Karinin, the Ataman of this Sech." His oval eyes were equally admiring as he studied her, putting one foot in his pony's stirrup, hooking his arm around his saddle pommel and lighting his curved, black pipe with a match which he struck on the sole of his boot. " You come from Auchinek, they tell me. You wish to make an alliance. Yet you know we are Christians, that we hate Jews worse than we hate Moslems and Muscovites." He removed his floppy grey and black sheepskin shako to expose his shaven head, the gold rings in his ears, to wipe his dark brow and thick moustache. A calculated set of gestures, thought Una Persson, but well accomplished.

" The alliance Auchinek suggests is an alliance of the Orient against the west." She spoke precisely, as if unimpressed by his style, his strength, his good looks.

" But you are — what? — a Russ? A Scandinavian, uh? A traitor? Or just a romantic like Cornelius? "

" What are you but that? "

He laughed. "All right."

The wind began to bluster, carrying with it the overriding smell of horse manure. The sky seemed to decide its direction and streamed rapidly eastward.

Karinin took his foot from the stirrup and slid the slim, scabbarded sabre around his waist until it rested on his left hip. He knocked out the pipe on his silver boot heel. " You had better come to my yurt," he said, " to tell me the details. There's no one much left for us to fight in these parts." He pointed into the centre of the sech, where the circles of yurts were tightest. His yurt was no larger than the others, for the Zaporozhians were touchily democratic, but a tall horsehair

47

standard stood outside its flap.

Una Persson began to see the farcical side of her situation. She grinned. Then she noticed the gibbet which had been erected near Karinin's yurt. A group of old Kuban cossacks were methodically putting a noose about the neck of a young European dressed in a yellow frock coat, lilac cravat, yellow shirt and a blue, wide-brimmed hat. The European's expression was amused as he let them tie his hands behind him.

" What are they doing? " Una Persson asked.

The ataman spoke almost regretfully. " They are hanging a dandy. There aren't so many as there were."

" He seems brave."

" Surely courage is a characteristic of the dandy? "

"And yet those old men plainly hate him. I thought cossacks admired courage? "

" They are also very prudish."

The tightening rope knocked the blue hat from the fair hair; it covered the face for a moment before falling to the mud. The dandy gave his captors a chiding glance. The Kubans slapped at the rumps of the two horses on the other end of the rope. Slowly the dandy was raised into the air, his body twisting, his legs kicking, his face turning red, then blue, then black. Some noises came out of his distorted mouth.

" Sartor Resartus." Karinin guided Una Persson past the gallows and ducked to push back the flap of his yurt and allow her to precede him. The yurt was illuminated by a lamp on a chest — a bowl of fat with a wick burning in it. The little round room was tidily furnished with a wooden bed and a table, as well as the chest.

Karinin came in and began to lace up the flap from the inside.

Una Persson removed her coat and put it on the chest. She unbuckled her ammunition belt with its holstered Smith and Wesson .45 and placed it on top of the coat.

Karinin's slanting eyes were tender and passionate. He stepped forward and took her to him. His breath smelled of fresh milk.

" We of the steppe have not lost the secret of affection," he told her. They lay down in the narrow bed. He began to tug at his belt. " It comes between love and lust. We believe in

48

moderation, you see."

"It sounds attractive." Much against her better judgement she responded to his caress.

NYE

Ironmaster House was built of grey stones. It was Jacobean, with the conventional small square-leaded windows, three floors, five chimneys, a grey slate roof. Around its walls, particularly over the portico, climbed roses, wisteria and evergreens. Its gardens were divided by tall, ornamental privet hedges; there was a small lawn at the front and a larger lawn at the back. The back lawn ran down to a brook which fed a pool in which water-lilies were blooming. In the middle of the lawn a water-spray swept back and forth like a metronome, for it was June and the temperature was 96°F.

From the open windows of the timbered sitting room it was possible to see both gardens, which were full of fuchsia, hydrangeas, gladioli and roses all sweetening the heavy air with their scent. And among these flowers, as if drugged, groggily flew some bees, butterflies, wasps and bluebottles.

Inside the shadowy house and seated on mock-Jacobean armchairs near a real Jacobean table, sat Major Nye in his shirtsleeves; two girls, one fair and one dark; and Major Nye's wife, Mrs Nye, a rather strong looking, weather-beaten woman with a contemptuous manner, a stoop and unpleasant hands.

Mrs Nye was serving a sparse tea. She poured from a mock Georgian, mock silver teapot into real Japanese porcelain cups. She sliced up a seed cake and slid the slices onto matching plates.

Major Nye had not bought Ironmaster House. His wife had inherited it. He had, however, worked hard to support the place; it was expensive to run. Since leaving the army and becoming Company Secretary to the Mercantile Charitable Association, he had lost his sense of personal authority. Many of his anxieties were new; he had previously never experienced anything like them and consequently was at a loss to know how to cope with them. This had earned him the contempt of his wife, who no longer loved him, but continued to command his loyalty. One of the girls in the room was Elizabeth, his daughter. He had another daughter, Isobel, who was a dancer in a company which worked principally on ocean-going liners, and he had a small son who had won a chorister's scholarship to St. James' School, Southwark, a school reputed to be unnecessarily brutal but, as Major Nye would explain, it had been the only chance ' the poor little chap had to get into a public school ', since the major could not afford to pay the kind of fees expected by Eton, Harrow or Winchester (his own school). In the army Major Nye had rarely had to make a choice, but in civilian life he had been given only a few choices and most of his decisions had been inevitable, for he had his duty to do to his wife, her house and his children. During the summer they usually took a couple of paying guests and they also sold some of the produce of their market garden at the roadside. Mrs Nye was seriously considering selling teas on the lawn to passing motorists.

Major Nye had to work solidly from six in the morning until nine or ten o'clock at night all through the week and the week-end. His wife also worked like a martyr to help keep the garden and the house going. Her heart was weak and his ulcer problems were growing worse. He had sold all his shares and there was a double mortgage on the house. Because he was insured, he hoped that he would die as soon as his son went up to Oxford in ten years' time. There were no paying guests at the moment. Those who did turn up never came for a second year; the atmosphere of the big house was sad and tense and hopeless.

Elizabeth, the dark-haired girl, was large-boned and inclined to fatness. She had a loud, cheerful voice which was patronising when she addressed her father, accusing when she spoke to her mother and almost conciliatory when she talked to the fair-haired girl with whom, for the past nine months, she had been having a romantic love affair. This affair had never once faltered in its intensity. The fair-haired girl was being very polite to Elizabeth's parents whom she was meeting for the first time. She had a low, calm, unaffected voice. Her name was Catherine Cornelius and she had turned from incest to lesbianism with a certain sense of relief. Elizabeth Nye was the third girl she had seduced but the only one with whom she had been able to sustain a relationship for very long.

It was Catherine who had asked Elizabeth to get Major Nye to collect Jerry Cornelius from Cornwall and deliver him to Ironmaster House where her brother had been picked up by Sebastian Auchinek's agents and transported to Dubrovnik. Catherine had come to know Sebastian Auchinek through Una Persson who had introduced Catherine to her first lover, Mary Greasby. Una Persson had once possessed mesmeric power over Catherine similar to that which Catherine now possessed over Elizabeth. Una Persson had convinced Catherine that Prinz Lobkowitz in Berlin would be able to cure Jerry of his hydrophilia and so Catherine had been deceived into providing the collateral (her brother) for the guns which had helped reduce Athens. She had also been instrumental in delivering Jerry into the hands of his old regimental commander, Colonel Pyat of the 'Razin' 11th Don Cossack Cavalry, who, for some time, had been obsessed with discovering the reason for Cornelius's desertion. He desperately wanted, once he had proved Jerry authentic, to revive the assassin and question him.

Catherine was only gradually becoming aware of her mistake. She had still not voiced the suspicion, even to herself, that Una Persson might have deceived her.

"And how is the poor blighter? " asked Major Nye, dolefully watching the water fall through the overheated air and rolling himself a thin cigarette. " Hypothermia, wasn't it? "

" I'm not sure, major. I haven't heard from Berlin yet. It's confused, as you know."

" It beats me," said Mrs Nye harshly, rising to collect the tea paraphernalia, " how your brother managed to get himself into that state. But then I suppose I'm behind the times." Her wide, cruel mouth hardened. " Even the diseases have changed since I

52

was a girl." She gave her husband a sharp, accusing glare. She hated him for his ulcers. " You haven't eaten your scone, dear."

" Old tummy . . ." he mumbled. " I'd better see to that weeding." His wife knew how to whip him on.

" The heat . . ." said Catherine Cornelius, and her bosom heaved. " Isn't it a bit . . .? "

" Used to the heat, my girl." He squared his shoulders. A funny little smile appeared beneath his grey moustache. There was considerable pride in his stance. " Drilled in full dress uniform. India. Much worse than this. Like the heat." He lit the cigarette he had rolled. " You're the cream in my coffee, I'm the milk in your tea, pom-te-pomm-pom-pom-pom." He smiled shyly and affectionately at her as he opened the door which led into the back garden. He gave her a comic, swaggering salute. " See you later, I hope."

Left alone, Elizabeth and Catherine looked longingly at each other across the real Jacobean table.

" We should be getting back to Ladbroke Grove soon if we're not to get caught in the traffic," said Catherine glancing at the door through which Mrs Nye had passed with the tea things.

" Yes," said Elizabeth. " We shouldn't leave it too late, should we? "

JC

Jerry's coffin was being rocked about quite a lot. The train carrying it stopped suddenly once again. It was about a mile outside Coventry. The awful smell always increased when the train was stationary. Was it the steam?

Colonel Pyat got up from the dirty floor to peer through the little hole in the armour plating of his truck. The light was fading but he could see a grimy grey-green field and a pylon. On the horizon were rows of red brick houses. He looked at his watch. It was nine o'clock in the evening; it had been exactly three days since the train had left Edinburgh. Pyat brushed at his torn and grubby uniform. He had nothing else to wear, yet it was now far too dangerous to be seen in military uniform outside London. He munched the last half of his stale sandwich and sipped a drop of vodka from his hip flask. There had been no change in Cornelius and Pyat had had no time to revive and question him. The colonel had given up his original ambition, anyway; now he hoped he might use the contents of the coffin as his safe-conduct, his guarantee of asylum, when he reached Ladbroke Grove and contacted one of the Cornelius relatives. Matters had not gone well in Berlin after Auchinek and his Zaporozhian allies had arrived. Somebody had told Pyat that no one could hold Berlin for more than a month and he hadn't believed them. Now this knowledge was his consolation — even

54

the Jew would not last long before someone else took over what was left of the city.

From within the coffin came a further succession of muffled shrieks and cries. Pyat heard a querulous shout from further up the train. Another voice replied in a strong Wolverhampton accent.

"Electricity failure, they think. Two other trains can't run. No signals, see."

Again the distant shout and the Wolverhampton voice replying: "We'll be moving shortly. We can't go until the signal says we can."

Pyat lit a cigarette. Sourly he paced the carriage, wishing he had thought of a better plan. A week ago England had seemed the safest state in Europe. Now it was in chaos. He should have guessed what would happen. Everything broke down so rapidly nowadays. But then, on the other hand, things came together quickly, too. It was the price you paid for swift communications.

The light faded and the single electric bulb in the roof glowed and then dimmed until only the element shone with a dull orange colour. Pyat had become used to this. He settled down to try to sleep, convinced that the sharp pain which had returned to his chest could only be lung cancer.

He began to nod off. But then the sounds from the coffin filled his head. They had changed in tone so that this time they seemed to be warning him of something. They had become more urgent. He stretched out his boot and kicked at the coffin. " Shut up. I don't need any more of that."

But the urgency of the cries did not abate.

Pyat climbed to his feet and stumbled forward with the intention of unstrapping the lid and putting a gag of some kind into Cornelius's mouth. But then the truck lurched. He fell. The big Pacific class loco was moving again. The cries stopped. Pyat remained on the floor of the carriage. He hugged his bruised body. His eyes were tightly shut.

It was dawn.

A green Morgan of the decadent Plus 8 period droned swiftly along the platform, passing the train as it pulled at last into an almost deserted Kings Cross station. The car followed the train for a moment, then turned off the platform into the main ticket office and drove through the outer doors and down the steps into the street. Through his peephole Colonel Pyat watched blearily, certain that the Morgan had some connection with himself. A strong smell, like that of a fair quantity of hard-boiled eggs, reached his nostrils. He spat on the boards and jammed his eye once again to the spy-hole.

Expecting a large crowd at Kings Cross, he had planned to lose himself in it. But there were no crowds. There was no one. It was as if all the people had been cleared from the station. Could it be an ambush? Or merely an air-raid?

The locomotive released a hugh sigh of hot steam and halted.

Pyat remembered that he was unarmed.

If he emerged from the carriage now, would he be shot down? Where were the marksmen hiding?

He unbolted the sliding doors of the waggon and slid them back. He waited for the other passengers to disembark. After a few seconds it became clear that there were no other passengers. A few small, innocent sounds came from various parts of the station. A clatter. A cheerful whistling. A thump. Then silence. He saw the fireman and the driver and the guard leave the train and swagger through the barrier towards the main exit, carrying their gear. They wore dirty BR uniforms; their caps were pushed back as far as possible on their heads. They were all three middle-aged, stocky and plain. They walked slowly, chatting easily to each other. They turned a corner and were gone. Pyat felt abandoned. Steam still clung to the lower parts of the train and drifted over the platform. Pyat sniffed the smoky air as a hound might sniff for a fox. The high, sooty arches of the station were silent and the glass dome admitted only a little dirty sunlight.

Because it was dawn, a bird or two began to twitter in the steel beams near the roof.

Pyat shivered and got down. Walking to the far side of the platform he took hold of a large porter's trolley. The wheels squeaked and grated. He dragged it alongside the armoured carriage. He felt faint. He looked warily about him. Silent, untended trains stood at every platform. Huge black and green steam engines with dirty brasswork faced worn steel bumpers

56

and the blank brick walls beyond. They were like monsters shocked into catatonia by a sudden understanding: this had been their last journey. They had been lured into involuntary hibernation, perhaps to remain here until they rusted and rotted to dust.

Pyat manhandled the heavy coffin onto the trolley. It bumped down and a somewhat pettish mewling escaped from it. Pyat took the handles of the trolley with both hands. He strained backwards and got it moving. He hauled it with some difficulty along the asphalt. The wheels squeaked and groaned. In his filthy white uniform he might have been mistaken for a porter who had been mysteriously transferred from some more tropical station, perhaps in India. He was not really as conspicuous as he felt.

He trudged through the ticket barrier, crossed the grey expanse of the enclave and reached the pavement outside. The streets and buildings all seemed uninhabited. Wasn't this the heart of London? And a Thursday morning? Pyat looked up at the bland sky. There were no aircraft to be seen. No dirigibles. No flying bombs. The bright early sunshine was already quite warm. It dulled his shivers.

A tattered horse-drawn lavender cab stood untended by the kerb outside the main entrance. Now that the Morgan had disappeared, it was the only form of transport in sight. The driver, however, was nowhere to be seen. Pyat decided that he did not care about the driver. With almost the last of his strength, Pyat got the coffin into the hansom and climbed up to the box. He shook the reins and the bony mare raised her head. He flicked her rump with the frayed whip and shouted at her. She began to walk.

Slowly the hansom moved away, the horse refusing to go faster than a walk. It was as if the hansom were the only visible portion of an otherwise invisible funeral procession. The horse's feet clopped mournfully through the deserted street. It reached Euston Road and began to head due west for Ladbroke Grove.

PROLOGUE (continued)

. . . and perhaps the greatest loss I still feel is the loss of my
unborn son. I was certain it would have been a son and I had
even named it, my subconscious coming up with a name I
would never have chosen otherwise: Andrew. I had not realised
what would happen to me. The abortion seemed so necessary
at the time if she were not to suffer in several ways. But it was
an abortion of convenience, scarcely of desperation. For a long
while I did not admit that it had affected me at all. If I had
ever had a son after that, I feel it would have banished the
sense of loss, but as it is it will go with me to my grave.

MAURICE LESCOQ, Leavetaking

THUNDER BRINGS COMA BOY BACK TO LIFE

Only a miracle could save nine-year-old Lawrence Mantle, said doctors. For four months he had been in a deep coma. Twice he 'died' when his heart stopped beating. There was no sign of life from his brain, surgeons told his parents. Then, in the middle of a thunderstorm, it happened. A flash of lightning and a loud thunderclap made nurses in the children's ward at Ashford hospital, Middlesex, jump . . . and Lawrence, still in a coma, screamed.

LONDON EVENING NEWS, December 3 1969

THE OBSERVERS

Colonel Pyat had first met Colonel Cornelius in Guatamala
City, in the early days of the1900-75 War, before the monorails,
the electric carriages, the giant airships, the domed cities and the
utopian republics had been smashed, never to be restored. They
met at some time during what is now called the Phoney War
period of 1901-13. They were both representing the military
establishments of two great and mutually suspicious European
governments. They had been sent to observe the trials of the
Guatamalans' latest Land Ironclad (the invention of the Chilean
wizard, O'Bean). Their two governments had been interested in
purchasing a number of the machines should the trials prove
successful. As it happened, both Pyat and Cornelius had decided
that the 'clad was still too primitive to be of much practical
use, though the French, German and Turkish governments, who
also had observers at the trials, had each ordered a small
quantity.

Their duty done, the two men relaxed together in the bar of
the Conquistador Hotel, where they were both staying. Next
day they would catch the aerial clipper *Light of Dresden* to
Hamburg. Once there, they would go their separate ways,
Cornelius to the West and Pyat to the East.

Through the tall, slightly frosted Charles Rennie Mackintosh
windows they could see Guatamala City's bright marble streets

61

and elegant mosaic towers with shopfronts by Mucha, Moulins and Marnez. Sometimes an ornate electric brougham would hum past, or there would be the somewhat anachronistic jingle of harness as a landau, drawn by high stepping Arab stallions, rattled by; sometimes a steam car would come and go, the hiss from its engines barely audible, the sun catching its brasswork and making its stainless steel body shine like silver. The steam car was now in use all over the world. Like the mechanical farming equipment which had turned South and Central America into such a paradise, it was the creation of O'Bean.

Colonel Pyat, leaning back in his black plush chair, signalled for the waiter to bring fresh drinks. Jerry admired his grace. The Russian had been wearing his white uniform for the best part of the afternoon and there was not a smudge of dust to be seen on it. Even his belts, his holster and his boots were of white kid, the only colour being the gold insignia on his collar and a touch of gold on his epaulettes. Jerry's dark green uniform was fussy in comparison, with a smear of oil evident on the right cuff. Some of the gold braid frogging on his sleeves, shoulders and chest was badly snagged, too. His belts, holster and boots were black. They were not quite as brightly polished as they might have been. Like Pyat's, his was a cavalry uniform, that of some Indian regiment by the cut of the long-skirted coat, but worn without a sash. (Pyat, who had seen some service on the frontier — largely courier work of an unofficial nature — could not place the uniform at all. He wondered if Cornelius might be a civilian given military rank for the sake of this assignment. Certainly Cornelius did not look much like an English cavalry-man. The way he had undone his coat at the first opportunity suggested that Cornelius found military dress uncomfortable.)

The drinks were brought by a haughty waiter who refused to respond to Pyat's friendly and condescending smile and left the proffered tip on the Husson silver salver he placed on the table. " Democracy gone mad! " said Pyat with a movement of his eyebrows and leaned forward to see what they had. There were Tiffany glasses. A bottle of Malvern water. A Glen Grant malt whisky and a Polish vodka. Jerry looked at them all resting on the Dufrêne inlay.

" They think we are barbarians," said Pyat, filling Jerry's glass with whisky and letting Jerry add his own Malvern water, " but they do not mind selling us weapons and war machines. Where would their economy be without us? "

Jerry reached his hand halfway to his drink. " They'd like us to get it over with, though. We disturb them by our continued existence. We've been staving off the apocalypse for so long. Suppose we turned on them? They have no army."

" Then they are fools. How long can this traumrepublik last? A few more years? "

" Months, more likely. Keep your voice down. They don't have to know . . ."

Pyat's ironic glance gave way to a look of introspection. " You speak like a priest. Not a soldier." It was a statement which hoped for a reply, but Jerry merely smiled and picked up his glass.

" To which regiment do you belong, colonel? " Pyat decided on a direct approach.

Jerry looked curiously at his uniform as if he himself hoped to find some clue to the answer there. " The 30th Deccan Horse, I think."

" You have been seconded, then? "

" Quite likely. No."

" You are a civilian! "

Jerry laughed. " Well, I'm not sure, you know." He shook his head. There were tears in his eyes now as his whole body trembled with mirth. " I'm simply not sure."

Pyat laughed too, because he enjoyed laughing. " Let's get a bottle each, shall we? I have a suite upstairs. And perhaps someone can find us a couple of girls? Or perhaps two girls will volunteer their services! Everyone is emancipated in Guatamala City! "

" Fine! "

When they had risen, Pyat flung his arm around Jerry's slender shoulders. " Do you feel like a girl, Colonel Cornelius? "

63

THE PERFORMERS

Dressed as a gentleman, Una Persson stalked the stage behind the green velvet curtain.

From the other side of the curtain came the noise of the crowd: shouts, laughter, screams, ironic cheers, groans, the clink of glasses and bottles, the rustle of heavy clothing. In the pit the orchestra was tuning up for the overture.

His paleness emphasised by the astrakhan collar of his chesterfield, Sebastian Auchinek raised a gold-tipped Unfiadis to his curved lips and coughed. He sat on a prop — an imitation rock — and looked through hooded eyes at the ballet girls in their frothy costumes as they took their places for the opening divertissement. Behind the girls was a backdrop showing Windsor Castle. The girls were dressed to represent *Rose, Shamrock, Thistle* and *Wales* (in a tall black hat and a pinafore because a Leek had been thought too indelicate a plant). The divertissement was entitled "Under One Flag". In the wings, waiting to go on, stood Sailors, Highlanders and Beefeaters. Una Persson was not appearing in the first of the two tableaux. She would feature in the second, 'Honour to the Queen", and lead the chorus in the closing cantata.

"You will be a success, Una!" Auchinek got up and caught her by the arm. "You are bound to be! Come, the curtain!" The gas flared brightly above the stage, the electrical spotlights began to come on. " It is going up! "

She walked swiftly into the wings. Auchinek hurried behind her. She pushed her way nervously past Mr Clement Scott, author of the opening Patriotic Ode. The orchestra began to play a rousing chorus of the satirical *Oh, What a Happy Land is England:*

We shall soon be buying Consols, at the rate of
Half-a-crown,
For like the Russian battleships, they're always
going down!
We have lately built an Airship and the only
thing it lacks,
Is the power to go on rising like the British
Income Tax!

Hip-hip-hooray!
Oh! what a happy land is England!
Envied by all Nations near and far!
Where the wretched Alien
Robs the British working men!
Oh! what a lucky race we are!
Oh! what a happy land is England!
Envied by all Nations near and far!
All Foreigners have found
This a happy dumping ground!
Oh! what a lucky race we are!

sang the audience and then began to cheer. The curtain rose.

Una reached the dressing room. Though she shared it with Marguerite Cornille, the comedienne, it was the best equipped dressing room she had ever used. This was her first time at the Empire, Leicester Square. It was one of the most respected of the newer, better class of music halls: a Theatre of Varieties. But it was the very reputation and respectability of the Empire which distressed Una so much. She was used to the friendlier, less ostentatious halls of Stepney, Brixton and Shepherds Bush.

" The atmosphere's a bit frosty." She entered the dressing room

65

and nodded to Mlle. Cornille who was making up already, with one eye on the mirror and the other on a magazine she held in her left hand, even though she was tenth on the programme.

" You get used to it, love. The crowd's all right. Same as any-where." The pert-faced girl was re-reading a short photographic feature about herself in *Nash's Magazine* which had just come out. " The rules and the snobs is the price you pay for regular work. It's my last week here. It'll be back to three different halls a night for me if I'm lucky and no halls at all if it's really bad. So my two weeks at the Alhambra over Christmas'll be like a holiday." She was boasting a bit, for a feature in *Nash's* usually meant a few good bookings at very least. Una wondered if *she* would ever go so far as showing her legs for a *Nash's* photographer.

Auchinek came in, closing the door softly behind him. "A good audience, by the sound of it."

" What I was saying," said Mlle. Cornille.

Auchinek offered them Unfiadis Egyptian cigarettes from his gold Liberty's case. Mlle. Cornille shook her head, but Una accepted one. As she lit it herself she looked closely at Auchinek, wondering what his real thoughts were.

" It's a step up, Una." He was her agent and in love with what he saw as her perfection, but he was embarrassed by the fact that he found Mlle. Cornille's brown curls and buxom charms more physically attractive. He was hoping that Una had not noticed. That Mlle. Cornille had noticed was evident in the attitude of friendly contempt she took towards him.

Una picked up her music and read over the lines of her songs as she finished the cigarette. There was a knock on the door. " Overture and beginners second tab."

Una felt her stomach muscles tighten. She spread her fingers wide as she ran her palms down the front of her thighs, over her trousers. Auchinek stepped forward and adjusted her bow tie. He handed her the cane and the silk opera hat, he flicked a speck of glitter from her tailcoat. "All right? "

She smiled. If she had had her own way she would have remained out of the West End, but she knew that he desperately wanted her to get to the top; and that was what performing at the Empire meant.

"Good luck, love," said Mlle. Cornille, both eyes now on her article.

"Stay here," said Una to Auchinek.

"I'd rather . . ." He glanced guiltily away from the comedienne. "Give you moral support."

"Stay here." She straightened her coat and put on her silk hat. "You can come to the wings and watch as soon as I'm on."

"Very well."

She walked down the corridor. Against a tide of returning Highlanders, Sailors, Beefeaters, Roses, Shamrocks, Thistles and Welsh girls, she made her way towards the wings. In the wings she saw that the chorus was already arranging itself on stage. There were eight girls, each dressed as a colony. There was India, Canada, Australia, Cape Colony, the West Indies, Malta, Gibraltar and New Zealand, each with her own verse to sing. In the opposite wings waited Art, Science, Commerce, Industry and a splendid Britannia, whose carriage they were to draw on stage. That was when Una would come on.

The curtain rose and the orchestra began a rousing accompaniment as the chorus sang together:

> *We, the children of the Empire, pay homage to*
> *our Queen!*
> *And we know she can be counted on where e'r her*
> *flag is seen!*
> *She's good, she's just, she's mighty and we know*
> *you will agree*
> *She's loved, admired and envied through all the*
> *seven seas!*

Una felt calm now. The music was jolly enough and the audience applauded loudly at the end of every verse and joined in each chorus. They weren't anything like as stuffy as she'd thought they'd be.

Art, Science, Commerce and Industry began to pull at Britannia's carriage. The float moved forward with a slight lurch. India, Canada, Australia, Cape Colony, the West Indies, Malta, Gibraltar and New Zealand fell back on two sides of the stage. The orchestra struck up with opening bars of Una's introduction. Una cleared her throat, took a deep breath and poised herself.

The gaslight dimmed.

At first Una thought it had been done for deliberate dramatic effect. But then the lights went out altogether, including the electrics, and the clapping faded, matches were struck, an anxious murmur began to fill the theatre.

Something exploded in the gallery. Someone shouted loudly. Women screamed. Una Persson was thrown backwards into the curtains and fell down. Feet struck her face and a body fell across her legs. The curtain collapsed over her. She heard muffled exclamations.

"Anarchists! "

"An air-raid! "

"Una? Una? " Auchinek's voice.

She tried to get up but could not fight free of the velvet folds.

" Sebastian! "

" Una! " His soft hands began to tear away the curtain.

She saw his face. It was bright red. There were flames leaping in the stalls. The crowd was a confused mass of flapping coat-tails, bustles and feather hats. It was climbing onto the stage, unable to use the ordinary exits.

Auchinek helped her to her feet. The heat from the flames was horrible. They were almost pushed into the orchestra pit by the panic-stricken audience. He held her tightly.

" What happened? " She let him guide her back to the wings. They were carried with the crowd towards the stage door. The fire roared behind them. Smoke made their eyes water and stung their throats. Props crashed down. Individual voices blended into one terrified wail.

" Incendiary bomb. Dropped from the gallery, I think. Why did it have to be tonight, Una? Your most important chance. The theatre will be closed for a week at least."

They reached the alley which ran beside the theatre. It was clogged with bewildered entertainers in flimsy, polychrome costumes, the frightened audience in heavy serge and scarlet and green velvet. At the end of the alley stood a tall, bearded police-man trying to calm the crowd and stop it from rushing headlong over the edge of the street and into the forty foot deep crater which, until the air-raids had begun a month ago, had been Leicester Square.

By the time the fire engines arrived at the front of the theatre, many of the people had been allowed to pass through the police cordon and the press had thinned. It was cold and there was a trace of fog in the air. The gas must have been turned off at a main, for none of the nearby streetlamps were alight. The only illumination came from the policemen's bullseyes and the fire itself. She felt full of relief. " Back to Brixton," she said. " What's bad luck for some is good luck for others, Seb, my boy."

He directed at her a mixed look of misery and malice. " Don't count on Brixton, Una. At this rate they'll be closing down all the halls." He regretted his spite. " I'm sorry." He took off his coat and placed it round her shoulders over the man's jacket she still wore.

More fire engines arrived — steamers this time — and the police let a substantial number of people through the cordon.

A sensation of being watched made her glance back at the theatre. She saw a young man leaning against the open stage door looking for all the world like a masher waiting casually for the appearance of his favourite chorus girl. He wore a dark yellow frock-coat with an exaggerated waist and flair, with brown braid at collar and cuff. He had a matching bowler with its brim tightly curled, a light brown cravat, and bell bottomed trousers cut very tight at the knee. The trousers were in a mustard check some would have considered vulgar. His gold-topped stick was in his left hand and an empty amber cigar-holder in his right. On the third finger of his right hand was a heavy gold signet ring. He seemed either unaware of the confusion around him or careless of it.

Una Persson regarded him with interest. His black, soft hair hung straight to his shoulders in the style of the aesthetes of some years earlier. His long, lean face bore an ambiguous expression which might have been amusement or satisfaction or surprise. His black eyes were large, deep-set, unreadable. Suddenly, with a nod to her, he stepped sideways and entered the burning theatre. Impulsively she made to follow him. Then she felt Auchinek's hand on her shoulder.

" Don't worry," he said. " This can't last forever."

She looked again at the stage door. The dark smoky interior of the theatre was now alive with red flame. She saw the young man's silhouette against the firelight before it disappeared, apparently marching without hesitation into the heart of the inferno.

" He'll die! " Una said softly. " The heat! "

Auchinek said anxiously: "Are you sure you're yourself, Una? "

THE SEDUCERS

Mrs Cornelius settled her pink feather boa around her broad shoulders and patted it down over the green and white fabric flowers decorating her fine big bosom. She wasn't doing too badly for thirty, she thought, giving her image a wink and dabbing at the rouge on her right cheek with a damp finger which protruded from her broderie anglaise cuff.

" 'And up me 'at, love."

The mean-faced boy of fifteen wiped his nose on the sleeve of his tattered Norfolk jacket and reached up to the mock Georgian mahogany chiffonier for the extravagant pile of artificial roses, peonies and sweet williams topped off by a yard or two of pink gauze, some wax grapes and a pair of pheasant's wings, which rested amongst her nicknacks. In both hands he carried the hat to where she stood before the full-length fly-specked wardrobe mirror in its gilded cast-iron frame.

"And the pins, love," she reproved, donning the hat as if it were the Crown of England.

He took the three long pins with their blue, red and gold enamelled butterfly wings and presented them in the flat of his unhealthy hand, his expression cool, like a nurse proffering a surgeon his instruments. One by one she picked them from his palm and slid them like a conjurer expertly into her hat, her hair and, apparently, her head.

71

" Cream! " She was satisfied. She tilted the brim just a fraction to the right. She flicked at a pheasant feather.

" Shall I be in this evening? " asked the boy. His accent while by no means educated was indefinably in contrast to the woman's. " Or not? "

" Better stay at Sammy's, love. I think I'll be entertaining tonight." She smiled comfortably at herself and admired her large, well-corsetted figure for a while, hands on hips. " You're looking prime, girlie." She gathered her pale green satin skirts and pirouetted on her matching patent leather boots. " You'll do, you will."

The boy put his hands in his pockets and swaggered about the untidy, over-furnished bedroom whistling, without irony, *I'm Gilbert, the Filbert, the Colonel of the Knuts*. He marched through the open door into the gaslit parlour. The parlour was a dark jungle of aspidistra and mahogany. Opening the front door of the flat he spread his arms, running and leaping down the lodging house's uncarpeted stairs and making a high-pitched whining sound as he pretended he was a fighting aeroplane making a death dive on its enemies. He rushed panting into Blenheim Crescent and was almost knocked over by the baker's motor van which hooted at him as it puffed past in the twilight. On the corner of the dowdy street, where it met Ladbroke Grove, under the unlit lamp and by the wall of the newly-built Convent of the Poor Clares, stood a group of younger urchins. They spotted him at once. They yelled at him, jeering insults which were more than familiar to him. He veered and began to walk in the opposite direction, pretending not to have noticed them, and went up towards Kensington Park Road and Sammy's pie shop on the corner. Some people thought Sammy might be the boy's dad, the way he favoured him. The boy always got first chance at shooting the rats in the cellar. Sammy kept a .22 pistol for the purpose. But, when pressed, the boy's mother usually claimed the Prince of Wales for the honour.

A thick, tasty smell of grease billowed from the warm shop and steam boiled in the yellow light from the street door and from the grating in the pavement under the window where, on gas burners, sat enamel trays of pies, sausages, bacon, faggots, saveloys and baked potatoes, heavy with shining, dancing fat.

72

At his stoves behind the wooden counter stood warm, greasy Sammy. With his thin assistant beside him he gave his attention to a score of long handled frying pans, each of which contained a different kind of food. The shop having just opened for the evening, the only customer was little frightened Mrs Fitzgerald, from round the corner in Portobello Road, getting her husband's dinner. Her shawl was drawn close to her face, but Sammy had noticed what she was hoping to hide. " That's a lovely shiner! " He grinned sympathetically as he wrapped the pies but Mrs Fitzgerald looked as if he had caught her in the act of some mortal sin. Her right eye was swollen green, blue and purple. She gave a barely audible but evidently embarrassed cough. The boy stared neutrally at her bruise. Sammy saw the boy. " Hello, there, nipper! " The colour of his own sausages, his fat, Jewish face ran with sweat. His striped shirt sleeves were rolled to his elbows and he wore a big white grease-spotted apron. " You come to give me a hand have you? " The boy nodded, stepping aside for Mrs Fitzgerald who seized her pies, left the correct number of pennies on the counter, and, like a mouse making for its hole, scuttled from the shop. " Mum says can I stay the night? "

Sammy's expression became serious and he said in a different tone, attending suddenly to his frying pans, " Yes, that's all right. But you gotta work for your keep. Get yourself an apron off the hook, son. We'll be busy in a minute."

The boy removed his threadbare Norfolk and hung it on the hook at the back of the shop. Taking down a sacking apron he pulled it over his head and tied the strings round his waist. He began to roll up his sleeves. Sammy's assistant was a young man of eighteen or so, his face gleaming with large, scarlet pimples. He said, " Go on up the other end. I'll do this end." The boy squeezed past Sammy's great bottom and went to stand near the window where the sizzling trays filled his nostrils full of the stink of frying onions. His eyes wandered past the trays and through the misted glass where they fixed on the street.

It was now dark and populated. Men, women and children came from all sides, bearing down on the pie shop, because it was Friday. They all had the glazed look of the really poor — the poverty trance had overtaken them, robbed them of their

73

wills and their intelligence, enabling them to continue life only in terms of a few simple rituals. There was little animation on even the faces of the children and their tired, heavy movements, their set expressions, their dull eyes made it seem that they all belonged to the same family, so strongly did they resemble one another. The boy felt a shudder of fear and for no reason that he could tell he suddenly thought, with some tenderness, of his mother. He turned to look at the pub on the opposite corner to Sammy's, the Blenheim Arms. The gas was being lit. The large crowd of out-of-work Irishmen and local loafers which had gathered outside its doors gave a ragged cheer. It was opening time.

Again the boy shivered.

"What's the matter, son," said Sammy noticing. "You catching something?"

THE INTERPRETERS

Captain Nye received an order to report to his barracks, the Royal Alberts in Southwark, where his C.O., Colonel Collier, informed him that the Black Flag had been raised in Argyll and that an anarchist army of some 8,000 men was camped in Glen Coe where it would shortly be joined by a force of French Zouaves (about a thousand) which had landed at Oban a week earlier, claiming to be independent volunteers. It was no secret that the French had territorial ambitions in Scotland, but this was the most blatant act of support to the rebel clans they had yet given. It was putting a distinct strain on the fiction of the Entente Cordiale.

"We do not want a direct confrontation with France for all sorts of reasons at the moment." Colonel Collier fingered his buttons and the cuffs of his tunic. "So this must be handled damned delicately, Nye. Neither, it seems, does the present government want any military action against the hill tribes if we can help it. You've had dealings with these people before, I gather?"

"I've some experience of the Highland clans, sir."

"I want you to go and talk to Gareth-mac-Mahon, their chief. He's a sly old devil, by all accounts. Used to serve with one of our native regiments. Learned all our tricks, needless to say, and took 'em back to the hills with him. I'm sure he knows he

75

can't beat us. Probably be satisfied with a few concessions. So find out what he wants and let us know as soon as possible. This is more in the nature of a diplomatic mission than a military one."

" I understand, sir."

" They're plucky blighters, but it looks as if their virtues have turned into vices." Collier stood up behind his desk. " It's the same with their pride. They're prepared to sacrifice all that they've gained under British rule in order to chase this chimera of ' independence '. Even if they should have some success, the French would move in at once. Mahon must realise this. They call him the Red Fox, I gather. Because of his cunning. Well, he's certainly no fool. Try to talk him round."

Captain Nye refused the offer of a squadron of motor escorted cavalry and instead asked for a single small dirigible flying machine which might be loaned by the Royal Airship Corps. " Let us impress them," he said, " with our science rather than our sabres."

Glen Coe was glorious in her autumn colours. Her bronze hills shivered with white streams which fell from scores of sources high up near the crest of the range. The dirigible hovered over the valley and Captain Nye peered through the observation ports in the large aluminium gondola and noticed, with some satisfaction, the consternation of the Zouaves in their blue tarbooshes, blue tunics and baggy red trousers as they became aware of the green and khaki camouflaged monster over their heads. The shadow of the ship moved implacably across the camp, its steam turbines purring as a hungry leopard might purr while stalking a herd of unsuspecting and succulent antelope. Down the glen sailed the aerial frigate, just a few feet above the tops of the tallest hills, following the boisterous river upstream to the falls at the far end of the valley. The bravest of the French mercenaries (if mercenaries they were) took a few pot-shots at the airship, but either they missed, fell short, or their bullets failed to penetrate the tough boron-fibre shell of the vessel.

Then the Zouaves were left behind and Captain Nye signalled to the captain to cut his engines to half-speed, for they were almost at their destination. The main camp lay ahead, a collection of semi-ruined crofts, hide tents, and peat or bracken shelters. They were clustered on the tawny hillside which shone like beaten gold as the sunlight struck it. Horses, tracked vehicles, Bofors guns and Banning cannon, as well as cooking and medical equipment, had been scattered apparently at random amongst the other paraphernalia of the camp. Broadswords, dirks and lances glittered beside pyramids of stacked rifles with fixed bayonets. Kilted clansmen sat talking in groups, passing bottles and cigarettes, or else wandered drunkenly about with no apparent purpose. Over this savage encampment fluttered the sinister black banner of Anarchy — Mahon's adopted standard. Gareth-mac-Mahon's own tent was easily spotted. It was a huge expanse of intricately woven blue, yellow, green and scarlet plaid. The scarlet was predominant. The folds of this great pavilion undulated slightly in a wind which blew through the hills from the west.

" Break out the flag now, sir? " The smart young second officer saluted Nye and the airship's captain, a man named Bastable. Bastable looked enquiringly at Nye. Nye nodded. They watched as the white parley flag billowed over the side, suspended from a line attached to the stern of the control gondola.

" Take her down a couple of degrees, height coxswain," said Captain Bastable.

" Two degrees down, sir."

The ship dropped lower. Its engines reversed to keep it steady against the wind. As it fell, a number of the savages dived for cover while their braver (or drunker) comrades ran forward waving their broadswords and howling like devils. They calmed down when they recognised the white flag, but they did not sheath their swords. They watched with glowering suspicion as the ship steadied less than fifteen feet over the Mahon's own tent. Captain Nye brushed his fine brown moustache with the back of his hand, waited a few moments and then stepped onto the outer gallery and stood with one hand on the rail, the other in a dignified salute of peace, speaking clearly in their own language. " I come to offer peace to the Mahon. To you all." There was a pause while the savages continued to glower and

77

then the flap of the pavilion was pushed back and a heavy Scot-lander emerged. For all his barbaric finery, the Mahon was an impressive man. He was clad in the traditional costume of the hill chieftain: the philabeg kilt, the huge, hairy sporran; the elaborately worked (if rather grubby) lace shirt, the plentitude of little leather straps and buttons and buckles and pins of bronze and silver, the big woollen bonnet secured by a hawk-feather badge; the green coatee with silver epaulettes; the black, buckled shoes; the clan plaid flung over his shoulder — the regalia befitting a great clain leader. All the cloth he wore, save for the coat and shirt, including the decorative tops of his green cross-gartered stockings, was of the same tartan as the tent. Nye recognised it as the red Mahon Fighting sett. The Mahon himself was short and broad-shouldered, with a red, belligerent face. He had a hooked nose, pale, piercing blue eyes and a monstrous grey-streaked red beard. With one hand on the hilt of his heavy, basket-hilted broadsword and the other on his hip he raised his head slowly, calling out in a proud growl.

"The Mahon acknowledges your truce flag. Do you come to parley?"

Although the Red Fox revealed nothing by his expression, Captain Nye was sure he was properly impressed by the aerial frigate. "My government wants to preserve peace, O Mahon," he said in English. "May I descend to the ground?"

"If ye wish." Gareth-mac-Mahon replied in the same language.

At Captain Nye's request, the rail was broken and a rope ladder rolled through the gap. Nye went down the ladder with as much dignity as was possible until he stood confronting the wily old hill fox. This was a man who had discovered the creed of anarchism while serving as a soldier in the capitals of the civilised world. He had brought the creed back to his native land, adapted it and turned it into a philosophy capable of bring-ing together all the previously disunited tribes. Nye was by no means deceived by the Mahon's appearance. He was well aware that he was not addressing a simple savage. If he had known nothing at all about the Mahon, he would still have recognised the look of profound cunning which glinted even now in those pale eyes.

78

" O Chieftain," began the captain in Scottish as soon as he had recovered his breath, " you have made the great Chief-of-us-All sad. I come to tell you this. He wonders why his children gather all these weapons to themselves." He spread his arms to indicate the camp. "And give hospitality to soldiers from other shores."

In the distance the autumn river roared down the narrow gorge, its flow altering constantly as it was fed by a thousand tiny streams which streaked the hills; white veins in yellow marble. Throughout the half mile radius of the camp the savage warriors stood and looked as their leader talked with the soldier who had come from the sky. Each of the men had a naked sword in his hand and Nye knew that if he made one mistake he would never be able to reach the airship before he was slaughtered beneath those shining blades.

The Red Fox's smile was grim and his eyes were like polished granite. " His Majesty will be sadder still, O Emissary, when he learns we intend to make war on those of his soldiers who are living in our land, that we intend to slay those of our own folk who are foolish enough to side with the soldiers. We have already razed Fort William IV."

" The Chief-of-us-All should punish you for that," said the captain, " but he is slow to anger. He understands that his children have been misled by the honeyed tongues of men from across the seas. Men who would make his children fight their battles for them."

The Mahon rubbed his nose with a large hand and looked amused. " Tell His Majesty that we are not his children. We are mountain warriors. We shall preserve our ancient ways. We would rather die than become the subject race of any foreigner."

" But what of your women? Your sons and your daughters? Do they wish to see their menfolk die? Will they be happy if the schools, the doctors, the medicines — aye and the merchants who buy their wares — disappear from this land? "

" We'll provide our own schools and doctors — and we'll have no more merchants ever again in the mountains of Argyll! "

Captain Nye smiled at the idea and was about to reply when he noticed a movement of the tent flap behind the Mahon.

A tall figure emerged to stand at the chief's side. He wore a

suit of heather-mixture tweeds. A shooting hat was pulled down
to shade his face, a monocle gleamed in his right eye. From his
mouth jutted a black cheroot. " I'm afraid you'll have no luck
with that argument, captain. The chief here has already decided
that the advantages of British rule are outweighed by the dis-
advantages."

For all the evidence of his eyes and ears, Captain Nye could
hardly believe that this was an Englishman. A renegade. He
tried to hide his astonishment. " Who the devil are you, sir? "

" Just an observer, old chap. And an advisor, of sorts, I
suppose." The man paused, his attention given to the faint humming which filled the air, drowning, eventually, the sound of the
water. He smiled.

" This is Mr Cornelius," said the Mahon. " He has helped
us with our fleet. Here it comes now." The hill chieftain pointed
behind Nye. The captain turned to look.

Over the brow of the farthest hills came swimming upwards
of a hundred massive aerial men-o'-war. They were airships of
a type far in advance of anything Nye had seen before. They
bristled with artillery gondoli. Their slender cigar-shaped hulls
were like the bodies of gigantic sharks. On each silver-grey side,
on each elevator fin was painted a livery which combined the
black flag of Anarchy and the blue cross of Scotland.

" Cornelius . . .? " Nye looked back towards the tent but the
tall man had gone inside. The Red Fox chuckled. "An engineer,
I believe," he said, " of some experience." He broke into English.
" Perhaps we shall meet again in Whitehall, will we not, Master
Emissary? "

" I'll be damned! "

Nye turned again to look at the massive battle fleet cramming
the sky, to notice the power of the guns, to speculate upon the
destruction they and the aerial torpedoes could accomplish. " I'm
dreaming."

" D'ye think so ? "

THE EXPLORERS

Catherine Cornelius left her brother's lodgings in Powys Square. She hurried back through the dark streets to her own house where she had heard Prinz Lobkowitz and his friends awaited her. One or two gaslamps glowed through the clinging fog but cast little light. There were a few muffled sounds, but she could identify none of them. It was with relief that she entered Elgin Crescent with its big overgrown trees and its tall comfortable houses; perhaps because the street was so familiar the fog did not seem so thick, though she still had to walk with some care until she reached Number 61. Shivering, she unlatched the gate and at last mounted her own steps, searching in her Dorothy bag for her key. She found it, unlocked the door and went inside. Fog drifted in with her. It filled the cold and gloomy hall like ectoplasm. Without taking off her coat she crossed the hall and opened the door to the drawing room. The drawing room was painted in a mixture of yellow and pale brown. She noticed that the fire was almost out. Removing her gloves she reached down and put several pieces of coal on top of the red cinders, then she turned and acknowledged the company. There were two others beside Prinz Lobkowitz; a man and a woman.

"These are the guests I mentioned," explained the Prinz softly. "I'm sorry about the fire." He indicated the woman. "Miss Brunner"—and the man—"Mr Smiles"—and sat down in the horseshoe armchair nearest the grate, one booted foot on the brass rail.

Catherine Cornelius looked shyly at Miss Brunner and then became wary. Foxy, she thought. Miss Brunner had neat red hair and sharp, beautiful features. She wore a well-cut grey travelling cape and a small pill-box hat perched over her right eye, decorated with a green feather, a tiny veil. Her clothes were buttoned as tightly as the black boots she revealed when seating herself on the arm of Prinz Lobkowitz's chair. Mr Smiles, bald-headed and large in a dark brown ulster, a long scarf wound several times round his neck, cleared his throat, fingered his mutton-chop whiskers as if they were not his own, unbuttoned the ulster and felt in the watch-pocket of his waistcoat, producing a gold half-hunter. He peered at it for a while before he began to wind it. " What's the time? My watch has stopped."

" Time? " Catherine Cornelius stared around the room in search of a clock that was going. There was a black marble one on the mantle, a grandfather in the corner.

" Nine twenty six," said Miss Brunner, referring to the plain silver pendant watch she wore about her neck. " Where are our rooms, my dear? And when shall we expect supper? "

Catherine passed her hand over her forehead and said vaguely, " Soon. I must apologise. My brother gave me very little warning, I'm afraid. The preparations. Excuse me. I'm sorry." And she left the room, hearing Miss Brunner say, " Well, it's a change from Calcutta."

Catherine found Mary Greasby, the maid-of-all-work, in the kitchen enjoying a glass of madeira with cook. Catherine gave instructions for beds and supper to be prepared. These instructions were received with poor grace by the servants. She returned to the drawing room with a tray on which were glasses and decanters of whisky, sherry and what remained of the madeira.

Mr Smiles stood with his back to the grate. The fire now blazed merrily. "Ah, splendid," he said, stepping forward and taking the tray from her. " You must forgive our manners, dear lady. We have been travelling in a rough and ready way in some rather remote parts of the world. Just the thing. We were reluctant to impose, but — well, fugitives, you know, fugitives.

Ha ha! " He poured whiskies for all save Catherine who raised her hand to decline.

" How is your dear brother, Miss Cornelius? " The red-headed woman's tone was patronising. " We have missed him so much while we have been abroad."

" He is well, I think," replied Catherine. " I thank you."

" You are very alike. Are they not, Mr Smiles? "

" Very."

" So I believe," said Catherine.

" Very alike." Reflectively Miss Brunner lowered her eyelids and sipped her drink. Catherine shivered and sat down on a hard chair near the piano.

"And how is old Frank," said Mr Smiles. " Eh? We've had some exciting times together, he and I. How is he? "

" I am sorry to say I have not seen him recently, Mr Smiles. He writes to Mother. The occasional postcard, you know."

" Like me, young Frank. Bit of a globe-trotter."

" Yes."

Prinz Lobkowitz rose. " I must be going, Catherine. It isn't very wise of me to stay here, considering the opinion the police hold of me at the moment. Perhaps we'll meet at the conference."

" Shall you find a cab at this time of night? If you would care to stay —"

" I dare say I'll find one. It's a long way back to Stepney. But I thank you for the offer." He bowed to Miss Brunner and kissed her hand. He shook hands with Mr Smiles. " Goodbye. I hope your stay is peaceful." He laughed. " For you if not for them! " Catherine helped him on with his old-fashioned Armenian cloak and saw him to the front door. He bent down and kissed her on the cheek.

" Keep your spirits up, *petite Katerina*. We are sorry to make use of your house like this, but there wasn't much choice. Your brother — give him my regards. We'll probably meet soon, tell him. In Berlin, perhaps. Or at the conference? "

" I think not the conference." Catherine hugged him. " Be careful, my dear, my own dear Prinz Lobkowitz."

He opened the door and drew his muffler about his mouth and chin as the fog surged in. He fitted his tall hat on his head. There came the sound of horses' hoofs on the road outside. "A cab."

Gently he squeezed her arm and then ran into the cold darkness. Catherine closed the door and started as the maid spoke from where she stood halfway up the stairs.

" Is it just the three of you now, mum? "

Miss Brunner appeared in the drawing room doorway. Her face seemed flushed, perhaps by the alcohol. She offered Catherine a look of considerable intimacy. " Oh, I think so," she said, " don't you? " She smoothed her red hair back, then she smoothed her straight flannel skirt over her thighs and pelvis. She stretched out and took Catherine's hand, leading her back into the room. Mr Smiles stood by the piano glancing through a Mozart Sonata.

" Do you play, Miss Cornelius? "

REMINISCENCE (C)

Someone singing

LATE NEWS

Two young boys who disappeared from Ballinkinrain approved school near Balfron, Stirlingshire, a month ago were found dead last night at the bottom of a gorge in the Frinty Hills, two miles from the school. The bodies of John Mulver, aged 10, of Balornock, Glasgow, and Ian Finlay, aged 9, of Raploch, Stirling, were found by a search party of police and civilians who have been combing the area for the past month.

GUARDIAN, April 13 1970

Two boys aged 15 and 9 were killed in Dacca today in the latest of a series of bombing incidents. A home-made bomb buried under rubbish in front of Pakistan's council building exploded. A man who was injured was seen riding frantically from the scene on his bicycle.

GUARDIAN, May 12 1970

A three-year-old boy found dead in a disused refrigerator in the garden of his home in Somerset was yesterday named as Peter Wilson, of Hillside Gardens, Yatton. It is understood the refrigerator was self-locking. Eight weeks ago three-year-old twins, Lynn and Caroline Woods, died of suffocation in a disused refrigerator in their home at Farley, near Thames Ditton.

GUARDIAN, June 2 1970

86

Paul Monks, aged 14, was found dead yesterday after an explosion in a wood near his home at High Street, Dawick, near Buckingham. The boy was seen on Sunday night with what appeared to be an unexploded mortar bomb.

GUARDIAN, June 2 1970

Four people were killed and six injured when a van and two cars collided at Wroot, Lincolnshire, yesterday. Two of the dead were children.

GUARDIAN, June 29 1970

An inquest was opened yesterday into the death at Eton of Martin Earnshaw, aged 14, son of Lady Tyneford and Mr Christopher Earnshaw. The boy was found hanging in his room at the school in the morning . . . Mr Anthony Chenevix-Trench, headmaster of Eton, had said earlier that Martin was extremely popular. " During the last few days he had been sent three times to me to be commended for his good efforts. We cannot account for this tragedy."

GUARDIAN, December 6 1969

The Alternative Apocalypse 3

Jerry turned the corner from Elgin Crescent into Ladbroke Grove. He saw that the ragpickers were still out. They had been working through the night, using stolen hurricane lamps, shuffling in and out of the huge banks of garbage lining both sides of the street. Here and there among the plastic bags and the piles of cans a discreet fire was smoldering.

Jerry made his way down the centre of the road, listening to the sly sounds, the secret scufflings of the people of the heaps, until at last he reached the corner of Blenheim Crescent and realised with a shock that the Convent of the Poor Clares was down. His headquarters lay in ruins. The walls had been demolished, as had most of the buildings. Bricks and rubble had been cleared neatly into piles, but for some reason a few of the trees had been preserved, protected by new white fences — an oak and two black, twisted, stunted elms. The rest of the trees had been sawn down and stacked in a pile in the centre of the site. The best part of the original chapel and the administration wing attached to it, on the Westbourne Park Road side, were still standing. The machinery of demolition was parked here and there: trucks and earth-movers cloaked in dark canvas glistening with drizzle. Jerry climbed over the rubble and plodded through the thick mud until he stood under the nearest elm. He reached up and touched the lowest of the gnarled branches; he kicked at the stake fence. It quivered. He stumbled up a pile of bricks and masonry and got through a gap in the chapel wall. Fragments of stained glass clung to lead frames. The pews had been torn up and scattered, the altar had been ripped out, the electrical wiring had been pulled down and everything was covered with plaster and white dust. High up, the light fell through the ruined roof onto a crude painting of the resurrection, its lurid greens, yellows and reds already faded by the action of the rain and the wind. On all the walls were patches the size and shape of the devotional pictures which had hung there. He walked into the administration wing; the first two floors of this had hardly been touched as yet. He noticed small piles of human shit in some of the empty rooms. In the Mother Superior's office, which had been his office, too, he saw the white outline of the big cross which had hung there when he had last visited the convent. All furnishings, with the exception of two sodden mattresses in one room, had been carried off; his friends, his employees, his pets had gone.

As the light improved he moved through the wreckage, picking up small things. A triangle of green stained glass, a fragment of wood from a pew, the bulb holder from a light fixture, a hook on which the nuns had once hung their habits, a key from a cupboard, a 1959 penny left on the floor of the chapel, a nail which had secured part of the large cross to the wall. He put them in the pockets of his black car coat. A few relics.

Then he climbed out the way he had come, trudging back to the road and noticing that his heavy Fry boots were coated with mud and shit.

On the other side of the garbage heap he heard the note of a taxi's engine. He clambered quickly over the refuse, waving urgently at the cab. Rather reluctantly it stopped and let him get in.

" The airport," he said.

As he had often suspected, the end had come quietly and the breakdown had been by slow degrees. In fact the breakdown was still going on. Superficially there was nothing urgent about it. As the weeks passed and communications and services slowly worsened, there always seemed to be a chance that things might improve. He knew they could not improve.

He remembered his old friend Professor Hira (who now some-times called himself Hythloday) escorting him through the chaos of Calcutta and saying " There *is* order in all this, though it's not as detailed as we're used to, I suppose. All human affairs can be seen as following certain basic patterns. The breakdown of a previous kind of social order does not mean that society itself has broken down — it is merely following different forms of order. The ritual remains."

The cab-driver glanced nervously at the rag-pickers. Some of them seemed to be eyeing the taxi as though it were an especially fine piece of carrion. The driver speeded up as much as he dared, for there was only room for a single line of traffic on what was still, officially, a two-way road.

Jerry stared reflectively at the shit on his boots.

The Alternative Apocalypse 4

You got to believe in something. You can't get excited about nothing, Colonel Cornelius, said Shakey Mo.

The four of them were squeezed into the cabin of a 1917 Austin-Putilov half-tracked armoured car. Beesley was driving while Cornelius, Shakey Mo Collier and Karen von Krupp manned the machine guns. The car was travelling slowly over the stony countryside of West Cornwall. In the distance a farm-house was burning. They were trying to reach St Michael's Mount, a fortified islet about ten miles down the South Coast, opposite the town of Marazion. Beesley believed he would find friends there.

Cornelius tried to make himself more comfortable on the pressed steel saddle seat, but failed. They went over a bump and everyone clung on to the hand-grips. It was very hot inside the half-track, even though they had lifted up the lid of the conning tower for ventilation. The original crews had worn gas-masks.

You're probably right, said Cornelius.

He saw a few figures, armed with rifles, move along the crest of the hill where the farmhouse burned. They didn't seem to offer a threat, but he kept his eye on them. His machine-gun was inclined to jam. He took out his Smith and Wesson .45 revolver, retrieved, like the rest of their equipment, from the

Imperial War Museum, and checked it over. There was nothing wrong with that.

He was worrying about his wife and children. It was years since he had last remembered them: There was a list in his mind:

One Woman

One Boy

One Girl

A woman had recently slashed her wrists in Ladbroke Grove after gassing her little boy and girl. All were dead. There was no reason why it should be his particular relatives. But there had been something about a Noël Coward and Gertrude Lawrence record on the gramophone and it seemed to him to be a clue to something even more familiar. He wiped the grime and the sweat from his face and glanced across the cabin to the opposite position. Karen von Krupp, her skirt hitched up, straddled her seat looking at him, her back to her gun. She was so old. He admired her stamina.

Whoever suggested the Highlands as a safe retreat was a fool, said Bishop Beesley, not for the first time. Those Scotchmen are barbarians. I said the Scilly Isles was a better bet and now we've wasted three months and nearly lost our lives a dozen times over.

The half-track droned on.

I think I can see the sea, said Karen von Krupp.

Jerry wondered how he had come to throw in with these three.

It's getting dark, said Mo Collier. He climbed out of his seat and stretched, making the stick-bombs at his belt rattle. What about making camp?

Let's wait until we reach the coast road, if it's still there, said Bishop Beesley. He looked over his shoulder, straight into Jerry's eyes. He smirked. Now what's wrong with you? Can guilt be anything more than a literary conceit, Mr Cornelius? He uttered a suggestive chuckle. What truly evil person ever feels guilty? You might almost argue that evil-doing is an honest reaction against that sham we call 'guilt'. Repentance is, of course, a rather different kettle of fish. He returned his attention to his steering.

Jerry considered shooting him and then seeing what happened

92

to the half-track without a driver. The bishop was always trans-
ferring his own problems onto others and Jerry seemed his
favourite target.

Speak for yourself, he said. I've never understood you, Bishop
Beesley.

Mo sniffed. You sound as bored as me, colonel. I could do
with some action, I don't know about you.

It's freezing. Karen von Krupp drew up the collar of her dirty
sheepskin jacket. Could we have the tower closed now?

No, said Bishop Beesley. It would be suicide with our exhaust
in the condition it is.

Karen von Krupp said sulkily: I'm not sure I believe you.

Anyway, it's still quite warm. Shakey Mo was conciliatory.
Chin up, Frau Doktor. He grinned to himself and began to move
his machine gun about in its slit. Brrrrr. Brrrrr. We might just
as well've come on bikes, the chances we've had to use these.

Portsmouth wasn't enough for you, eh? said Karen von Krupp
bitterly.

Mine was the only bloody gun working, Collier pointed out.
I maintain my equipment. All the others jammed after a couple
of bursts.

We were nearly killed, she said. She glanced accusingly at
Jerry. I thought that Field-Marshal Nye was a friend of yours.

Jerry shrugged. He's got his duty to do just like me.

Law and Order freak, explained Collier, lighting a Players.
Groovy. I wish we had some music.

An explosion rocked the car and the engine whined miserably.

Bloody hell! yelled Collier in relief. Mines!

93

LATE NEWS

A 14-year-old boy died after falling 60ft from the roof of a block of shops near his home in Liverpool on Saturday night. He was William Brown of Shamrock Road, Port Sunlight.

GUARDIAN, December 29 1969

A boy of 13 was remanded in custody until February 16 at Ormskirk, Lancashire, yesterday accused of the murder of Julie Mary Bradshaw, aged 10, of Skelmersdale. The girl's body was found on Monday night in the loft of a house.

GUARDIAN, February 11 1969

A boy aged 12 found murdered on a golf course at Bristol yesterday was killed by four or five savage blows on the head it was said after a post mortem last night. The blows could have been made with a tree branch, said police. Martin Thorpe, of Rye Road, Fulton, had gone to Shirehampton golf course to search for golf balls.

GUARDIAN, April 2 1970

A schoolgirl was killed and five other children and three adults wounded when Arab guerillas fired Russian-made Katyusha rockets into the Northern Israeli town of Beison yesterday. Three of the rockets fell in the playground of the school. Two of the injured children were in a serious condition.

GUARDIAN, April 2 1970

Schoolboy Michael Kenan, aged 12, was drowned in a reservoir at Durford, near Chelmsford, Essex, yesterday while bird nesting with friends.

DAILY EXPRESS, June 8 1970

Police tightened security in Warsaw yesterday as a curfew was again clamped on the port of Szezecin, the scene of violent street fighting on Thursday . . . A Swedish radio reporter, Mr Anders Tunborg, said, " The tanks repeatedly charged the crowds who sprang out of the way to avoid being run down. A mother and her young daughter did not get out of the way in time and an onrushing tank hit them both. A young soldier stood watching nearby and crying."

THE SCOTSMAN, December 19 1970

REMINISCENCE (D)

You are killing your children

THE LOVERS

With her chemise pulled up to her navel, Una Persson pressed her slim self to Catherine Cornelius who lay beneath her. Catherine's clothes were neatly folded on the stool near the dressing table. Una Persson's summer shirtwaist frock, stockings, drawers and corsets were scattered on the carpet. The bedroom needed painting. It was a bright summer afternoon. Sunlight crept through the tatttered net and the dusty glass of the windows.

With passion Una said:

" My own dear love. My darling sweet."

And Catherine replied:

" Dear, dear Una."

She arched her perfect back, quivering. Grasping her buttocks, Una kissed her roundly in the mouth.

" Love! "

Una gave a long, delicious grunt.

" Oh! "

" Una! Una! "

Later the door rattled.

In stepped Miss Brunner, trim and prim.

"All girls together." She laughed harshly. She made no apology because it was obvious she relished interrupting and embarrassing them. " We must be about our business soon. This place needs a tidy."

Una rolled clear, directing a muted glare at Miss Brunner who was crisp in linen and lace, like an ultra-fashionable bicyclette.

"The new chambermaid's arrived," said Miss Brunner. She began to fold Una Persson's dress. "She wants to clean in here."

Catherine was puzzled. "There's no need . . ."

"Come now," said Miss Brunner, flinging open the door, "we mustn't let ourselves go." She revealed the maid, a huge, red figure in a green baize overall and a sloppy cap, a bucket in one hand, a mop in the other. Her hair hung down her face. "This is Mrs 'Vaizey'."

Una pulled up the sheets.

"Oh, my gawd! " said the cleaner, recognising her daughter.

Catherine turned over.

Mrs 'Vaizey' gestured with the mop and bucket. She was miserably upset. She looked ashamed of herself. "This is on'y temp'ry, Caff," she said. She looked wretchedly at Miss Brunner, who was smiling privately. 'Could I — ? " Then she realised that Miss Brunner had known all along that her name hadn't been Vaizey (one of her post-Cornelian husbands) and, more-over, that Miss Brunner had known Catherine was her daughter.

Mrs Cornelius sighed. "You bloody cow," she said to Miss Brunner. She glanced at the pair in the bed. "Wot yer up ter? " She remembered how she had looked like Catherine once. She recalled the money she might have had if she had not been so generous, so soft. Her heart went out to her daughter then. She dumped the mop into the bucket of water, pointing the handle at Miss Brunner. "You watch this one, love," she said to Una Persson, since only Una Persson was now visible above the bed clothes. "She'll 'ave yer fer sure if she gets a chance."

"You're not being paid for cheek, you know," Miss Brunner replied somewhat feebly, striding towards the door, "but to clean the rooms. Your type, Mrs 'Vaizey', are ten a penny, as I'm sure you know. If you're not happy with the position . . ."

"Don't come it wiv me, love." Mrs Cornelius began to splash about the linoleum with her mop. "Not everybody'll work in a third-rate whorehouse, neither! " Her anger grew and she became proud. "Fuck it." She picked up the bucket and threw the contents over Miss Brunner. As the starch ran out, the linen and the lace sagged and the Lily Langtry wave fell apart over her forehead.

Una grinned, sitting up with interest.

Miss Brunner hissed, clenched her hands, began to move with staring eyes upon Mrs Cornelius, who returned the stare with dignity so that Miss Brunner paused dripping.

" Yore nuffink, yer silly little tart. I've 'ad too much. Caff! " Catherine peered out from the bed.

" You comin', Caff? "

Catherine shook her head. " I can't, mum."

" Jest as yer like."

Una Persson said: " I'll look after her, Mrs Cornelius."

Mrs. Cornelius removed her cap and apron and threw them at Miss Brunner's feet. " I'm sure yer'll do yer best, love," she said softly. " Don't let Modom 'ere shove yer abaht! "

Miss Brunner seemed paralysed. Hands on fat hips, Mrs Cornelius appeared to grow in stature as she waltzed around the drenched figure. " I know yer! I know yer! " she chanted. " I know yer! I know yer! Ya ya ya! "

" Everything all right at home, mum? " said Catherine desperately.

" Not bad." Mrs Cornelius was pleased with herself, although later she might regret this action. She'd taken the joB because of the boy, after she and Sammy had had words. But tonight it would be feathers and frills again and a trip to the Cremorne Gardens. Her right hand swept down on Miss Brunner's sodden and corsetted rump. There was a loud bang as flesh struck whalebone. Still Miss Brunner did not move. Mrs Cornelius giggled. " Don't let 'er wear yer aht." She circled Miss Brunner once more and then waved at her from the door. " Ta, ta, Lady Muck."

In terror, Catherine murmured to her mother. " See you soon."

" Keep yerself clean and yer carn't go wrong," advised Mrs Cornelius as she closed the door. The last Catherine saw was her leering wink.

Miss Brunner came alive with a snort. " Dreadful woman. I was forced to sack her. I'll get changed. Can you two be ready by the time I've finished? "

Una was amused by Miss Brunner's attitude. " This is a farce. Whom are we to entertain this evening? "

" Prinz Lobkowitz and his friends will arrive at six."

" Oh," said Catherine, reminiscently.

" Silly creatures," said Miss Brunner.

Una Persson raised her lovely eyebrows. "Aha."

" Our success depends on tonight's meeting," Miss Brunner said as she left. The door slammed.

Una stroked Catherine's thigh beneath the sheet. " I wonder if this is the ' big meeting '? "

Catherine shook her golden head. " That isn't for a while."

" For all we know it's already happened. And what comes after the meeting? This identity's getting me down. Not enough information. Do you ever think about the nature of Time? "

" Of course." Catherine twisted so that she could place her delicate lips on Una Persson's flat stomach and at the same time her hand rose lightly to touch her friend's clitoris. Una sighed with pleasure. From where she lay she could see the abandoned mop, the fallen bucket, the apron and the cap. " Your mother has spirit. I hadn't expected that."

" Neither had I." Catherine's tongue fluttered like a trapped butterfly, the pressure of her hand increased. Una made a noise.

" I was terrified of them both," said Catherine. " I still am."

" Forget it."

Una gave a coarse, satisfied grunt.

" Good? " whispered Catherine Cornelius.

THE BUSINESSMEN

"Molly O'Morgan with her little organ
Was dressed up in colours so gay,
Out in the street every day,
Playing too-ra-la-oor-a-li-oor-a-li-ay.
Fellows who met her will never forget her,
She set all their heads in a whirl.
Molly O'Morgan with her little organ
The Irish-Aye-talian girl!"

sang Major Nye, twirling his splendid moustache and swirling
his huge, tartan ulster as he strode over the moor with Sebastian
Auchinek in tow. Auchinek was miserable and sought desperately about him for some sign of human habitation, preferably
an inn. But there was none; just grass and gorse and boulders,
the occasional bird and a few shy sheep. If Major Nye had not
been the largest shareholder in a chain of well-appointed pro-
vincial halls, Auchinek would have complained. But he had to
get Una a good year's bookings, at least thirty weeks, outside
London (for as he predicted they had closed the London halls),
if he was going to make it up to her for the disappointment she
must feel at losing the Empire.

"One of Ella Retford's," explained Major Nye, pausing in his
stride and looking with relish at the dark green Exmoor heather.

" Has your girlie got anything like that? "

" Better," said Auchinek automatically, staring at the vast moor with disgust and resignation. " She has the real quality, major." He whistled a complicated melody. " That's one of hers. *Waiters get me going.*"

" It will mean a trip to London for me," Major Nye said, stalking on. "And London's not the safest place in the world these days, is it? "

" No really exciting place is, major."

" I heartily dislike London, Mr Auchinek."

" Oh, well — yes, I suppose so." Uncertainly, Auchinek watched a large bird flap into the sky. Major Nye lifted his ashplant and pretended to sight down it at the bird.

" Bang! " said the major.

" Well," he continued, " I have, as a matter of fact, got to be in London on some pretty important business fairly shortly. Not quite certain of the date, but ask my office. They'll keep you posted."

"And you'll give her an audition."

" That was the idea, old boy. If I've time. By the way, what is the time? "

Auchinek stared at him in surprise.

Major Nye shrugged. The sky was deep blue, bland and warm. " I'm kept pretty busy," he said. " What with one thing and another."

" You have many interests," Auchinek said admiringly.

" Oh, many. I play," the major laughed, " a wide variety of parts, you might say." He put a hand to the knot of his Ascot cravat. " But then we all do, really . . ." His moustache tilted upwards on the right side as he gave a mysterious smile. Auchinek determined to get himself a suit of solid tweed, like the major's, and a good ulster, and aim towards the acquisition of a small estate somewhere in Somerset or Devon. He hated the country, but these days there was hardly any choice. They came to a hill overlooking the winding white road to Porlock. Beyond the road lay the sparkling sea. On the dusty, unpaved road a carriage, drawn by two pairs of bays, was struggling, making poor time. The carriage was old and much in need of an overhaul.

102

Major Nye leaned on his ashplant and stared in amusement as the carriage slowly climbed the hill. " Could this be the vicar on his way to see me? He travels in style, our vicar. Used to ride. One of the best hunting men in these parts. He fell off his horse, though. Ha, ha."

A white head appeared at the window and a pale hand hailed the couple. " Major! Major! "

" Vicar! Top o' the morning to ye! "

" Your son, major, have you heard? "

" What about the young rip? " Major Nye smiled at Auchinek. " He's in the army, you know."

" Captured, major. A prisoner-of-war."

" What? The eldest boy? "

" Yes, major. I have the telegram here. I was in town when it arrived. I told them I'd deliver it."

Auchinek knew that his luck hadn't changed yet. He sighed. He had picked a bad time to see Major Nye.

"Armoured steamrollers of some kind," continued the vicar, growing hoarse, "broke their lines and cut them off. Almost all were killed. He fought bravely. It will be in tomorrow's press."

" The devil! "

" He's wound-ay-ed! " The vicar's voice cracked completely as the carriage hit a rock and bounced. His coachman shouted at the horses.

" You'll be returning to London on the seven-twenty won't you, Mr Auchinek? " said Major Nye.

" Well . . ." Auchinek had hoped to be invited for the night. " If that's the most convenient train."

" I'll come with you. Quickly, get a hold on those leading horses and make 'em move. We'll take the vicar's carriage back to the house and I'll just have time to pack a bag."

" In what engagement was your son captured? " Auchinek asked as they clambered down the hill towards the road.

" Damn! " said Major Nye, catching his sock on a piece of gorse and stopping to free himself. " Regiment? 18th Lancers, of course."

" Engagement? "

" What? My boy? Never! "

THE ENVOYS

Prinz Lobkowitz was almost sure that he had been followed all afternoon by a police agent. He hoped that he was wrong. He glanced at his watch, waiting outside the remaining gate to Buckingham Palace. He looked out of the corners of his eyes to see if he could recognise the agent; surreptitiously he inspected each of the passers by (there were few) but none was familiar. He turned to inspect the palace. It had been boarded up for a year now, but there were still redcoated and bearskinned Guardsmen standing in sentry boxes at various points. This had seemed as good a place as any to meet the other envoy. And surely it must be some of the most neutral soil in the world at the present moment. The watch, a Swiss hunter with an alpine scene decorating the inner case, was a gift from Miss Brunner. He had never been able to find the catch. As soon as the big meeting was over, he thought, he'd buy himself a twenty-four-hour digital wrist-watch of the kind the French were now making. He loved gadgets. It was what had led him into politics, after all.

The other envoy was late.

Prinz Lobkowitz took a rolled copy of *The Humorist* (' Typically British, but not old-fashioned ') from his Prince Albert frockcoat pocket and began to study it intently, displaying the cover which sported a Bonzo dog cartoon. This had been arranged earlier and the specific issue of the specific magazine agreed upon. Prinz Lobkowitz was fond of *The Humorist*. Already he was becoming absorbed in it, smiling involuntarily at the jokes.

A few moments later a distinguished middle-aged man of military bearing bumped into Lobkowitz and pretended to recognise him. In slightly accented English he cried with delight: " Good heavens! Why, it's old Henry, isn't it? "

For a second or two Lobkowitz feigned puzzlement. Then he said: " Could you be George? "

" That's right! Spiffin', seeing you again! "

Lobkowitz frowned as he tried to recall his lines. A little reluctantly he rolled up his magazine and replaced it in his pocket where it made a noticeable bulge in the line of the overcoat. " Come and have a drink, old boy." Lobkowitz clapped the man on the shoulder. " We've a lot to talk about."

" Yes, indeed! "

As they crossed the road and entered St James's Park, which was filled with the noise of a dozen different calliopes from the nearby fairground, a man said softly: " I am Colonel Pyat, our Embassy sent me."

"And I'm Prinz Lobkowitz, representing the exiles. I hope this will be a fruitful meeting at long last."

" I think it might be."

They had reached the fairground which occupied both sides of the ornamental lake. Bunting and banners and candy-striped canvas, brass and steel and luridly painted wood, moved round and round and up and down as the people screamed or giggled or laughed aloud.

Pyat stopped at a stall on which sat a miserable monkey tended by an old Italian in a stovepipe hat. The Italian grinned and offered to sell Pyat an icecream. Pyat reached out his hand and stroked the monkey as if looking for fleas, yet the touch was tender. He shook his head and moved on. " Icecream! " shouted the Italian, as if Pyat had forgotten something. " Icecream! "

In his frock coat and top hat, Pyat moved with dignity away.

" Icecream? " said the Italian to Lobkowitz who was a few paces behind Pyat. Lobkowitz shook his head. Pyat spoke over his shoulder. "Any news of Cornelius? "

"Jeremiah, you mean? "

"Yes."

"None. He seems to have vanished completely."

"Perhaps it's for the best. Yes? "

"His insight's useful."

"But he could foul things up. And we don't need that at present, with the big meeting coming along."

"No."

Under the low-hanging willows, where young prostitutes showed off their soft, painted flesh, they went, through the happy crowds, between the merry-go-rounds, the swing-boats and the helter-skelters.

"How jolly the peasants are," said Pyat in an attempt at irony which somehow failed. "Alas! regardless of their doom, the little victims play."

"Were you at Eton? So was I," said Lobkowitz grinning back at a cheeky girl. "Don't you enjoy fairs? "

"I've hardly ever seen one of this kind. In Finland once. With the gypsies, you know. Yes. Near Rouveniemi, I think. In Spring. I didn't attend. But I remember seeing the gypsy women by the river, breaking the Spring ice to wash their clothes. The sideshows were very similar, though there was more wood and less metal. Bright colours." Colonel Pyat smiled.

"When were you last in Finland? " Lobkowitz avoided the guy rope of a sideshow tent. He took a deep breath of the air which was heavy with motor oil, candy floss and animal manure.

Colonel Pyat shrugged and waved his hands. "When there was last a Finland." He smiled again, more openly. "I used to like Finland. Such a simple nation."

An old woman selling lavender appeared. She wore a bright red shawl which clashed with her flowers. She whined pathetically at them, holding out her sprigs. "Please, sir. Please, sir." She nodded her head as if she hoped, by sympathetic magic, to make them nod back. "Lucky, sir. Sweet lavender, sir. Please buy some, sir."

Pyat was the first to reach into his trouser pocket and pull out a half-crown. He handed it to her, receiving the sprig in return. Its stem was wrapped in silver paper. Lobkowitz gave her two shillings and received a similar piece. The woman tucked the money away in the folds of her thick, dirty skirt. 'Thank you, gentlemen."

The lavender forgotten in their right hands, they walked on.

" But you people had to take Finland out," said Lobkowitz.

" Yes." Pyat raised his hand to his face and noticed the lavender there. He began to adjust it in his buttonhole. " It was a question of widening the available coasts."

" Expediency." Lobkowitz frowned.

" Does anyone act for another reason? Come now, Prinz Lobkowitz. Shall we confine ourselves to schoolboy moralising? Or shall we discuss the real business at hand? "

" Perhaps that, too, involves schoolboy morals? " Lobkowitz flung his lavender from him. It fell into the mud near the water's edge.

Colonel Pyat said sympathetically, " Forgive me. I know . . . I know —" He gave up.

A crowd of urchins ran past them shouting. One of the urchins gave Lobkowitz a brief, piercing glance before running on. Lobkowitz frowned and felt over his pockets to see if he had been robbed. But everything was there, including *The Humorist.*

They mounted a boardwalk which led through the mud to the jetty which stretched out into the lake. There were two couples on the jetty. They stopped.

" The sides change," said Prinz Lobkowitz. They stood side by side watching the ducks and flamingoes. On the opposite bank promenaded a score of belles in pretty dresses, arms linked with a score of beaux, dressed to the nines, their curly-brimmed bowlers tilted at exaggerated angles. A hurdy-gurdy played sentimental tunes. a bear danced. A punt passed.

They could see the shell of Buckingham Palace outlined against the evening sky in the west and, to the east, the shell of the Treasury Garrison, bristling with big naval guns.

" It's growing colder," said Colonel Pyat, adjusting the collar of his elegant coat. Prinz Lobkowitz saw that Pyat had a silk handkerchief tucked into his left sleeve. Clouds of red-tinged grey streaked the sky and streamed north.

" Everyone's leaving now." Pyat stopped and picked up a pebble. He threw it into the dank water. Sluggish ripples

107

appeared for a few seconds. A fish put its lips to the surface and then submerged. " There are hardly any of our old friends left. Dead singers."

THE GATHERERS

"It's nice ter go away, but it's nicer ter come 'ome, innit?" said Mrs Cornelius as she sharpened the carving knife against the steel and looked with loving pride upon her roast pork.

The table had been laid with a red plush cloth. There were big blue tassels on the cloth. Over this had been laid a white linen cloth, its edges stitched with broderie anglaise. On the linen rested the vegetables in their monstrous china serving dishes with roses painted on the sides. There were large knives with weathered bone handles, solid forks, big spoons, napkins in rings of yellowed ivory, a silver salt cellar, a silver mustard pot, a silver pepper pot. Around the table sat Mrs Cornelius's children and their guests. They had all come for one of Mrs Cornelius's 'special' Sunday luncheons. Sammy, who always stood in as 'man of the house' on these occasions, sat in his tight best black serge suit beside her, sweltering as ever, but this time the quality of his swelter was different; the swelter of fear had replaced the swelter of work. The boy, pinch-faced and hungry, sat next to Sammy, his mouth watering as he waited for his share. His mother's huge red lips rounded as she scraped metal against metal. She had had her hair done in a pompadour coiffure with a Marcel wave and she was wearing the purple princess gown with the yellow imitation Valenciennes lace on it. The padded shoulders added to her already impressive size.

" Pass yer plates along," she said, preparing to cut.

There was a clatter as the plates were picked up and passed. Catherine, seated on the other side of her mother, stacked her brother Frank's plate on top of her own. Frank took his friend Miss Brunner's plate and passed it to Catherine. Frank and Miss Brunner were dressed in rather similar suits of severe grey. Frank, however, wore a rose. His ravaged face was set in a smirk which showed he was on his best party manners. Miss Brunner, too, was doing her best to be affable.

" It's a loverly bit o' pork," said Mrs Cornelius as she sliced.

" It looks nice and juicy," said Miss Brunner. She winked across the table at Mr Smiles, who was dressed as the vicar he had once been.

" Shall I be barman? " asked Mr Smiles, indicating the beer barrel on the sideboard and gesturing at the same time towards their glass mugs. He grinned nervously through a black beard.

" Good idear," said Mrs C.

" Light? " said Mr Smiles.

" Suits me," said Sammy.

Mr Smiles got up and put the first mug under the spiggot.

For all that it was lunchtime, the heavy velvet curtains were drawn and the gas lamps were full on at either side of the littered mantelpiece. Mrs Cornelius was suspicious of the neighbours who overlooked her rooms at the back. She suspected they might be burglars. If they saw a spread like this, they could easily guess there'd be money in the house. As there was, at this moment.

The air was close. The smell of the meat filled the room. The vegetable dishes steamed.

Slice by slice the pork and the crackling and the stuffing was heaped on the plates. Mrs Cornelius was a generous hostess, if an indifferent cook.

The noise increased as vegetables were ladled out.

" Gravy? " Miss Brunner passed the gravy boat to Frank.

"Apple sauce? " Sammy passed the sauce dish to the boy who helped himself to a large portion. He loved apple sauce.

" There's more spuds in the oven," said Mrs Cornelius as Mr Smiles considered the almost empty bowl. " Go an' get 'em, love," she told the boy. He sprang up, anxious to get the job over with so that he could tuck in.

" Greens? " said Catherine to Frank.

" Swedes? " said Miss Brunner to Mr Smiles.

" Parsnips? " Sammy held the bowl inquiringly.

" Marrer? " Mrs C asked, looking for it.

"All the marrow's gone, mum," said Catherine in a small voice.

Mrs Cornelius loved marrow. But she contained her fury and lifted her glass of light ale, toasting them all. " 'Ere's ter the lot o' yer, then! " She drained the glass, spluttered thickly behind her red hand, and delicately picked up her knife and fork. "Ah, this is ther life! "

Her son came back with the extra potatoes and put them on the table. Hurriedly he clambered into his place and began to wolf the food. Miss Brunner, eating rapidly but discreetly, eyed him as he ate. She dabbed at her thin mouth with napkin. He did not notice her.

" It's a pity yore friend couldn't come," said Mrs Cornelius to her daughter, " Ill, wos she? "

" Yes, mum."

" Shame."

Save for the noise of the cutlery, they ate in silence for a while until Frank said, " I heard there were some people looking for Jerry, mum."

" Don't talk ter me about 'im! " she said.

The boy, who had almost devoured his whole meal, looked up in interest. " What's 'e done, then? "

" We won't go into that, will we? " said Mr Smiles laughing. He glanced at Mrs Cornelius. " No offence."

" None taken," said Mrs Cornelius grimly. " Yore quite right. We won't go inter it."

" They'll never find 'im," said the boy.

" It's unlikely." Catherine looked tenderly and with some admiration at her little brother.

" Who were they? " said the boy. " These people that was looking for 'im."

" Foreigners," said Frank, " mainly."

Miss Brunner tapped his sleeve with her fork and left four tiny points of grease there, like little teeth-marks. " Maybe they

111

want to give him a job? "

"And maybe they don't," said Frank.

" Seconds? " said Mrs Cornelius.

Everyone, except the boy and Miss Brunner, refused.

" Yer get ter miss good 'ome cookin', I shouldn't wonder," said Mrs C to Miss Brunner. She laid two small slices of meat on Miss Brunner's plate.

" Tasty," said Miss Brunner. She offered Mrs Cornelius a secretive smile, as if she referred to some shared experience about which only they knew.

Mrs Cornelius gave the boy what was left of the joint and then, without reference to him, piled the cooled vegetables onto his plate.

Miss Brunner quickly finished and leaned back with a contented grunt.

Catherine began to take the dirty plates into the kitchen.

" See 'ow the duff's doin', luv, will yer? " requested her mother. She confided to Miss Brunner: " It's a loverly duff."

" I'm certain of that."

After the plum duff and the cheese and the port, the family and its friends, with the exception of the boy, who had gone to sleep, smoked their cigarettes, pipes and cigars.

' Well, that was a bit of all right," said Sammy. " Makes a change from meat pies, I can tell you."

Mrs Cornelius smiled complacently. " Not arf, yer cuddly ole fat pig." She bent from where she was helping herself to a pint from the barrel on the sideboard. She kissed his bald head. He snorted and blushed.

Mr Smiles, who had hated the meal, stroked his gravy-stained beard and said, with some strain, " You are a splendid cook, dear lady."

"A plain cook," Mrs Cornelius replied, by way of confirmation and amplification of the compliment. " Oh fuck." The beer mug had overfilled. She dabbed at the sides with her finger, raising the finger to her mouth and sucking it. " Sorry, vicar."

Sammy had taken out his spectacles and was polishing them. He inspected one side carefully.

" Lens," he said. " Cracked."

112

" 'Ave yer seen the rest o' the 'ahse? " Mrs Cornelius inquired of Miss Brunner. " Not," she laughed raucously, " that there's a lot ter show."

" I'd love to see it."

" Come on, then." The two women left the room.

"Any news from America at all? " Mr Smiles packed tobacco into his pipe.

Frank was staring at the door through which Miss Brunner and his mother had passed. He looked worried. " Do what? " he said.

"America? What's going on over there? Much doing? "

" No, nothing much." Frank got up, glancing absently at Mr Smiles. He leant against the mantelpiece. " How's business? "

" Which business? " Mr Smiles winked at him. It was a sad old wink. Frank, staring again at the brown door, didn't notice. He began to move towards the door.

Catherine put her hand on his arm. " Cheer up, Frank. It's not the end of the world."

This idea seemed to frighten him. She said quickly, "A shilling for your thoughts."

" Cheap at arf the price! " desperately guffawed Sammy from the easy chair in which he now sat. He was feeling very lonely. As he had expected, nobody responded.

Mr Smiles felt sick. "Ah, where's the you-know-what? " he asked Sammy.

Sammy pointed at the brown door. " Through there and on yer left," he said. He picked up an old copy of *The Illustrated London News* which had a coloured supplement on the Jubilee headed *The Glory that is England*. Sammy smiled. It was such a short time ago. He wondered what would have happened if the old queen had lived on.

On the landing Mr Smiles turned right by mistake and found himself outside the bedroom door. There were peculiar sounds coming from inside. He stopped to listen.

"At least yer don't run ther risk o' 'avin' babies," he heard Mrs Cornelius say.

" Don't count on it, dearie," said Miss Brunner.

Mr Smiles remembered about the bathroom.

In the dining room Frank was saying, " If she doesn't hurry

113

up soon, I'm off without her."

"Calm down, Frank," said Catherine.

But Frank was glaring now. "Why does she always have to spoil everything? The fat old bag."

"Oh, don't Frank."

His head among the used dishes on the table, the boy stirred. He groaned.

They all looked at him.

"Poor little sod," said Sammy. "Let's not have a row, eh?"

"Well . . ." said Frank, reluctant to stop before his climax. "I mean . . ." He felt nothing for the boy, but he did not wish to offend his sister at that moment, particularly since there was a likelihood that she knew where Jerry was.

Catherine's perfect features bore an expression of infinite sympathy as she went to stroke the sleeping child's hair. "He's having a nightmare, I expect."

THE ROWERS

Considering that he was a prisoner of war, Captain Nye was having quite a good time. It was almost like a holiday. His captors had proved to be courteous and allowed him considerable freedom within the reservation. Even now he was boating on Grasmere Lake with a very pretty girl. Save for the basic facts of his circumstances, he couldn't have imagined a more perfect situation. The sky was a beautiful deep blue and the surrounding hills were a rich, varied green. The lake was absolutely still, reflecting in impressive detail the oaks and willows on its banks.

Captain Nye pulled vigorously on the oars and the boat shot away from the little landing stage at the end of the tea-gardens with their comforting wrought-iron balconies overlooking the water. All the iron was painted green, to blend in with the hills and trees.

The girl was called Catherine. She made a lovely picture as she sat in the stern with a Japanese silk parasol over her shoulder, a wide-brimmed Gainsborough straw hat on her golden curls, her filmy summer frock cut low at the neck and high on the ankle. With touching lack of expertise she gingerly held the rudder rope and pulled it to left or right when Captain Nye directed.

Soon they were alone in the middle of the lake. Far away on

115

the other side there were one or two more boats. Captain Nye rowed towards a little island, eager to get a better look at the rather picturesque ruined bell-tower which stood on it. A system of these towers had once covered the area, the work of an eccentric clergyman who had erected them so that travellers or boatmen would hear them through the fog and thus be able to find their bearings. Unfortunately there were a number of tragic accidents and the flaws in the system became more than obvious when the clergyman had himself drowned on Derwent Water under the impression he had reached the sanctuary of his own churchyard. Now the towers were merely romantic and a source of speculation amongst those who knew little of the local history of the Fell country.

"What mysteries shall we discover, I wonder, in Merlin's castle? " asked Catherine, in a fanciful mood.

Captain Nye looked back over his shoulder at the remains of the building. "Perhaps we'll find Arthur's sword and with it bring peace where today there is nought but strife." She alone could elicit these fantasies from him. He wished very much that they were on the same side. He knew that essentially Catherine was his gaoler and that therefore she must be highly trusted by his enemies. It was a damned shame.

"Nearly there," he said. "Standby for landing! " He shipped the oars as the bottom scraped on the tiny beach. Leaping into the shallow water, careless of wetting his white flannels, he took the painter and hauled the boat up to the point where Catherine, gathering her skirts about her, could reach the prow and take his hand, descending prettily to the land. She twirled her parasol and smiled at him.

"But if we find the sword," she said, "will you be able to pull it from the stone? "

"And if I could, what would you think then? "

She frowned. "I don't know. People play such awful tricks on one, these days."

He laughed. "I know that." He held out his hand. "Come. To the castle! "

They climbed the grassy slope to the tower but were less than halfway there before the smell struck them.

"Ugh! " Captain Nye wrinkled his nose.

116

" What could it be? " she asked. " Sheep droppings? "
He was a little shocked by her outspokenness. " Maybe. Or a
dead animal, even? "
" Shall we look? " Her face became concerned. " In case it
isn't a sheep or something? "
" What . . .? "
" I mean — "
He understood what she meant now. Reluctantly he said,
" You stay. I'll go."
She stood, heels together, holding her parasol, while he forced
himself to the top of the hill and disappeared behind the wall
of the ruin. She was puzzled by the peculiar briny aspect of the
smell. They were a good forty miles from the coast, surely?
She knew that she should have stayed with the captain. It was
her job. But the smell disturbed her more than physically. She
felt extremely nervous and depression was swiftly creeping in.
The perfect day was over.
When Captain Nye returned he was pale and he could hardly
look at her. He had a handkerchief over his mouth. Wordlessly,
he took her arm and guided her back to the boat.
She climbed in and he shoved off. All his movements were
disorganised, hasty. The boat almost turned over as he got
aboard and swung the oars into the water, rowing back towards
the tea-gardens. But he had only gone a few strokes when he
was forced to abandon the oars and lean over the side, vomiting,
as discreetly as he could, into the water.
Catherine came forward and took the oars before they could
slip from the rowlocks. She did her best to keep the boat on
course.
Captain Nye wiped his lips, then dipped his handkerchief into
the water, wiping his whole face. " I must apologise."
" Good heavens! Why? What was it you saw? " With a
steady, accomplished stroke, she began to row for the shore.
" I must report it to the pol — to your authorities. A man,
I think. Or something that had been a man. Or — I'm not
sure . . ."
" Murdered? "
" I don't know."
The really awful thing about the dead creature was that it

117

had had a certain apelike cast of features and yet at the same time the remains of the face had reminded him unmistakeably of the girl who now rowed so smoothly away from the island. Every time he looked at her frank, blue eyes, her full, pink lips, her well-shaped nose, he saw the ape face of the rotting creature which had lain amongst the debris and sheep-dung in the gloomy interior of the tower.

He began to wonder if the whole thing had been deliberately arranged for him. Perhaps his captors had other reasons than kindness for allowing him so much freedom. But what could they possibly want from him, anyway? He knew no secrets.

"Do you — ? Did you expect to find anything like that in the tower? " he asked her.

Her body moved rhythmically back and forth as she rowed. She shook her head.

"Intimations," she said. "I couldn't explain."

THE PEACE TALKS

Preliminary Speech

In his speech to the Court of Appeal, shortly before his exile, Prinz Lobkowitz said:

" In our houses, our villages, our towns, our cities, our nations, time passes. Each individual will be involved, directly or indirectly, in some 150 years of history — before birth, during life, and after his death. Part of this experience will be received from parents or other adults, from old men; part will be received from his own life, and his experience will, in time, become part of his children's experience. Thus a generation is 150 years. That is how long we live. Our behaviour, our prejudices, our opinions, our preferences are the produce of the fifty or sixty years before we were born and in the same way do we influence the fifty following our deaths. Such knowledge is apt to make a man like me feel that it is useless to try to alter the nature of his society. It would be pleasant, I think, if we could somehow produce a completely blank generation — a generation which has not acquired the habits of the previous generation and will pass no habits on to the next. Ah, well. I thank you, gentlemen, for listening to this nonsense with patience. I bid you Au Revoir."

AT THE PEACE TALKS

The Ball

The major social event during the Peace Talks was the Gala Ball at San Simeon. Hearst's monstrous white castle had been bought for the nation by an unknown benefactor some years before and re-erected on the site of the old Convent of the Poor Clares at Ladbroke Grove, where it was now a familiar local landmark and a favourite tourist attraction, more impressive, in the opinion of many, than the buildings of Versailles, Canberra or Washington.

Everyone had been invited. Commentators said that it was equal in magnificence to the Great Exhibition, the Diamond Jubilee, the New York World's Fair or the Berlin Olympics. In a mood of immense optimism (for the Peace Talks could be said to be going splendidly) the castle was prepared for the Ball. Illumination of every sort was used. There were tall Berlage candelabra of silver and gold in which were fitted slender white and yellow candles; Schellenbühel crystal chandeliers holding thousands of red candles; Horta flambeaux in brackets along the walls; huge globular gas mantels, electric lights of a hundred different shades of colour, neon of the subtlest and brightest, antique oil lamps the height of a man, and little faceted glass globes containing fireflies and glow-worms, strung on threads through the grounds of the various ' casas ' which made up the whole of the original Hearst complex. Hearst himself had always called his castle The Enchanted Hill. Now, of course, it was, if anything, an Enchanted Dale. The Casa Grande, with its twin Hispano-moresque towers containing thirty-six carillon bells, its hundred rooms and its ornate bas reliefs carved from white Utah limestone, dominated the other three ' guest castles ' arranged before it, north, south and west — Casa del Monte,

Casa del Sol and Casa del Mar. Tall cypresses, willows, poplars and firs had been planted thickly among the buildings, replacing the Californian palms which had once grown there. Within the branches of the trees and the privet hedges had been buried more tiny lights to make the gardens sparkle like fairyland. Rhododendrons, poinsettias, orchids, chrysanthemums, roses and azaleas grew in well-ordered profusion and the overall appearance reminded at least one visitor of the old roof garden at Derry and Toms blown up to an enormous scale (' and none the worse for that '). Bas-reliefs decorated the Spanish walls of the gardens and there were copies of famous statues from all over the world, in marble and granite or cast in terra cotta or bronze, one of the grandest being Boyar's copy of Canova's ' The Graces ' in St Petersburg. This statue, in the classical manner, was permanently illuminated and showed Joy, Brilliance and Bloom, representing, in the words of the guide book, ' all that was beautiful in Nature and that which was gracious and charming in Mankind '. The Times, in its leader for the day of the ball, had written: " It is to be hoped that this lovely statue will symbolise to the guests the rewards which they can win if their talents are devoted to the pursuit of peaceful endeavour, rather than to Strife and her attendants, Greed and Envy." Many newspapers had echoed these sentiments in one form and another and even the weather, which had been singularly delightful for several weeks, seemed to make a special effort for the occasion. All through that day hundreds of footmen, housemaids, cooks, butlers, kitchen-maids and pages had hurried to and from among the lavish rooms preparing them for the ball. There was to be available every kind of culinary delight. In the ballrooms (or those rooms which had been turned into ballrooms for the occasion) musicians practised many styles of music. The flags of all nations, embroidered in threads of precious metal on the finest silks, glittered from the walls. Tapestries in rich brocades proclaimed the glories of those nations' histories and the set pieces of the buffet tables were the great national dishes of the world. In the grounds were mixed forces of soldiers, arranged there both for ceremonial and for security reasons, their dress uniforms dazzling in the variety of their colourings, their swords, pikes and lances shining like silver.

123

Through rooms lush with mosaics, murals, carvings and bas reliefs, with gilt and silver and enamelling, with paintings and sculpture from Egypt, Greece, Rome, Byzantium, China and India, from Renaissance Spain, Italy and Holland, from 18th century France and Russia, from 19th century England and America, with tiled floors and inlaid floors set with mother-of-pearl and platinum, with wall-hangings and curtains from Persia, with carpets from Afghanistan, with carved wooden ceilings from 16th century Italy and 17th century Portugal, all polished so that they shone with a deep, warm glow, crept the smells of roasting ox and sheep and pigs and calves, of delicious curries and dhansaks, of Chinese soups and fowl, of paellas, strudels and bouillabaises, of succulent vegetables and subtly spiced salad dressings, of pies and cakes and patés, of glazes and sauces and gravies, of bombes surprises, of lemon, orange, pineapple and strawberry water-ices, of peacocks and quails, grouse, pigeons, ortalons, chickens, turkeys, wild ducks, turning on spits or stewing in pots, of rottkraut and kalter fisch, of syllabubs, of sausages and baked ham, of tongue and salt beef, of fruits and savoury roots, of carp and haddock and halibut and sole, of mushrooms and cucumbers, of peppers and bamboo shoots, of syrups, creams and crêpes, soups and consommes, of herbs and fats, of venison and haggis, of whitebait, mussels and shrimps, of hares and rabbits and caviar, of livers and tripes and kidneys. There were wines and spirits and beers from every province of the world. There were glasses and steins and goblets of the clearest crystal and the most exquisite china. Cups and plates and dishes of gold, pewter, silver and porcelain stoody ready to receive the food; pretty girls and handsome men in national costumes stood ready to serve it. Only one tradition would not be kept tonight: there would be no host or hostess to receive the guests. The first guests to arrive would make it their business to receive the others and introduce them after the Master of Ceremonies had announced them in the main ballroom. This peculiar arrangement had been considered the most diplomatic. And now the sun was setting. The ball was about to begin.

" I do hope," said Miss Brunner, curling her ermine robe over her arm as Prinz Lobkowitz helped her from the carriage, " that we are not the *first*." Up the marble staircase they went, between rows of rigid soldiers holding flickering candelabra, to where, from behind colonnades, two footmen appeared and took their invitations, bearing them through the great gold doors into the anteroom of lapis lazuli where they were handed to a head footman, in scarlet and white with a tall, many-waved white wig which curved outwards over his head, who gave them to the Master of Ceremonies who bowed, read the cards, bowed again and ushered them through doors of crystal and filigree into the blazing splendour of the great ballroom.

" Prinz Lobkowitz and Miss Brunner! "

" But we *are*." Miss Brunner glowered furiously as her name and his echoed through the empty expanse. She smoothed her green velvet gown and fingered the pearl collar at her throat.

" Is it my fault, dear lady," Prinz Lobkowitz was equally put out, " if you are obsessed with time? We are always too early."

"And, consequently, always too late," she sighed, making the best of it. They walked slowly towards the far end of the hall. They inspected the servants; they went to the sideboards and tasted a morsel or two while glancing rather disdainfully about them at all the opulence. " What a lot of gilt."

He turned solicitously to listen, his many orders dazzling her for a moment. " Mm? "

" Gilt."

"Ah." He nodded thoughtfully, his patent leather toe tracing whorls of mother of pearl on the floor. " Quite so. A great deal of it. Still, perhaps we'll be able to do something about that now. We mustn't quarrel. That would not be in the spirit of the occasion."

" I'm reconciled to that," she said.

Footsteps sounded in the distance. They looked towards the doors. They saw the Master of Ceremonies raise a scarlet sleeve and read the card before him :

" The Right Reverend, Father in God, Denis, by Divine permission Lord Bishop of North Kensington! " intoned the M.C.

" He's overdoing it a bit, isn't he? " Miss Brunner prepared to receive Bishop Beesley. The corpulent priest had dressed himself in his cloth of gold cloak, his most ornate mitre and held a crook so rich in engravings and curlicues that it outdid anything San Simeon could offer. The bishop's pale face broke into a smile as he saw his old friends. He waddled slowly forward, his eyes wandering over the cakes and trifles on the buffet tables. At last he reached the pair and, with his attention still on the food, held out a beringed hand, either to be kissed or to be shaken. He did not seem offended when they did neither. "My dear Miss Brunner. My dear Prinz Lobkowitz. What a scrumptious feed they've laid on for us! Oh! "

From the gallery, musicians began to play selections from Coward's *Private Lives*.

" How charming," said Bishop Beesley, leaning forward and scooping up a handful of syllabub in his palm and sliding it gracefully into his maw, licking each of his little fat fingers and then both his little fat lips. " How nice."

Again the great voice echoed:

" My Lady Susan Sunday and the Honourable Miss Helen Sweet! "

" Well! " whispered Miss Brunner. " The S.S. I hadn't expected *her*. Her friend looks worn out."

" Captain Bruce Maxwell! "

"And I thought he was dead," said Bishop Beesley.

" His Excellency the President of the United States."

"And he looks it," said Miss Brunner. She smiled as Lady Sue and Helen approached. " How delightful."

Prince Lobkowitz noticed how alike the two older women were. Miss Brunner had been right about Helen Sweet. The girl had faded. Even her ball gown was a faded blue in comparison with the royal blue of Lady Sue's.

" My dear! " Lady Sue was saying. She embraced Miss Brunner. A slim, well-corsetted woman in a dress by Balenciaga, she wore six strands of blue diamonds at her powdered throat, with matching pendant earrings and tiara. It was to be an evening of ostentation, it seemed. " Good evening," said Helen Sweet mildly.

The band was now playing an instrumental version of *Little Red Rooster*.

Captain Maxwell was shaking hands with Prinz Lobkowitz. The captain's hands were cool and damp. There was sweat on his brutish forehead. His great backside, much heavier than any other part of him, seemed to waggle in sympathy. " Good to see you, old boy," he said in a military accent (though in fact he was a Salvationist).

" Professor Hira! "

In impeccable Indian dress, the small professor crossed the floor, nervously fingering his white turban. His coat was of deep pink silk with little round panels of a lighter pink stitched into it. The trousers matched the panels. The buttons were perfect pearls.

" Professor Hira! " Miss Brunner was genuinely pleased to see the physicist. " How long has it been? " She scowled. " Will it be? " She smiled. " Well, how are you, anyway? "

" So so, thank you." He did not seem to share her pleasure at the meeting.

" Mr Cyril Tome." Thin, pale, with white hair but with lips so red they seemed rouged, his hornrims glittering, the critic and would-be politician stood in his monkish evening dress for a second or two beside the Master of Ceremonies before braving the floor. Nobody greeted him.

" Mrs Honoria Cornelius and Miss Catherine Cornelius."

" Good God! " said Captain Maxwell, chewing a stick of celery, " Who d'you think put her on the list? " Largely because it was what they had all been wondering about him, nobody answered. " Honoria, eh? I bet! "

" Major Nye and Captain Nye."

" They do look alike, don't they? " murmured Lady Sue to Miss Brunner. It was true. Save for the obvious difference in ages, father and son might have been the same man. The impression was sharpened by the fact that they wore the uniform of the same regiment.

The guests began to spread themselves a little more evenly around the perimeters of the room.

" The Right Honourable Mr M. Hope-Dempsey."

" He's drunk! " murmured Prinz Lobkowitz as the young Prime Minister looked vaguely around him, then weaved genially in the general direction of the others, his long hair waving behind him. He seemed to have a live animal of some sort hidden under his coat.

" It's a cat," said Miss Brunner. " Where on earth did he get hold of it? "

The guests were now arriving thick and fast. Vladimir Ilyitch Ulianov, resident in China and extremely old and bad-tempered now, wearing a baggy black suit, hobbled in. Following him was his friend and protector the Eurasian warlord General O. T. Shaw, ruler of North China. Beside Shaw was Marshal Oswald Bastable, renegade Englishman and chief of Shaw's airforce. After them came Karl Glogauer the Revivalist, small, shifty, intense; a tall, moody albino, whose name nobody caught; the ex-Literary Editor of the Oxford Mail; a score or so of assorted conference delegates; Hans Smith of Hampstead, Last of the Left Wing Intellectuals; the Governor-General of Scotland; the Viceroy of India, the King of North Ireland, the recently abdicated Queen of England; Mr Roy Hudd, the entertainer; Mr Frank Cornelius and his companion Mr Gordon 'Flash' Gavin; Mr Lionel Himmler, the theatre impressario; Mr S. M. Collier, the demolition expert; Mr John Truck, the transport expert and Minister of Controls; the Israeli Governor of Central Europe; Admiral Korzeniowski, President of Poland; General Crossman (Crossman of Moscow) and Lady Crossman; Miss Mitzi Beesley and Dr Karen von Krupp; Miss Joyce Churchill, the romantic novelist; the cathedral correspondent of *Bible Story Weekly* and his son and daughters; the Paris correspondent of *Gentleman's Quarterly* and his friend Sneaky John Slade, the blues singer; Miss Una Persson and Mr Sebastian Auchinek, her agent; a Lapp parson called Herr Marek; Colonel Pyat with Miss Sylvie Landon, Presidente of the Academie Francaise; more than a hundred of the finest male and female film stars; a round thousand politicians from all over the world; thirty American deserters; five fat field-marshals; eighty-six ex-nuns from the original Convent of the Poor Clares; some Arabs and a German; Spiro Koutrouboussis, the Greek tycoon, with a group of other Greek millionaires; a bank manager and a television script writer; a Dutch soldier, the King of Denmark and the King of Sweden; the Royal Canadian Mounted Police rugby team; Mr Jack Trevor Story, the jazz band leader, and Miss Maggie Macdonald, his star singer; the Queen of Norway and the ex-Emperor of Japan; the Governor of England and his

128

chief advisor General K. G. Westmoreland; Mr Francis Howerd, the comedian; a number of dons who wrote children's novels at Oxford; the most corrupt and feeble-minded paperback publisher in America; Mr Max Miller, the comedian; a number of television producers; Nik Turner, Dave Brock, Del Dettmar, Robert Calvert, Dik Mik, Terry Ollis: members of the Hawkwind orchestra; some advertising executives, pop music critics, newspaper correspondents, art critics, editors and recording artistes and show biz personalities including Mr Cliff Richard, Mr Kingsley Amis, Mr. Engelbert Humperdinck and Mr Peter O'Toole; the Dalai Lhama, some Trades Union officials; thirteen schoolmasters; Mr Robert D. Feet, the pedant (who had thought it was a Fancy Dress Ball and had come as G. K. Chesterton); Miss Mai Zetterling and Mr David Hughes; Mr Simon Vaizey, the society wit, and a host of others. They ate, they conversed, they danced. The mood became gay and the worst of enemies became conciliatory, claiming with sincerity and passion that they had never really disliked one another. Peace was just around the corner.

" We could all be said to be prisoners, Mr Cornelius," Bishop Beesley was saying as he munched a piece of shortbread, " and these revolutionists are perhaps the most hopeless of all prisoners. They're prisoners of their own ideas."

" I'll drink to that, bishop." Frank Cornelius raised his champagne glass. " Still, abolish war and you abolish revolution, eh? "

" Quite so."

" I'm all for the good old status quo."

Miss Brunner was laughing. Gordon Gavin, for all he was dressed in evening clothes, still managed to give the impression that he was clad from neck to knee in an old gaberdine raincoat. The seamed and seedy face, the hot, guilty eyes, the hands that rarely left the pockets of his trousers or else hovered helplessly near his flies, all contributed to the impression. ' I'm flattered," said Miss Brunner, " but I'm afraid all my dances are spoken for." Flash looked relieved.

The musicians were playing Alkan's *Symphony for the Piano on the theme ' Five '* to waltz-time. Mrs Cornelius was having marvellous fun. All the boys were after her! She clutched the little Lapp parson, Herr Marek, to her and raced him round the

129

floor. He was scarcely visible, buried, as he was, in her bulk, but he seemed to be enjoying himself. He had an evil glint in his eye as his muffled, heavily accented English came from the region of Mrs Cornelius's bosom. "Morality, my dear lady, what is that? If it feels good, do it. That's my philosophy. What do you say? "

"Yore naughty, that's wot I say! " She laughed comfortably, completing a pirouette which took him off his feet. He giggled. They just missed colliding with Colonel Pyat and one of the most beautiful of the ex-nuns, Sister Sheila.

The dance ended and the laughter and the conversation swelled. Not only the main ballroom was packed, now. All the subsidiary ballrooms and many of the guest rooms were crowded. As Dick Lupoff was to report to the *L.A. Free Press* ' the world's finest were letting their hair down that night '.

The band struck up with *A Bird in a Gilded Cage* and many of the guests began to sing the words as they took their partners for the dance. The babble of voices grew gayer and gayer. Champagne corks popped and glasses clinked.

Prinz Lobkowitz was commiserating with the ex-Queen of England as they waltzed discreetly in the shadows beneath the musicians' gallery. "My dear Eva, it is a situation one can never really get used to. Training, you know, and background. Not, of course, that you were expecting anything, I suppose, at the beginning."

" The epidemic . . ."

" Exactly. At least Lady Jane was executed. Poor girl."

" It's a bit warm in here, isn't it? " Frank Cornelius was saying on the other side of the ballroom as he danced inexpertly with Helen Sweet. " You look thoroughly washed out."

" Oh, it's all right." Helen Sweet glanced timidly into the gap between his chest and her breasts.

Lady Sue swept past in a flash of crystalline blue. " Don't overdo it, Helen! " Lady Sue was dancing with her friend the ex-Emperor of Japan. Dressed in traditional Japanese costume, the old man was finding the waltz steps a bit difficult.

Catherine Cornelius, feeling a trifle dizzy, leaned against a buffet table. She was a picture of beauty and well-supplied with beaux. They crowded round her. She brushed a lock of fair hair from her forehead, laughing as Captain Nye, who had brought her another drink, said: "I'm afraid they've nothing non-alcoholic left. Will champagne do? " She accepted the glass, but put it down on the table. All of a sudden she began to shiver. "Are you cold? " asked three Austrian hussars solicitously and simultaneously.

" I shouldn't," she said. " Is anything speeding up? "

Captain Nye was filled with foreboding.

They started to play *The Wind Cries Mary* as a foxtrot. Captain Nye held out his hand to her and smiled kindly. " This must surely be mine." She gave him her hand. It was ice cold. He could barely hold on to it. With an enormous effort of self-discipline he drew her freezing body close to his. She had turned very pale.

" If you are not well," he said, " perhaps I might have the honour of escorting you to your door."

" You're kind," she said. Then she almost whispered: " But it is not kindness I need."

Major Nye had already had three dances with Miss Brunner. This was the fourth. Major Nye asked Miss Brunner if she knew anything of the theatre.

" Only what I see," she said.

" You must let me take you backstage sometime, at one of my theatres. You'll like it."

" I'm sure."

" You're a very lovely woman."

"And you're a very handsome man."

They stared into each other's eyes as they danced.

In the third bedroom of the Casa del Monte, seated on a black walnut panelled Lombardy bed, covered in 17th century carvings, the most corrupt and feeble-minded paperback publisher in America sipped his vodka and tonic and stared sourly at his tennis shoes while one of the Oxford dons bored him with a long and enthusiastic description of the joys and difficulties involved in doing *Now We Are Six* into Assyrian. It was what they both deserved. Of all those at the ball, only the publisher was not enjoying himself.

Colonel Pyat and Prinz Lobkowitz smoked their cigars and strolled in the gardens, stopping on the terrace of the Casa del

Monte. " Peace at last," said Colonel Pyat, breathing in the richly-scented air. " Peace. It will be such a relief, don't you think? "

" I, for one, will be happy," the Prinz agreed.

" It will give us so much more time to enjoy our lives."

" Quite."

Miss Brunner and Major Nye found themselves by the Venetian fountain outside the Casa del Sol. Most of the security guards had gone, withdrawn discreetly as the ball progressed. The house itself glowed with light and the waters of the fountain, topped by a copy of Donatello's David, were illuminated with a dozen different soft colours. Miss Brunner put her hand into the water and watched it run up her threequarter length evening glove and drip from her elbow. Major Nye gently stroked his moustache. " Lovely," he said.

" But imagine the expenditure." Miss Brunner smiled to show that she was not really being vulgar. "And no one knows who paid for it. What a splendid piece of tact. Who do you think it is? "

" It's hard to guess who's got that kind of money in England today," he said without much interest.

Miss Brunner's eyes became alert. " That's true," she said. And she was thoughtful. " Oh, dear." She removed her hand from the fountain and placed it lightly against Major Nye's hip. " What a kind man you are."

" What kind? Oh, I don't know? "

The night was full of music, laughter, witty conversation. It came at her from all sides. " It's a magic night! I need someone, I think," she murmured to herself. She decided she would be wise to stick with the material at hand. " I want you so much," she breathed, propelling herself into the major's arms. He was astonished and took a little while responding.

" By God! By God! You beauty! "

The German band on the nearby terrace struck up with a selection of Buddy Holly favourites.

Miss Brunner looked round Major Nye's shoulder, scanning suspiciously the privet hedges. It was just a feeling, but it was getting stronger all the time.

" My dear! " Bishop Beesley lay on a yellow bedspread in

the yellow-draped Yellow Room of the Casa del Sol. The room was furnished largely in early Jacobean style and the bed-posts were topped by carved eagle finials. On the Bishop's right was a Giovanni Salvi *Madonna and Child*. Lying on the Bishop's left, and facing him, was the beautiful ex-nun with whom Colonel Pyat had lately been dancing. She had turned out to be an Australian. Now she had no clothes on. Bishop Beesley's mitre had fallen to the pillow and his hands were completely covered in chocolate. He had brought the girl and the chocolate mousse up here together and was intently covering her body with the stuff. " Oh, delicious! " The girl seemed uncomfortable. She put her hand between her legs, frowning. " I think I'm feeling a little crook."

Dr Karen von Krupp was dancing in the main ballroom with Professor Hira. Professor Hira had an erection because he could feel Dr Karen von Krupp's girdle and garter-belt through her gown. He hadn't had an erection since Sweden (and then it had proved his downfall). " The rhythm of the quasars, doctor," he said, " is, essentially, a lack of rhythm." He pressed his erection tentatively against her thigh. Her hand slipped from around his waist and patted him tenderly. His breathing grew more rapid.

" Quasars," said Dr von Krupp romantically, closing her eyes, " what are they, compared with the texture of human passion? "

" They are the same! That is it! The same! Everything is the same. My argument exactly."

" The same? Are we the same? "

" Essentially, yes."

The music finished and they wandered out into the garden.

Everyone was smiling, shaking hands, patting one another on the backs, exchanging addresses, laughing uproariously at one another's jokes, making love, resolving to be more generous, more tolerant and to learn humility. The Peace Talks and the Gala Ball would not be forgotten by most of them for a long time. The whole spirit of the talks had been crystallised here. Nothing but improvement lay ahead. Strife would be abolished and heaven on earth would be established.

Only Miss Brunner, Catherine Cornelius and Captain Nye were beginning to wonder if there wasn't a snag. Bishop Beesley and Frank Cornelius, who would normally have been swift to spot the signs, were both too absorbed in their own activities to notice anything.

Frank Cornelius had locked the door of the movie theatre (done in gold and crimson, with silk damask wall hangings and copies of Babylonian statues holding electric lights made to look like lilies) and sat in the back row with Helen Sweet with his hand up her skirt as they watched one of the prints of *Yankee Doodle Dandy* with James Cagney as George M. Cohan and Walter Houston as his father Jerry Cohan. Frank loved the feel of Helen's lukewarm, clammy thigh; it made him nostalgic for the childhood he'd never had. Shakey Mo Collier, operating the projectors, tried to peer through his little window and get a good look at what Frank was doing.

Bishop Beesley and his ex-nun were now completely covered in chocolate and were prancing around the Yellow Room in an obscene version of the Cake Walk.

Lady Sue Sunday, still in the ballroom, was doing the tango with Clive Tome who had just proposed marriage to her. She was considering his offer seriously, particularly since he showed an unexpected aptitude for the tango. " We could probably both live on Sunday's money, I suppose," mused Lady Sue. " I have a certain income from my writing, moreover," said Cyril Tome. "And there would be so much we could clean up together."

' Flash ' Gordon was in the garden taking a happy interest in the azaleas. Nearby, Mrs Cornelius was wandering hand in hand with Professor Hira while Herr Marek hovered jealously in the background, planning to murder the Indian. In the Games Room, where billiard and pool tables rested on travertine floors and where the walls were decorated with rare Gothic tapestries and antique Persian tiles, with its 16th century Spanish ceiling showing scenes of bullfights, Dr von Krupp and Una Persson were playing billiards while Sebastian Auchinek and Simon Vaizey looked on. " I used to be rather good at this," said Dr von Krupp, making an awkward shot awkwardly. The spot ball struck the red with a click. " Isn't that a foul? " asked Una Persson politely. " I mean, I thought I had the spot." Dr von Krupp smiled kindly at her. " No you didn't, dear." Simon Vaizey was seized by a fit of hysterical giggling. " I shouldn't really be here, you know. I think I'm a gatecrasher."

The President of the United States and the Prime Minister of England were completely and happily drunk and were dancing round and round the otherwise deserted marble Morning Room together, making the huge silver sanctuary lamps on the ceiling jingle and shake with their merriment. A small black and white cat sat on the window sill, licking its paws.

" You look much nicer without your make-up," said the President. " I'm glad it's you who's Prime Minister now."

Holding a rather grotesque Tiffany lamp above her head Mitzi Beesley, the bishop's daughter, was trying to limbo with Lionel Himmler, who had learned the dance in Nassau during his brief stay there. They were getting on well together. " I've never enjoyed myself so much," Mitzi told him. " I love you."

"And I love you," he said. His normally morose features were beaming. " I love *love*! "

Spiro Koutrouboussis had just shaken hands on a satisfactory business deal with his fellow Greek millionaires when he saw Catherine Cornelius standing in a dark corner of the Main Library, looking through a rare copy of *Paradise Lost*. He crossed the huge Meshed carpet and presented himself. "Are you free for the next dance, Madamoiselle Cornelius? " he asked in careful French.

" I'm afraid I'm feeling a trifle unwell, m'sieu." She tried to smile. " My escort has gone to find my cloak."

" May I put my landau at your disposal? "

" Thank you. You are very kind. M. Koutrouboussis. I was sorry to hear of the unfortunate collapse of your —" she shivered uncontrollably — " project."

" No matter. A new one is developing. That's business. *On mourra seul*, after all." His own smile was full and charming.

" *Il n'y a pas de morts, M. Koutrouboussis!* " She closed her eyes.

" Could I offer you my coat? "

" I — thank you." Gratefully Catherine accepted his heavy jacket, pulling it around her. " I'm very sorry to . . ."

" Please." He raised a gentle hand.

One of the carved cabinets swung out from the wall and nearly struck Spiro Koutrouboussis on the shoulder. He leapt back.

From the space behind the bookcase emerged a tall figure

135

with long, straight black hair, a pale, voluptuous face. He was
wearing a short black overcoat with wide military lapels. His
black trousers had a slight flare. His shirt was of the purest
white silk and there was a broad, crimson tie at his throat. One
long-fingered hand held an oddly shaped gun. " Hello, Cathy.
I see you were expecting me."

" Oh, Jerry! I'm cold."

" Don't worry. I'll deal with all that. What are these people
doing in my house? "

" Dancing."

" You might have dressed for the occasion," said Koutrouboussis, eyeing the gun. Jerry put the gun in his big pocket.

" It took some time getting warm, myself," he said, by way
of apology. " How's tricks, Koutrouboussis? "

" The tricks are over. I am back in legitimate business now."

" Just as well. God, you go away for a little while and you
come back to find the place crammed with guests. Is this my
party, then? "

" I suspect so."

Jerry laughed. " Oho! You know me of old, don't you? But
this isn't Holland Park. It's Ladbroke Grove. I'm reformed. I
lead a very quiet life, these days."

" Jerry! " Catherine had turned quite blue and seemed on
the point of collapse. " Jerry! "

He wrapped his arms around her. " There. Is that better? "

"A bit."

" I can see I'm going to have to take steps." Jerry poured
himself a large whiskey from the decanter on the ebony and
marble table. " I suppose Frank's about? "

"And mum."

" Fuck."

" She's all right, Jerry. Tonight."

" I haven't got a lot of time, either," said Jerry to himself.
" Still . . ."

" How long are you staying for, Jerry? "

" Not long. Don't worry." He smiled at her, full of misery.
" This is like the old days. I'm sorry."

" It's not your fault."

Miss Brunner came into the Games Room. " I knew it. You'd

better not try anything, Mr Cornelius."

" Oh, I don't know. This is my place, after all."

" Sod you, You set it up."

Jerry shrugged.

" Christ! " She spat on the rug.

In the Morning Room, the Prime Minister of England and the President of the United States were sitting side by side in the same big chair. " Culturally, of course," said the President, " we have always been exceptionally close. That must stand for something."

The Prime Minister laughed happily. " Me? I'll stand for anything. What's the score? "

The lights went out. The President giggled.

In the main ballroom the music went on for some time, until the candles and the flambeaux also began to dim, to gutter and finally extinguish themselves. Everyone murmured with delight, expecting a surprise. Laughter filled the great hall as men and women speculated on the nature of the treat.

At the entrance, the gold doors swung back; the glass doors swung back. A cold wind blew.

In the gardens the glow-worms and the fireflies were still, but there was one light, from the beam of a large flashlight held in the hand of a shadowy figure who swung up the steps into the Casa Grande. The figure wore a short top-coat with its wide lapels turned up to frame a long, pale face. The eyes gleamed in the reflected glare from the flashlight. The figure entered the ballroom and pushed its way through the silent throng until it stood beneath the musicians' gallery.

The voice was cool: " There's been a mistake. It's time to call it a day, I'm afraid. You are all on private property and I advise you to leave at once. Anyone still here in half-an-hour will be shot."

" Good God! " Prinz Lobkowitz stepped forward. " Who on earth? "

" This is difficult for me," said the figure. It directed the flashlight upwards. " It's to do with the third law of thermo-dynamics, I suppose." The musicians had replaced their instruments with a variety of sub-machine-guns and automatic pistols. " But I won't bore you with a speech."

137

" Do you realise what you are doing? " Prinz Lobkowitz swept his hands to indicate the crowd. " You could wreck everything."
" Perhaps. But things have to keep moving, don't they? Now you must leave."
A machine gun sounded. Bullets struck the chandeliers and glass flew. The guests began to scream and mill about. The ex-Queen of England went down, her shoulders cut by several shards. Mr Robert D. Feet, the pedant, clutched a bleeding eye. Others sustained less important injuries. The scramble for the exit began. It was almost dignified.

As the guests flooded from the Casa Grande, others began to arrive from the various guest castles. They wanted to know why the lights had gone out. Car engines started up. Horses stamped and snorted. Wheels churned in gravel. There was a smell of May.

In the cinema, Frank Cornelius began to guess that something was up. Abandoning Helen Sweet, he crept to the doors and gingerly unlocked them. " Jerry? "

In the Yellow Room Bishop Beesley was struggling to get his surplice on over the hardening chocolate, leaving the half-eaten ex-nun on the floor where she lay. He adjusted his mitre, picked up his crook, stooped for one last lick and then hurried out.

In the Morning Room the President of the United States and the Prime Minister of England had already left. Only the cat remained, sleeping peacefully in a warm chair.

Captain Nye found the library and opened the door. "Are you there, Miss Cornelius? "

" Yes, thank you. I'm feeling awfully better."

" We must go."

" I'm afraid we must."

" This will be the ruin of the talks."

" Quite a good ruin, though."

Laughing, they left the library.

Mrs Cornelius, Professor Hira and Herr Marek were already in Ladbroke Grove. " It'll be nice to get back." Mrs C felt in her reticule for her key. " It's only round the corner, luckily."

The three of them were unaware that anything had happened to

138

mar the ball.

"Can you smell velerian?" asked Flash Gordon as Helen Sweet, weeping, stumbled into his hedge. "You're a little darling, aren't you?" He gathered her up. "Come and see Holland Park with me."

She sniffed. "All right."

Trembling with a mixture of fear and anticipation, Flash led her towards the main gate.

"What's bad news for some is good news for others," said Lady Sue as her carriage raced past the couple. She had lost her tiara but had gained Bishop Beesley. She didn't know at that point that he wasn't a negro.

Slumped in the far corner of the brougham, the bishop groaned. He had horrible indigestion.

Cars and carriages erupted into Ladbroke Grove, scattering in all directions, some colliding in the gloom (for the gas lamps had also been extinguished). A small boy was run over by Colonel Pyat's Lamborgini.

In the third bedroom of the Casa del Monte, several Oxford dons and the most corrupt and feeble-minded paperback publisher in America were blown to bits by explosive shells from the big Schmeisser in the hands of the second cellist. The publisher, for one, was almost grateful for this change of pace.

Some, mostly those who had walked to the gates and were now strolling up Westbourne Park Road towards the Portobello Road looking for taxis, had taken the events with a certain amount of amused relish. They chattered and laughed as they walked along, listening to the distant sounds of machine-gun fire.

"Well," said Dr von Krupp, who was of this party, "it's back to square one, I suppose."

"Do you live in London?" asked Una Persson, her arm around Sebastian Auchinek's neck.

"Oh, I think I'll want to now," grinned the doctor.

In Spiro Koutrouboussis' landau, which had been the first carriage to get away, Captain Nye and Catherine Cornelius embraced in a long and tender kiss. They were already half-way to the Surrey border, heading for Ironmaster House.

Spiro Koutrouboussis was still in the Casa, having survived the massacre of his colleagues. He had a gun and was looking

139

for his host. He bumped into Frank on the stairs, mistook him for Jerry, and shot him. Frank, thinking that he had been shot by Jerry, returned the fire. The two bodies tumbled down the stairs together.

Miss Brunner and Major Nye gave up any thoughts of revenge and clambered into the major's camouflaged Humber Snipe. As they roared away, one of the violinists emerged on the steps and lifted his Tommy gun to his shoulder, firing after them, but the bullets bounced off the car's armour and then they had turned a corner and were safe.

Easing the car into Ladbroke Grove, Major Nye asked Miss Brunner: " Well, what did you make of all that? "

" Now that I look back," she said, " I suppose it seems inevitable. But not to worry."

" I must say you know how to make the best of things," he said admiringly.

Slowly the great house grew still until the only sound that could be heard anywhere was the purring of the small black and white cat as it stretched itself, licked its whiskers, then settled back to sleep again.

THE PEACE TALKS

Concluding Remarks

Upon his return from exile at the request of the new revolutionary junta, Prinz Lobkowitz made a short speech as he stepped off the airship. The speech was addressed to Colonel Pyat and an ecstatic crowd. He said:

"The war, my friends, is ceaseless. The most we can expect in our lives are a few pauses in the struggle, a few moments of tranquility. We must appreciate those moments while we have them."

PROLOGUE (continued)

. . : the ghosts of the unborn. And the ghosts of the unknown: the wardead and those who died in the concentration camps. Dying in anonymity, without witnesses, they are never decently brought to rest. It's hard to explain. And yet the birth of every new child is a kind of resurrection. Every child welcomed into the world helps to lay a ghost to rest. But it takes so long. And these days, it's hardly a lasting solution. Perhaps we should simply stop killing people.

MAURICE LESCOQ, Leavetaking

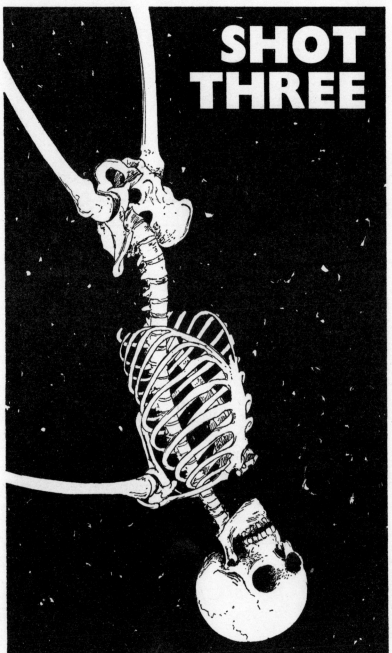

SHOT
THREE

'MIRACLE CURE' OF FRANCES, 6

The Pope has been asked to declare that six-year-old Frances
Burns is a miracle girl. Three years ago, she was dying of cancer.
Surgeons who had been fighting for her life gave her only a few
days to live. Now she is a happy, laughing tomboy of a girl. And
the consultant who treated her admits: "A miracle is not too
strong a term for her recovery." The astonishing cure of Frances
Burns began when her mother, Mrs Deirdre Burns, took her
pain-racked daughter from Dennistoun, Glasgow, to the Roman
Catholic shrine of Lourdes in Southern France. Frances was
bathed in the waters of the mountain spring where thousands of
invalids have sought a cure. Back in Glasgow, after two days in
the Sick Children's Hospital, Frances sat up and asked for food.
A week later the tumours on her face had disappeared. She was
on the road to an amazing recovery. The panel of 31 specialists
who make up the Lourdes Medical Bureau have asked the Pope
to consider pronouncing Frances's cure a miracle.

THE SUN, August 23 1971

145

THE THEATRE

Una Persson was on stage. She was playing Sue Orph, latest of
Simon Vaizey's sophisticated heroines, in Vaizey's most successful musical comedy to date — *Bright Autumn* — at the Prince
of Wales' Theatre. The house was full and Una noticed her old
agent, Sebastian Auchinek, in the front stalls. Auchinek was in
politics now and writing thousands of articles and pamphlets.
His latest production was called "A New Deal for Britain's
Jews."

Draped in a light pink silk Chanel pyjama suit, Una leaned
against a grand piano and confronted her leading man, Douglas
Crawford, as he said:

" I never guessed you kept a diary, darling,"

Una held the book insouciantly in one long hand and said
lightly: " Oh, darling, it's hardly a *real* diary."

The line had become a catch-phrase everywhere now.
Comedians imitated it on the wireless. It might have been
written especially for her rich Rs.

" But it *is* secret, I suppose," Douglas continued. " Is it
awfully secret? "

" It is rather."

" I thought we weren't to have secrets, you and I. I thought
we had agreed it wouldn't be that kind of marriage." He was
offended.

146

She was eager to reassure him. "Darling, it *isn't* — it's just that —"

Icily remote, he said: "Yes?"

"Oh, darling don't be a *bear*!" She turned away from him, looking down at the keys of the piano.

"A prig, you mean, don't you?" He folded his arms and stalked to the cocktail cabinet at the far end of the stage. "Well, what if I am a prig? What if I love you so horribly I can't stand to think of you keeping secrets from me? You know, people who keep diaries are usually afraid of something. Isn't that what they say? What are *you* frightened of, Susan? What have you written about that man you saw last night — you know — that man? What's his name?" He pretended he didn't care, but it was obvious to the audience that he was barely in control of his passions.

Una replied in a high, offended tone, speaking rapidly: "You know perfectly *well* what his name is. It's Vivian Gantry." She paused, becoming reminiscent. "We were lovers — years ago ..."

"And you still love him? Is that what you're frightened to tell me? Is that what you've written in your damned diary?" Douglas wheeled round, his face tortured with emotion.

Una dropped the diary and swept towards him. "Oh, you fool, you fool, you sweet, precious fool! How could I love anybody but *you*?"

"Tell me?"

She stopped suddenly, lowering her head. Then she turned to point at the fallen diary. "Very well, read it if you like."

He hesitated. He started to mix himself a drink at the cabinet. "What does it say?"

"That I love you in so many ways that I can't even say it to your face."

"Oh?" It was possible to see now that he wanted to believe her but was still cautious.

Her voice was almost a whisper and yet it reached the back of the theatre. "Yes, Charles. I suppose I'm too much in love with you, really ..."

He put the drink down and seized her shoulders. Her face remained averted. "Swear it?" he said, almost savagely. "Do

147

you swear it, Sue? "

She recovered her composure and stared him directly in the eyes. Mockingly, spreading her fingers over her heart, she said lightly, but with something of an edge to her voice. " Very well, if you think it necessary. There! I swear it." Her tone softened. She took his hand. " Now stop all this — this *silly* jealousy."

By now he was completely miserable for having doubted her. " Oh, darling I'm sorry." He folded her in his arms. Softly the orchestra started the introduction to the most popular song of the show. " I *am* a bear! An utterly boorish bear! And a prig! How could I possibly, possibly doubt you. Forgive me? "

Her voice was warm and soft when she breathed:

" Forgive you."

" Oh, darling! "

He began to sing:

> " *You know I'd be blue dear,*
> *With someone new, dear.*
> *I'll never weary — of you.*
> *Heartbreak and sorrow,*
> *Will never spoil tomorrow,*
> *And I'll never be blue, dear, again . . ."*

As the curtain fell on the act, Sebastian Auchinek, his eyes full of tears, clapped and clapped until a hand fell on his shoulder and he looked into the grave, polite faces of two plain-clothes policemen. " Sorry to interrupt your evening out, sir. But we wonder if you wouldn't mind coming with us to answer one or two questions."

It was like a bad detective story compared with the fantasy he had just been watching. He said almost pathetically and with an attempt at levity:

" Can't I answer them here? "

" I'm afraid not, sir. We've a warrant, you see."

" What are you arresting me for? "

" Wouldn't it be less embarrassing if we answered that when we're in the street, sir? "

" I suppose so. Can I get my coat? "

" That's waiting for you in the lobby, sir." The policeman

scratched his little moustache. " We took the liberty."

Sebastian Auchinek looked around at the other people in the stalls, but they were all involved in getting to the bar, studying their programmes or chatting amongst themselves.

" I see," he said. " Well . . ." He got up, shrugging. " I am Miss Persson's manager, you know. The papers will know you've arrested me."

" Not an arrest, as such, sir. A request for help. That's all."

" Then surely I can see the play through? "

" It's urgent, sir."

Auchinek sighed. He darted one last look at the curtain, drew one last breath of the atmosphere, and then left by a side exit.

THE FLYING BOAT

The great grey flying boat manoeuvred on her two outer forward-facing propellers, slewing round in the shallows until she faced the main expanse of the blue lake. Save for the ripples which spread from the flying boat's massive angular floats, the lake was flat, shining and still. In the early morning air the growling Curtiss Conqueror engines drowned every other sound. The boat was a Dornier DoX with twelve 600 hp liquid-cooled back-to-back engines mounted on her 160ft wing.

There was space on the ship for a hundred and fifty, but, with the exception of Captain Nye, who was piloting the plane, there were only three people aboard.

Even the snow-capped grandeur of the Swiss alps failed to dwarf the monoplane as she coursed over tranquil Lake Geneva, all twelve props twirling when Captain Nye flicked the toggle-switches which brought them to life.

"We're flying light. We'll make time, everything else being equal." He chatted casually to Frank Cornelius who lounged seedily in the roomy co-pilot's chair and stared through the glass at the glare from the rising sun, a ball of pulsing brass whose rays pierced the morning mist.

The boat surged across the deserted lake and headed towards the ruins of the city on the far shore. Captain Nye waited until the very last minute before taking her up, flying playfully low over the collection of shanties near the lakeside. A few children scattered in fright; then the Dornier was climbing steeply, banking into the sun, going East.

"She's an ugly bitch, but she's fast." Captain Nye levelled out. They were doing at least 130 mph. "Go and check if the ladies are all right, would you, old man?" They were now well clear of all but the highest mountains.

Frank unstrapped himself and slid the cabin door open. He crossed Joubert and Petit's 60ft Art Deco ballroom and descended the angular staircase to the first class deck where Miss Brunner and his sister Catherine were already seated on high bar-stools having Pimms Number Ones prepared for them by Professor Hira. The physicist was to be their guide on this expedition.

"Everything okay?" said Frank. "Isn't it smooth?"

"Beautiful," said Miss Brunner, dabbing at her Eton crop and winking. Catherine looked away. Through the observation ports she could see the clean, shimmering peaks. "It's a lovely day," she said.

"We'll make Rowe Island by Monday easily," said Frank. "Six thousand miles, just like that. It's incredible!"

"Aren't you flinging yourself rather too hard into the part, Frankie, dear?" Miss Brunner fingered her lip-rouge.

"Dear Miss B. You've no enthusiasm left at all. I think I'll stroll back to the pilot's cabin." Frank blew a kiss to his sister and another to Professor Hira. Pointedly he ignored Miss Brunner. They were always quarrelling; even the Indian physicist paid no attention, placing the tall slab-sided Vuitton glasses with a click on the zig-zag black and white inlay of the Kroll bar. He didn't drink himself, but he was a wizard at mixing things up.

"It'll be nice to visit the island again," said Catherine. "So warm. People go there for their health, I hear."

"Just as we are, dear, really." Miss Brunner adjusted her white cardigan over the blue and black silk day dress, offering Catherine a Gold Flake from her thin silver cigarette case. Catherine accepted. Professor Hira leaned over the bar and lit the cigarettes with the big table lighter which had been built to resemble a heavy Egyptian sarcophagus, but which was really

151

made of aluminium and, like so much of the flying boat's equipment, a spin-off from the airship industry. Miss Brunner found
airships not sufficiently *chic* for her taste; indeed, even Catherine thought them a trifle gross. Still, they did enable ordinary
members of the public to travel from country to country for
comparatively little money, if that was a good idea. She was
disturbed, however, by the prediction that they would one day
take the place of the flying boat. Progress was progress, but she
was sure that people of taste would always prefer the elegance
of an aircraft like the Dornier, with her lovely Joubert and Petit
and Josef Hoffman interiors. Catherine leaned her elbow on the
bar, her hand curving back at the wrist, the jade cigarette holder
gripped loosely between her forefinger and middle finger perfectly matching the plain jade bangle on her slim arm. She wore
the minimum of make-up, the minimum of clothing on her torso.
Miss Brunner gave her an admiring once-over. " Frank is vulgar,
but you, dear, are more than perfect."

Catherine smiled a private smile, her foot tapping to the
rhythm of the Ipana Troubadours record Professor Hira had
just placed on the Victorphone. The muffled sound of the Curtiss Conquerors seemed to be beating to the same time. " I'll get
by — as long as I have you," sang Catherine with the record.

"But Frank, I think, is more in tune, eh? " said Professor
Hira, breaking both their moods.

Miss Brunner was frosty. "Should that be a compliment, I
wonder? " She slid from her stool. " I'm going to the powder
room. I feel a mess."

Catherine watched her go through the door marked *Damen*.
Sometimes Miss Brunner could be a real stickler for form.

Left alone with Catherine, Professor Hira was ill at ease. He
cleared his throat, he beamed, he played with the cocktail
shakers, he looked vaguely up at the roof. Once, when they
struck some mild disturbance, he made a move to help her
steady herself, then became embarrassed, changing his mind
half-way through the motion.

Catherine decided to check the cargo. With a pleasant nod
to the professor, she gathered up her Worth skirts and walked
aft. The companionway led down to the second-class lower deck,
which Hoffman had redesigned as a galley and dining cabin.

She went through the galley and into the cool forward cargo hold. Aside from their yellow and black pigskin luggage, there was only one piece of cargo, a cream-coloured box about five feet long, three feet wide and three feet deep. The lid of the box was padlocked. Catherine took a key from the side pocket of her little gold Delaunay bag and inserted it into the lock, turning it twice. Then she opened the lid. Inside was the shiny white skeleton of a child, aged between ten and twelve. The skull was damaged. In the bone of the forehead, just above and between the eye sockets, was a large, regularly-shaped hole.

As a mother might move a sleeping child before drawing the covers over it for the night, Catherine rearranged the skeleton on its red and white leather cushions. She leant with a fond smile into the box, kissing the skull just above its injury; then tenderly she closed the lid and padlocked it up, murmuring: " Don't worry."

She sighed, pressing her palms together in front of her lips. " The Indian Ocean is the friendliest in the world, Professor Hira says. And Rowe Island is the friendliest island in the Indian Ocean. We'll all be able to rest there." She staggered as the plane hit more turbulence, banking steeply. She managed to grasp the yellow and green silk safety rope secured to the bulkhead. The Dornier righted herself almost immediately. Catherine checked that the box hadn't shifted in its moorings and then carefully she began to make her way back to the bar.

THE PIER

"It's the 'ottest summer in years," Mrs Cornelius was saying as she waded back to the shore, her jazzy print dress hitched above her red, dumpy knees. She was sweating like a sow, but she was happy, out of breath, having a high old time at Brighton. She'd been to the races, been on the sea-front miniature railway, had two sticks of rock, some winkles, five pints of Guinness, a bit of skate and chips and a sing-song in the pub just before she'd been sick. Being sick had cleared her system and now she felt like a million dollars. It did you good. Colonel Pyat, in perfect civilian summer dress, a white linen suit, a panama hat, two-tone shoes and a malacca cane over his arm, stood on the pebbles holding Tiddles, Mrs Cornelius's small black and white cat, which, of late, she had taken to carrying everywhere she went, even to the shops, the pictures or, like today, on their honeymoon day excursion to the seaside.

"Wot abart th' pier?" Mrs Cornelius panted. She cocked her thumb over her damp shoulder at the East Pier, an affair of rusty scaffolding holding a dance hall, a theatre, a penny arcade and a fun fair. From where she stood on the bank she could hear the dodgems clattering and crashing. Every so often, there came a high-pitched giggle, an excited yell.

Colonel Pyat shrugged his acquiescence. It was his duty. He would do it.

154

" 'Ere, give us th' cat! " She seized the limp beast from his arms. " Looks daft, a man carrying a cat. They'll reckon yore a fairy or somefink if you ain't careful! " She laughed raucously, nudging him playfully in the ribs. " Not that there aren't a few o' *them* darn 'ere. Brighton! I should think so! " She cast an eye over the jolly crowd which covered the beach, as if vetting them for signs of sexual deviation. Deckchairs, newspapers, raincoats, fairisle pullovers, jackets, towels, were scattered everywhere and on them lay or squatted mums and dads and adolescent boys and girls, the sun shining on their Brylcreemed crops and their permanent waves. The younger kids wandered around eating ice-cream bricks from the Walls Stopme-and-buy-one man who pedalled his refrigerated bin up and down the front. Other children, clutching their scratched metal buckets and chipped wooden spades, sought wistfully for some sand. The noise of a barrel-organ came closer. Far away, on the promenade overlooking the beach, open-top double-decker buses sailed slowly along, crammed with men in white Oxford bags and open-neck shirts, or girls in snazzy summer frocks, their hair tightly curled or waved, their lips blossoming with scarlet and cerise. The smell of brine, of grease, of chips and jellied eels drifted languidly on the still air.

" Phew! " She wriggled her toes into her emerald-green slingback sandals and led the way through her fellow holidaymakers and up the shingle towards the pier. " It could get yer darn, too much o' this, eh? The 'eat, I mean."

On the pier, having paid twopence each to go through the turnstile, Colonel Pyat found to his relief that the wind had changed direction and was blowing all the smells, save that of the sea, back towards the town where the Chinoiserie Pavilion's green domes could be seen among the more down to earth Regency terraces. It certainly was hot and the sun hurt his eyes, making him wish he had brought his tinted spectacles. The cat struggled for a moment in his coat and then was still again.

" Wot a marf, wot a marf, wot a norf an' sarf," sang Mrs Cornelius. " Lumme, wot a marf 'e's got. When 'e was a nipper, Cor Lord Lovel, 'is pore ol' muvver use ter feed 'im wiv a shovel! Wot a gap (pore chap), 'e's never bin known to larf — 'cos if 'e did it's a penny ter a quid, 'is face ud fall in arf! "

155

Colonel Pyat looked apprehensively at Mrs C. The last time she'd sung that particular song, it was just before she'd been violently sick in the gutter outside The Ship.

" This is wot I *corl* a Bank 'Oliday Mondy," continued Mrs Cornelius, taking the cat from him, raising it close to her face and stroking it. " Let's go on the ghost train now, eh? "

" You don't want to overdo it, you know," said Colonel Pyat.

" Wot? Me? " She shook with mirth. " You must be joking! "

They went on the ghost train. Colonel Pyat was frightened by the monsters and witches and skeletons which sprang at him from all sides, the screechings, the howls, the cackling laughter, the clammy stuff that touched his smooth-shaven cheeks, the spider-webs, the flashing lights, the rush of cold air, the mirrors, the awful darkness through which they passed, but Mrs Cornelius — although she yelled and shrieked incessantly — had a lovely time.

They took a cup of tea and a bun each in the pier cafeteria, looking out over the sparkling sea. All the waitresses gathered round to stroke Mrs Cornelius's cat. " Innit *tame,*" said one. Another offered it a bit of biscuit, which it refused. Another girl, with a scrawny face and a wretched body, brought it a saucer of milk. " 'Ere, pussy. Pussy? Pussy? " The cat lapped the milk and the girl felt grateful all day.

They got on the dodgems. Mrs C went in one car, with the cat stuffed down her bosom with only its little head sticking out, looking really comical, and Colonel Pyat went in another. Mrs Cornelius's car was bright red and gold with a number 77 on it. Colonel Pyat's car was green and white with a number 55 on it. The power arms cracked and flashed and sparks flew as the cars started up. Mrs C leaned forward, driving her car head-on at Colonel P who resigned himself to the thump which shook his bones and grazed his knee. Through the loudspeakers came the distorted voice of Nat Gonella singing *If I had a talking picture of you.* " Yer too effin' slow! " screamed Mrs C delightedly, and off she went to deal damage to other unsuspecting drivers. Even the cat seemed to be enjoying himself on the dodgems. " Oo! Muvver! " shouted Mrs Cornelius as she flung back her turbanned head and took another victim.

Colonel Pyat began to feel queasy. As soon as the cars stopped moving, he got out and stood on the side while Mrs Cornelius had another turn. He was amazed that so much violent activity could take place on such an apparently flimsy structure as the pier. It must be considerably stronger than he thought. He lit a cigarette and strolled towards the rail, looking down through the gaps in the planks at the sea swishing below, listening to the distinctive noises of the woman he had married, wondering if, after the destruction of the town, this pier would still survive.

The cars had stopped again and Mrs Cornelius was clambering out and waddling across the floor to the boardwalk which ran round the outside of the dodgem arena. She was sweating and grinning when she joined him and she had picked up some of the oily aroma of the cars.

" Come on," she said, seizing him by the arm and leading him further up the pier, " we still got time fer a dance."

THE HILLS

A smoky Indian rain fell through the hills and woods outside Simla and the high roads were slippery. Major Nye drove his Phantom V down twisting lanes flanked by white fences. The car's violet body was splashed with mud and it was difficult to see through the haze that softened the landscape. In rain, thought the major, the world became timeless.

Turning into the drive outside his big wooden bungalow, he brought the limousine to a stop. A Sikh servant gave him an umbrella before taking over the car.

Major Nye walked through the rain to the veranda, folding the umbrella and listening to the sound of water on the leaves of the trees. It was like the ticking of a thousand watches. It smelled so fresh. Simla hadn't changed much. That was something.

His wife and two little girls were still in Delhi. They had been reluctant to make this journey of return with him. But there had been people he wanted to see. He had felt the need to reassure the servants that he was still in the land of the living.

Inside, the house was cold; all the furniture was draped in white dust-covers. There were no smells and, save for the rain, no sounds. The place was dead. He felt tired, borne down by responsibility, by the sudden understanding that all his dedication had been pointless. How much longer could the Raj last, with the Chinese, the Russians and the Americans hammering at the gates?

He saw that a fire had been lit in the grate. Someone had been burning books. He picked up the poker and turned over the covers, which were only partially burned. *How Michael found Jesus* was one title, and there were others: *Ragnarok and the Third Law of Thermodynamics, Time Search Through the Declining West, Bible Stories for Little Folk, A Cure for Cancer, How to Avoid Heat Death.* All religious and medical stuff, plainly. Who on earth could have bothered to set fire to them? He was crossing to the bell-pull when he was distracted by a sound from outside. On the veranda servants were shouting. He went to the window and opened it.

" What is it, Jenab Shah? " he asked the big Afghan butler.

The man shrugged and grinned in his thick beard. " Nothing, sahib. A mongoose killing a cobra. See." He held up the limp body of the snake.

Major Nye nodded and closed the window. He went to the door and into the shady hallway. He walked up the uncarpeted stairs. He entered the bedroom which he and his wife had once shared. The bed and the rest of the furniture was also draped in white sheets. He grabbed the edge of a sheet covering a massive teak wardrobe and yanked it down. Dust filled the room. He coughed. He pulled a bunch of keys from his pocket and selected one, putting it into the lock of the wardrobe. The door creaked open, revealing a mirror in which, for a second, he regarded himself with surprise. He had aged. There was no doubt of it. But he had kept his figure. He reached into the wardrobe and selected an Indian coat of silk brocade. It was blue, with circular panels of slightly lighter blue stitched at intervals all over it. The buttons were diamonds and the cloth was lined with buckram. The high, stiff collar was fixed at the throat by two hidden brass buckles. There was also a scarlet sash. Major Nye took off his own jacket and drew the Indian coat over his white silk shirt. Carefully he did up all the buttons and then clipped the collar together. Finally he tied the sash about his waist. With his greying hair and white moustache, his clear blue eyes and his tan he could still look impressive; as impressive as when he had received the coat. It had been a

159

present from his defeated enemy Sharan Khang, the old hill fox. Was Sharan Khang still perpetuating the fiction that his Himalayan Kingdom was independent? Major Nye smiled.

Wearing the coat, he went downstairs to the gunroom. With another key he unlocked the door. Lying on the table was the Mauser FG42 where he had left it last. Closing the door behind him, he went over to the gun and picked it up, brushing away the dust which had settled on the barrel. He slotted the telescopic sight into its mount, checked the magazine and cradled the gun in his left arm. A small drop of oil now stained his silken sleeve. He opened a drawer and found a box of cartridges. He put these into his left hand and then went out, locking the door again.

He looked at his wrist-watch, checking the time. The rain had stopped for a moment. He began to smell the grass, the rhododendrons, the trees. He went outside and walked across the lawn which still had croquet hoops sticking in it from the last game, years before. On the far side of the lawn and partly obscured by foliage was the white ruin of the mansion he had built when he had first come to Simla.

Major Nye had always had a superstitious reluctance to visit the ruin, the result of a single Tibetan bomb dropped from a Caproni Ca 90 B.B. during the brief Italian crisis some years earlier. It had been the only plane ever to get as far as Simla.

The mansion's roof had collapsed completely now and part of the front wall bulged outwards. All the windows were smashed and the double doors at the front had been thrust out by the force of the blast. The only occupants of the house had been an aya and Major Nye's small son. They had both been killed.

Major Nye took a firmer grip on his rifle. He fitted shells into the magazine and then continued to stalk forward, but it was becoming harder to move at all. He mounted the first two broken steps, making himself look at the door. He was sweating.

Until this moment, he had never considered himself a coward, but he stopped dead before he reached the last step to the doorway. He shuddered at what his imagination made him see behind the doors. Trembling, he lifted the Mauser to his shoulder and, without bothering to sight, fired the whole magazine into the timber. Then he dropped the gun and ran, his face twisting in terror.

He shouted for his car. The Phantom V was ready. He got into it and drove away from Simla, his eyes wide with self-hatred.

In Delhi he booked a passage on a ship leaving Bombay a few days later. He didn't see his wife or children, but stayed at his club. Next morning he took the train to Bombay and, even when his ship, the SS *Kao An,* was well out into the Arabian Sea, he was still weeping.

THE STATUE

Prinz Lobkowitz straightened his uniform and stood shakily up in the open staffcar as it rolled into Wenzslaslas Square in the early afternoon. The troops, in smart black and gold uniforms, stood in their ranks, straight and tall and ready for review. On all sides of the square the watching crowd was eight and ten people deep. The Mercedes reached the rostrum erected below the statue of the martyr-king. The crowd cheered, the soldiers presented arms. A whistle sounded and the statue blew up. A chunk of stone rushed past Prinz Lobkowitz's head and he flung himself down into the car. General Josef, his aide, seated opposite the Prinz, drew his revolver and shouted for the driver to accelerate quickly, but the driver's nerve was gone and he was having trouble getting the Mercedes back into gear.

Save for the dead and wounded, the troops remained in reasonably good order, but the crowd had panicked. The air was filled with its screams as it tried to escape from the square. Two or three shots sounded. This increased the tension. People ran in all directions.

The smoke and dust was clearing now. Lobkowitz saw that the entire statue had been destroyed. Hardly a stump of the pedestal had survived the blast. The temporary rostrum had become a heap of shattered wood and twisted metal. Prinz Lobkowitz's standard lay half-buried in the rubble near a

162

smashed, bloody corpse which he couldn't identify.

General Josef, the aide, began shouting hoarse orders to his troops. Rifles ready, squads of soldiers broke from the square and drove their way through the terrified civilians, pouring into the surrounding buildings, occupying them and searching for the assassins. Suddenly something cracked above Lobkowitz's head. A banner had unfurled itself from a bouncing telephone wire. The banner bore a single word:

FREIHEIT

Lobkowitz pursed his lips. Terrorists. And it wasn't as if he'd taken the country by force. He felt let down.

The Mercedes was in gear now, reversing towards the street by which it had entered the square. Lobkowitz tried to straighten up and see what was happening. Old General Josef pushed him down again. On the roof of a house on the far side of the square some figures appeared. They wore civilian dress but they had bandoliers of cartridges criss-crossed on their chests and there were rifles in their hands. They looked a bit like Slovak brigands. The men and women on the roof began to fire indiscriminately into the square. Some soldiers fell; some ran for cover.

" There'll be hell to pay," General Josef kept muttering. Lobkowitz wasn't sure whether his aide was frightened of losing his job; whether Josef intended to sack his security officers; or whether he was vowing to take reprisals on the terrorists, whoever they were. Lobkowitz knew the terrorists could be anyone. They could be the disguised ' volunteer' soldiers of half-a-dozen different foreign armies; they could be anarchists; or mercenaries in the pay of some extreme right-wing group; they might be communards; they could even be Czech nationals. Time would tell.

Now the driver had swung the Mercedes round in a circle and headed down the broad, treelined Avenue Mozart, making for the Presidential Palace where they might still find safety. General Josef let the Prinz sit up. Josef put his revolver away, buttoning the holster.

" That's the last time we use an open car," he growled as he tidied his white hair and re-adjusted his cap. " It'll be an

163

armoured half-track next. The devil with public relations! "

"They didn't do much damage." Lobkowitz spoke mildly. He was unhappy in his uniform. It was too severe. He preferred the more comfortable and colourful uniforms of his native land. How much longer should he go on listening to these advisors?

"Freiheit! " muttered the aide bitterly. "What do they know of freedom? They think it means license — self-expression. A little freedom is bought at great cost. I know. I was in the original Corps which made this damned city safe. You should have been here, Prinz, before we sent for you. The stink alone would have knocked you out. It wasn't a city of liberty: it was a city of libertines."

A feeling of intense boredom swept over Lobkowitz. He had heard this remark made by a score of men in a score of different cities.

"That's finished, at least," Josef went on. "But it could all be ruined again. We must work fast."

"Do you know what the terrorists are? " Lobkowitz asked. "Do you know what movement they support? "

"Not yet. That's the least of our worries." The aide tapped his teeth with his cane and became reflective. Prinz Lobkowitz asked him no further questions.

Back at the Presidential Palace, Prinz Lobkowitz felt lonely. He sat in his huge, impressive office and looked at no one and nothing. At his back were the crossed flags of both their nations, hanging over the 18th century fireplace. From a window which opened onto the balcony he contemplated the street. In the middle of the avenue, waving a sword and mounted on a horse, stood a granite statue of some other antique hero. Even as Lobkowitz looked, it blew up. It was as if every statue he glanced at immediately burst into fragments. The noble stone head rose towards him and then, as he covered his eyes, burst through the window, taking both glass and frame into the room and bouncing, chipped but unbroken, into the empty fireplace.

For a second Prinz Lobkowitz thought it was his own head. Then he smiled. He crouched down behind his massive desk, keeping it between him and the window in case there were further explosions. After all, he thought, he had no axe to grind.

If they didn't want him, fair enough. He'd be glad to get home.

The telephone began to ring. Lobkowitz felt for it on top of the desk and found it. " Lobkowitz."

"Are you hurt, sir? " It was General Josef's voice.

" No, not at all, but the firedog's a bit bent."

" I'll be up right away."

As he waited for Josef's arrival, Lobkowitz sat on the edge of the desk and lit the last of his Black Cat cigarettes. Before he crumpled the packet and threw it into his wastepaper bin, he took the brightly coloured card (one of a series of 50 given away free with the cigarettes) and tucked it into the top breast pocket of the civilian waistcoat he had always worn under his uniform. It was a picture of a triceretops, number eighteen in a series of dinosaurs.

The red and black packet was the only piece of scrap in the otherwise clean steel wastepaper basket. He felt for it.

The gilded doors swung open. Una Persson stood there, dressed all in black, a rifle slung over her back, a beret on her shining curls. She opened her arms to him, smiling.

" Darling! I have defeated you again! "

REMINISCENCE (E)

In the early hours of a summer morning a cat kills a mouse in the kitchen, letting it run a little way and then stopping it again. Outside in the garden large black slugs crawl over the iron furniture. There is movement in the toolshed. There is a whisper from beyond the trees.

LATE NEWS

A crowd of about 200 attacked two Army scout cars and a Land Rover in Belfast last night after one of them ran over and killed a five-year-old girl. Cars, vans and lorries were set on fire and there were bursts of machine-gun fire which injured four young children. The girl was one of a crowd of children playing on the street corner. An Army spokesman said she jumped under the wheels of the leading scout car.

MORNING STAR, February 9 1971

A widow, her five children and an uncle died in a fire at a cottage in Pontypool yesterday. Firemen found the bodies of Mrs Patricia Evans, aged 34, Jacqueline, 13, Garry, 11, Joanne, eight, Martin, six, and Catherine, two, in a bedroom. On the stairs was the body of Mr John Edwards, aged 63, the uncle who came to rescue them.

GUARDIAN, February 9 1971

George Lasky, aged four, was drowned when he fell into an ice-covered pond in a field at Slough yesterday. He had gone on the ice to pick up a ball.

GUARDIAN, March 2 1971

Murder squad detectives set up headquarters in a holiday beach café in Cornwall yesterday after the badly-battered body of a 17-year-old high school girl had been found near the entrance to a cliff-top camp site.

GUARDIAN, March 15 1971

A three-year-old boy was found dead in a disused refrigerator last night.

GUARDIAN, June 29 1971

Lynn Andrews, aged 10, was stripped almost naked and punched and kicked to death while her mother looked on helpless, it was said in court at Woolwich yesterday. Raymond John Day (31), unemployed, was sent for trial charged with murdering the girl.

GUARDIAN, June 30 1971

The Alternative Apocalypse 5

Jerry Cornelius was in Sandakan when the news came of the resumption of hostilities. The news was brought by Dassim Shan, Jerry's major domo, while Jerry swam in the cool waters of the palace pool, all pink and blue marble and tinkling fountains.

Rajah? Dassim, feet together, stood uncertainly on the edge of the pool, one hand against a jade pillar. Jerry was some distance out in the middle of the pool, hidden in the shade. Milky light filtered down from the semi-transparent dome in the roof. Dassim's voice echoed a little.

They are fighting again, rajah.

Oh? A splash.

Does it not concern you, rajah?

Dassim peered into the water, searching every inch of it for his master, but he could see only goldfish.

The Alternative Apocalypse 6

Bishop Beesley, Mitzi Beesley, Shakey Mo Collier and Jerry Cornelius stood on the footbridge staring down at the railway as the train passed beneath their feet. Through the steam they could see the open trucks piled high with stiffening corpses. Dead troops.

Jerry pushed his helmet back from his forehead and eased the strap of his pack. Well, he said, our luck's still holding.

The smell! Mitzi Beesley, dressed in a complete ARP uniform, circa 1943, held her nose.

Her father sorted through his tin of emergency rations to see if there was any chocolate he'd overlooked. That's not the half of it, he said. He wore khaki battledress with his dog-collar rather ostentatiously displayed at the throat.

I remember a train like that when I was a kid, said Mo Collier nostalgically. On'y in that case the soldiers on it was alive.

Same difference, said Mitzi with a wink. She rubbed busily at her blue flannel thigh as the last truck went under the bridge.

Jerry looked at his left watch. Well, back to work. Not far to Grasmere now.

They all climbed on to the lightweight Jungle Bug, with its motorbike saddle seats and its canvas windshield. Jerry settled himself in front of the driving gear and started the engine. For a moment the machine reared, its front wheels spinning, and then they were off down the narrow lane as a thin cloud of rain drifted from the fells to the west and the green hills turned suddenly black.

We've never fully been able to reproduce World War Two conditions, Bishop Beesley yelled over the screech of the engine and the slap of the wind. I sometimes consider it a personal failure.

Your moral dilemmas always resolve themselves sooner or later, dad, Mitzi comforted. She reached over from where she sat alongside him on the pillion behind Jerry and straightened his M60 on his shoulder for him. Is that better?

He nodded gratefully, munching a piece of Nut Crunch he had found in the breast-pocket of his battledress. They bounced on towards Grasmere and, as the rain passed, glimpsed the lake on the far side of a hill lying almost directly ahead of them. They had heard that what was left of an enemy division was hiding out in Wordsworth's cottage. It was a long shot, but it was something to do.

The road went through a pine wood and then bent along the eastern shore of the lake, leading directly into the town of Grasmere. The town was a ruin of looted gift shops and tea rooms. In one or two places they were forced to steer round small craters in the road. Elsewhere a sack had burst and been abandoned, leaving a litter of plaster Wordsworth busts, oven gloves and daffodil vases.

They headed for the main road with its cracked and weedgrown concrete and at last sighted Dove Cottage and, a few doors away, another cottage that was the Wordsworth Museum. There were signs of fighting in the stone, half-timbered buildings. One or two cottages had been destroyed completely, but Dove Cottage, with its roses round the door, was intact. They climbed off the Jungle Bug and readied their weapons, approaching cautiously.

Dove Cottage seemed deserted, but Jerry didn't take any chances. He ordered Bishop Beesley forward. The bishop lay down behind a hedge and raked the windows. There was a musical tinkle as the glass broke. Bishop Beesley waited for a while and then stood up, munching a Mars Bar.

A Webley .45 sounded from an upstairs window and the bullet went past him, hitting the ground. He turned, his Mars Bar half-raised, and darted an enquiring glance at Jerry, who shrugged.

There was another shot. Bishop Beesley eased his bulk to the ground again, put a new clip in his M60 and fired at the window.

When there was no further answering fire, the four of them spread out and approached the cottage. Jerry noticed that the plaque on the door reading ' Wordsworth's Cottage ' had been holed a few times by shells larger than Bishop Beesley's. The door opened easily for the lock had already been blown off. They went in. An American teenage girl, with long black hair and a red mou-mou pulled up around her waist, lay on the polished timber floor. Her blood had dried on her face and her left hand was missing. Apart from the girl, the downstairs rooms, with their glass cabinets of Wordsworth and Lake Poets trophies, were empty. Pictures of Southey, Coleridge, De Quincy and the Lambs smiled down at them. Shakey Mo broke one of the cabinets with the butt of his Sten and lifted out an oddly shaped object of carved ivory. He squinted at the label. Look at this! De Quincy's drug balance. Look at the size! What a head! He put the balance into the gamebag he had slung over one shoulder and rummaged through the rest of the cabinet's contents. He found nothing else of interest. More glass broke in the next room and the three of them trooped in to see what Mitzi was doing. She had smashed the glass partition behind which had been arranged a typical sitting room of Wordsworth's time. She had stripped off her ARP uniform and was draping herself in the dead poet's clothes, his hat, his jacket, his shawl and one of his waistcoats. She held his umbrella in one hand. With her Remington tucked under her arm, she tried to open the umbrella. They all laughed as she paraded round the room pretending to read from one of Dorothy Wordsworth's diaries.

Jerry heard a footfall upstairs and raised his Schmidt Rubin 5.56 to rake the ceiling. The footfall stopped.

I suppose we'd better get upstairs, said Shakey Mo.

Jerry led the way.

The upstairs rooms were much the same as the downstairs rooms, with more cabinets and more trophies, some of which

172

had been smashed by Bishop Beesley's M60 bullets coming through the windows. In the front room sat a woman of about sixty. She was tall, dressed in a plain blue dress and her hair was grey. The empty Webley was still in her hand. She was evidently upset. There are guided tours, you know, she said. You only had to ask.

Bishop Beesley grinned with relish as he advanced on her. I'm going to fuck the life out of you, he said.

Jerry and the rest made a tactful retreat.

Bishop Beesley joined them later in the Wordsworth Museum where Shakey Mo was inspecting an old shot-gun labelled 'Wordsworth's Gun'.

My God, said Beesley in disgust, even this place has a tinge of vitality. Bishop Beesley argued that since too much life had led to their present difficulties (overcrowding and so forth), then life meant death and was therefore evil. Therefore it was his duty to wipe out the evil by destroying life wherever he found it. He was a wizard at that sort of thing. Jerry had his eye on him.

Are we all finished here? Jerry asked.

They padded away, turning only to watch when Shakey Mo lobbed a couple of Mills bombs into the cottage and the museum.

Damn! said Mitzi as the buildings went up. I left my uniform behind.

She wrapped Wordsworth's shawl more tightly around her, pursing her lips in rage as she tripped, on Cuban heels, back to the Jungle Bug. Bishop Beesley, Shakey Mo and Jerry Cornelius took the opportunity to piss against a hedge; then the rain came on again.

In improved spirits, they mounted the Bug and headed towards Rydal and the high, green hills beyond.

173

LATE NEWS

Lt. William Calley, charged with massacring 102 South Vietnamese men, women and children at My Lai hamlet, testified at his court-martial at Fort Benning, California, yesterday, that the army taught him children were even more dangerous than adults. He was taught that ' men and women were equally dangerous, and children, because of their unsuspectingness were even more dangerous '. The army also taught him that men and women fought side by side and women for some reason were better shots. He was told that ' children can be used in a multiple of facets. For example, give a child a hand grenade and he can throw it at an American unit. They were used for planting mines. Basically they were very dangerous.'.

MORNING STAR, February 23 1971

Three boys died when a house caught fire in Cemetery Road, Telford, Salop. They were Keith William Troop, aged five, Peter John Green, aged three, and Matthew Percival Green, aged two. They were the sons of Mrs Joan Green, aged 22.

GUARDIAN, May 3 1971

Mrs Valerie Ridyard, aged 25, pleaded guilty to the manslaughter of Darren, aged five months, Michael, aged three, and

174

Barbara, aged four, on the grounds of diminished responsibility. Her pleas of not guilty to murder were accepted. The children died in separate incidents between October 1970 and January 1971. Mr Arthur Prescott, QC, prosecuting, said the facts were short and tragic. There had been a history of conduct by Mrs Ridyard resulting in illness to the children through partial suffocation and poisoning.

GUARDIAN, June 10 1971

The West Indian immigrant parents of seven children admitted at Berkshire assizes, Reading, yesterday to killing one of their sons in a ritual sacrifice. Olton Goring (40), of Waylen Street, Reading, was committed to Broadmoor after the prosecution accepted his plea of not guilty to murdering the boy, Keith, aged 16, but guilty to manslaughter on grounds of diminished responsibility. Goring's wife, Eileen (44), pleaded guilty to manslaughter and was ordered to be sent for treatment in a mental hospital. It was said the Gorings were members of a Pentecostal mission in Reading — a revival sect widely supported in the West Indies. Followers believed themselves possessed by the Holy Spirit while in a trance and felt they were in direct communication with God.

GUARDIAN, June 10 1971

A boy aged 14 will appear in court at Tamworth, Staffordshire, today in connection with the death of a man aged 19 whose body was found in a house on Saturday.

GUARDIAN, August 23 1971

A girl aged 14 was charged on Saturday with the murder of Roisin McIlone, aged five, whose body was found beside an overgrown bridle path near her home in Brook Farm Walk, Celmsley Wood, near Birmingham. A bloodstained stick was found nearby.

GUARDIAN, August 23 1971

REMINISCENCE (F)

The black, burning warehouses of Newcastle.

THE AIRSHIP

During the First Night Dance on board the L.S. *Light of Dresden,* bound for India via Aden, Mrs Cornelius went out onto the semi-open observation deck to get some air. She felt a little queasy; it was her maiden trip on a zeppelin, but she was determined to enjoy herself, come what may. All she had to do was clear her head and let herself get used to a feeling that was like being permanently in a slightly swaying descending lift that was also moving horizontally. She stood outside the big hall where the spotlights played beams of red, blue, yellow and green on the dancers. The band was called The Little Chocolate Dandies. Their saxophones wailing, they launched themselves into their next number, *Royal Garden Blues.* Mrs Cornelius wasn't too sure she was that keen on jazz, after all. At present she felt like hearing something just a teeny bit more restful. But the only thing she could think of was *Rock-a-by-baby*: in fact, she couldn't get it out of her head. She looked down at the lights of Paris (she thought it was Paris) and imagined the drop. Though she had been assured that it was completely rigid and part of the main frame containing the helium bags, she was sure she could feel the catwalk swaying below her. The music from the dance floor now seemed much more friendly. She reeled back in again.

Everyone was really jazzing it up tonight. She was nearly

knocked down twice by couples as she moved towards the bar. She grinned. Ah, well! She felt a hand on her shoulder.

"Are you perfectly well, dear lady? "

It was that bishop she'd met earlier. She'd liked him from the start, with his nice, jolly fat face, though she hadn't taken to his wife in the baggy pink evening dress, frizzy hair, with her thin, pale, nervous head constantly grinning in a way Mrs C personally found offensive. If you asked Mrs C, the bishop's wife fancied herself a bit. Lady Muck. The bishop, on the other hand, was a real gentleman, he could mix with anyone at any level. Mrs C could go for him in a big way. She smiled to herself at the thought, wondering what it would be like with a bishop.

" Quaite well, thank yew, bishop, love," she said. " Jist gittin' me air-legs, thet's hall."

" Would you care to dance? "

" Oh, charmed Ai'm shewer! " She put her left arm round his ample, black clad waist and folded her dumpy right hand in his. They began to fox-trot. " Yore a lovely dancer, bishop." She giggled. Over the bishop's shoulder she saw his wife looking on, nodding to her with that same set, patronising smile, though you could tell she wasn't pleased. Mrs C defiantly pushed her bosom against the bishop's chest. The bishop's red lips smiled slightly and his little eyes twinkled. She knew he fancied her. She went all warm and funny inside as his hand tightened on her corset. What a turn up.

"Are you travelling alone, Mrs Cornelius? "

" Well, Ai've got me littel boy wiv me, but 'e's no trouble. Got a cabin to 'imself."

"And — Mr Cornelius? "

" Gorn, unforchunatly."

" You mean? "

" Quaite. R.I.P."

" I'm sorry to hear it."

" Well, it was a long time ago, you see."

"Aha." The bishop looked upwards, towards the gigantic gas-bags hidden behind the dance hall's aluminium ceiling. " He's in a happier state than we, all in all."

" Quaite."

Well, thought Mrs C, he's not slow. Maybe he was the original bishop in the jokes, eh? Again she couldn't stop herself from smiling. Her queasiness had completely disappeared, to be replaced by that old feeling.

"And how are you travelling? First class, I assume? "

"Ai should fink so! " She roared with laughter. " No such luck, Ai'm afraid. It's second class for me. It's not cheap, the fare to Calcutta."

" I agree. I, too — that is to say my wife and I — am forced to travel second. But I must say I've no complaints, as yet, though it is only our first night aloft. We are in cabin 46 . . ."

" Oh, reahlly? Wot a coincidence. Ai'm in number 38, Just deown the passage from you. Mai littel boy's in 30, sharin' wiv a couple of other littel boys."

" You have a good relationship with your son? "

" Oh, yes! 'E's devoted! "

" I envy you."

" Wot, me? "

" I wish I had a good relationship with my — my sole relative. Mrs Beesley, I regret, is not the easiest woman with whom to be joined in holy matrimony."

" She seems a naice sort o' woman, if a bit, you know, out of things, as you might say."

" She does not take pleasure, as I do, in making new friends. Normally I travel alone, and Mrs Beesley remains at the rectory, but she has a sister in Delhi and so she decided, this time, to accompany me." Now the bishop's stomach pressed against her stomach. It was so cosy, it made her legs feel like jelly.

" P'raps she should rest more," said Mrs C. "Ai mean she could take the chance to relax before we get to India, couldn't she? It would probably do 'er good." She hoped the bishop hadn't noticed the rather savage delivery of that last sentence. He certainly seemed unaware of the change in her tone and only smiled vaguely. The music stopped and, reluctantly, they broke their embrace and clapped politely at the coloured men in tuxedos on the bandstand. One of the musicians stepped forward, his black hands running up and down the keys of his saxophone as he spoke.

"And now, ladies and gentlemen, we'd like to give you my own *That's How I Feel Today*. Thank you."

Tuba, banjo, three saxophones, drums, piano, trumpet and trombone all started up at once and, oblivious to the other dancers, Mrs Cornelius and Bishop Beesley began to Charleston, still holding each other very close. When Mrs Cornelius next noticed Mrs Beesley, the bishop's wife was quietly leaving through the exit onto the main corridor. Mrs C felt triumphant. Po-faced bitch! Didn't she believe in a feller enjoying himself?

"Ai'm afraid yore waife 'as decided to leave us," she said into his plump, red ear.

" Oh dear. Perhaps she's gone to lie down. I wonder if I shouldn't . . .? "

" Oh, come on, bishop! Finish the dance! "

" Yes, indeed. Why not? "

The lights dimmed, the tone of the music sweetened and Mrs C and Bishop B began to fox-trot again. It was very romantic. Everyone on the floor sensed the mood and got smoochy. Mrs Cornelius's bosom began to heave and she wriggled her bulk against Bishop Beesley's, who responded by moving his hand over her bottom.

She murmured, as the music subsided, " You feel like it, don't you? "

He nodded eagerly, smiling and clapping. " I do, dear lady. I do, indeed."

" Would you like to escort me to mai cabin door? "

" I should like nothing better." The old dog was almost panting with lust. She winked at him and put her arm in his.

" Come on, then."

This was what she called a ship-board romance.

They went into the passage and turned left, searching for the right cabin number in the dim, blue light.

They slipped surreptitiously passed number 46 and Mrs Cornelius searched hastily for her key as they approached number 38. She produced it with a flourish and inserted it delicately into the lock, turning the levers with a soft double click. She stood there coquettishly, a hand on her hip. " Would you care for a nip of something to keep out the cold? "

He snorted.

He darted a quick look up and down the corridor, and dived into the cabin, his mouth closing on hers, his hands caressing her huge breasts. His breath was oddly sweet, almost sickly, but she quite liked it.

She hitched up her skirt and lay down on the bunk. He pulled down his gaiters and flung his sticky body on top of her. Soon they were bouncing up and down in the narrow bunk, all the aluminium work creaking. They were shouting and grunting in unison as orgasms shook their combined thirty-eight stones of flesh when the door opened and blue light filtered in from the corridor. A spotty youth stood there, peering in. Evidently he couldn't see clearly. " Mum? "

" Oh, fuck me! It's orlright, son. Git along will yer? I'm busy at the minute."

The boy, who was probably in his mid-teens, continued to stand there, his mean, ratlike features those of an idiot, his large eyes dull and uncomprehending.

" Mum? "

" Bugger off! "

" Oh," he said, as his eyes got used to the dark, " sorry."

The door closed.

Mrs Cornelius clambered from the bunk, scratching her pelvis. " Sorry abart, that, bishop. Fergot ter lock it." She pulled the bolt into its socket, then stumbled back, her knickers still around one ankle. She unbuckled her corsets and let them drop and was above to remove her dress when the bishop seized her by the hair and pulled her head down towards his penis which rolled back and forth like the mast of a storm-tossed ship. His eyes continued to stare thoughtfully at the door.

In the passage the boy grinned at his mum's antics and, dressed only in his raincoat, boots and socks, continued to search for a vacant lavatory. He listened to the vibrations from the vessel's great engines, listened to the faint sound of the wind as it slid over the monstrous silver hull, listened to the distant music of the jazz band. He ran his hand through his long, greasy hair and wished that he had a monkey suit he could wear. Then *he'd* go to the dance and the janeys had better look out for their virginity! He shuffled down a side-passage and then slid open the door onto the observation deck. The lights of the city were past now and the airship seemed to be flying over open countryside. Here and there were a few flickering lights from small villages or farmhouses. Even from this height he didn't much fancy the country. It made him nervous.

He looked up at the blackness above. There were hardly any stars out at all and a thin rain seemed to be falling. Well, at least the weather would be better in Calcutta.

The ship shivered as it turned a degree or two, correcting its course. The distant music wavered and then continued at full strength. The note of the engines altered. There was something almost hesitant about the way the ship moved. The youth stared forward and thought he saw in the distance the white-topped waves of the Mediterranean. Or was it the Bay of Biscay? Whatever the name of the sea, the sight of it meant something to him. For no reason he could understand, the sight filled him with a sense of relief. They were leaving Europe behind.

The youth watched eagerly as they began to move out above the water. He grinned as he saw the land fall away. Apart from the crew, he was the only one to notice this change.

THE LOCOMOTIVE

Wondering how he had come to be involved in this revolution
in the first place, Colonel Pyat swayed forward to have a word
with the driver of the armoured train. Dirty steam struck his
face and he coughed painfully, his eyes watering. He tried to
rub at his eyes with his free hand, but the train snaked round
a bend and forced him to reach out and grab the other steel
hand-rail on the observation platform. The train travelled over
a vast plain of burned wheat. In all directions the landscape
was flat and black, with the occasional patch of green, white
or yellow which had somehow escaped the flames. Colonel
Pyat would be glad to get into the hills which he could just see
on the horizon ahead. He opened the plate-armour door of the
next compartment and found that it was deserted of soldiers.
Here there were only boxes of ammunition and light machine
guns. He made his way cautiously between the stacks. Perhaps
military responsibilities were the simplest a right-thinking man
could shoulder without feeling feeble. Certainly, the responsibility of commanding an armoured train was preferable to the
responsibility he had left at home. On the other hand, he could
have been helping the sick in some relatively safe hospital behind
the lines, not heading willy-nilly towards the Ukraine and the
worst fighting of the whole damned civil war. 193- had not
been a good year for Colonel Pyat.

He tried to brush the soot off his uniform and succeeded only in smearing more of the stuff over the white buckskin. He sat down with a thump on an ammunition box and, scraping his match on the barrel of a machine gun, lit a small cheroot. He could do with a drink. He felt for the flask in his hip-pocket. It was there, all slim brass and silver. He unscrewed the top and raised the lip to his mouth. A single drop of brandy fell onto his tongue. He sighed and put the flask back. If they ever got to Kiev, the first thing he would do would be to requisition a bottle of Cognac. If such a thing still existed.

The thin strains of a piano accordion drifted down the length of the train from behind him. The vibrant, gloomy voices of his troops began to sing. He got up, the cheroot held tightly in his teeth, and continued on his way.

' I should have stayed in the diplomatic corps,' he was thinking as he opened a door and saw the huge log tender looming over him, its chipped black enamel smeared with streaks of green and yellow paint where someone had tried to obscure the previous owner's insignia. There was a door in the tender, leading to a low passage through which he had to pass to get to the engine footplate itself. He heard the logs thumping and rattling over his head and then he had emerged to find the fireman hurling half a tree into the yellow, roaring furnace. The driver, his hand on the acceleration wheel, had his head sticking out of the observation port on the left of the loco. Two guards sat behind him, their rifles crooked in their arms, their legs dangling over the edge of the footplate. They were half asleep, their fur shakos tipped down over their foreheads, and they didn't notice Colonel Pyat's arrival. The footplate smelled strongly of the cedar wood which was now their main fuel. Overlaying this was the well-defined odour of human sweat. Colonel Pyat leant against the tender and finished his cheroot. Only the fireman knew he was there and the fireman was too busy to acknowledge his presence.

Throwing the butt of his cheroot at the blasted fields, he stepped forward and tapped the driver on his naked shoulder. The thickset man turned reluctantly, showing a face covered in dirty fair hair; his red-rimmed eyes glared through the black mask of soot. He grunted when he saw that it was Pyat and tried to look respectful. " Sir? "

" What sort of time are we making? "

" Not bad, sir, considering everything."

"And Kiev? When should we get there now? "

" Less than another eight hours, all things being equal."

" So we're not much more than half a day behind schedule. Splendid. You and your crew are working wonders. I'm very pleased."

The driver was wondering why they were bothering to go to Kiev in the first place, but wearily he responded to his commander's attempt at morale-building. " Thank you, sir."

Colonel Pyat noticed that, having tried for a second to look alert after they had noticed him, the guards had resumed their earlier slumped postures. " Mind if I stay on the footplate for a little while? " he asked the driver.

" You're the commander, sir." This time the driver couldn't stop the sardonic, edgy note in his voice.

"Ah, well." Pyat turned. " I won't bother you, then."

He ducked into the passage under the tender and stumbled through to the other side. As he tried to get the door open, he heard a faint cry from behind him. A rifle shot sounded. He went back through the passage. Now both guards were on their feet, shooting into the air.

" Look, sir! " One of them pointed ahead.

They were almost upon the lowest of the foothills and something was moving just behind the nearest ridge.

" Better take it easy, driver." Pyat grabbed for the cord to ring the alarm bell through the rest of the train. " What do you think they are? "

The soldier answered. " Land 'clads, sir. At least a score of them. I saw them better a moment ago."

Pyat tugged the alarm cord. The driver began to slow the train which was now about half-a-mile from a tunnel running under a high, green hill. Even as they watched, a pair of racing metal caterpillar tracks appeared on the roof of the tunnel, pointing directly at them. Then they saw a gun-turret above the tracks as they descended. The long 85mm cannon swung round until it pointed directly at the engine. Pyat and the rest threw themselves flat as the gun flashed. There was an explosion

185

nearby, but the locomotive was undamaged. The driver looked to Pyat for his orders. Pyat was inclined to stop, but then he decided to risk a race for what might be the safety of the tunnel (if it hadn't been mined). There was a chance. The tank barbarians rarely left their vessels. Some hadn't seen direct sunlight for months. " Maximum speed," he said. The fireman stood up and dragged more logs off the tender. Pyat yanked open the firedoor. The driver pulled his acceleration wheel all the way round. The train hissed and bucked and lurched forward. Another 85mm explosive shell hit the ground, this time on the other side of the train. The tunnel was very close now. On either side of it there emerged a motley collection of land ironclads, half-tracks and armoured cars, mobile guns, all armed to the teeth. The vehicles were painted with streaks of bright, primitive colour and decorated with shells, bits of silk and velvet, strings of beads, strips of ermine and mink, bones and severed human heads. Pyat's suspicions were confirmed. This was the roving Makhnoite horde which, months before, had swept down from beyond the Volga, bringing terror and nihilism. The horde was virtually invulnerable. It would be pointless, now, to stop.

The train entered the darkness of the tunnel. Already Pyat could see daylight at the other end. Then, from behind, came a massive explosion and the locomotive was hurled forward at an incredible speed. They came out of the tunnel with wheels squealing, with the whole loco rocking, and in a few seconds had left the tank barbarians far behind.

It was only later, as the driver began to slow the locomotive, that they realised they had also left the greater part of the train behind at the tunnel. Evidently a shell had broken the coupling between the first carriage and the tender.

Pyat, the driver, the fireman and the two guards laughed in relief. The train sped on towards Kiev. Now there was a very good chance that they would not be off schedule at all.

Pyat congratulated himself on the democratic impulse which, originally, had led him to join the men on the footplate. There were some advantages, it seemed, to democracy.

THE STEAM YACHT

Una Persson shivered. She wrapped her heavy black mink more tightly around her slim body. The silk Erté tea gown beneath the coat was cold and unpleasant against her flesh. She was feeling old. It was as much as she could do to stay awake. She smiled to herself and made a few long strides through the clinging fog, over the deck to the rail of the yacht.

She could see nothing at all of Lake Erie and she could hear nothing but the dull flap of the waves against the *Teddy Bear's* white sides.

They were fogbound. They had been lying at anchor for days. The wireless had broken and there had been no reply to signal rockets, sirens or shouts. Yet Una was sure that a dark launch had passed close to the yacht at least twice in the last twenty-four hours. She had heard the purr of its engine several times during the previous night.

The yellow-white fog shifted and swirled like something sentient and malevolent. It was as if she were trapped in some dreadful Munch lithograph. She hated it and wished bitterly that she had not accepted the owner's offer of this cruise. It had been so boring in New York, though. She really disliked Broadway much more than she disliked the West End.

She drew the red and black silk scarf off her tightly-waved, short-cropped hair and wiped the moisture from her hands and

187

face. Why was everything so frightfully bloody?

She went back to the companionway behind the wheelhouse, paused, shivered and then daintily began to descend on high-heeled slippers, trying to make as much noise as possible on the iron steps.

Arriving in the corridor leading to the guest cabins, she noticed that some wisps of fog had at last managed to creep in. Now it was scarcely warmer here than it had been on deck. A 'brooding' silence. Were they to die here, then? It began to seem likely.

She tried to pull herself together, straightening her shoulders, putting a bit of bounce into her long step, bearing up manfully.

She went into the owner's large cabin, remarking, not for the first time, the incredible American vulgarity of it. It had been designed to look like a Tudor hall, with oak beams on the roof and pewter plates on the walls, claymores and tapestries. An electric Belling heater, built to resemble a log fire, only barely managed to take the chill off the cabin. The cabin had looked like this when the yacht had been purchased from its previous owner, but no attempt had been made to change it. It made her feel ill. It made her nervy.

The owner stood with his back to the cabin, staring out of the square, diamond-leaded porthole, into the fog. Once he leaned forward and, with his handkerchief, wiped condensation from the glass.

" Do you see any faces you recognise? " asked Una, attempting to sound friendly.

" Faces in the fog? " He glanced back at her and smiled. "All faces are foggy to me, my dear. It's my loss, I suppose."

Una gave vent to a dramatic sigh. " You and your old angst, darling! What would you do without it, I wonder? " She bent forward and pecked him on the cheek with her carmine lips. " Oh, it's so *cold*." She crossed to the genuine Tudor sideboard and picked at a dish of mixed nuts. " When *will* this boring fog lift? "

" Why don't you make the most of it? Relax. Pour yourself a drink."

"A tot of rum? I can't relax. The fog's so *sinister*." She ended this sentence on her famous falling note but then she let it rise again, almost without pause. " I like to *do* things, Lob." The pathos and the warmth in her voice was so strong that Prinz Lobkowitz was quite startled, as if he had found himself once again at the theatre where he had first seen her act. " I don't mean silly things," she continued. " Worthwhile things."

" Good causes? " He was ironic.

" If there's nothing else."

There was a sound on the water. The faint putter of a motor.

She crossed eagerly to the window and, standing beside him, peered out. She moved her head this way and that as if there was a particular angle at which she would be able to see through the fog. She saw a gleam of water, a shadow.

He put his arm around her shoulders. She was so womanly at that moment. But she shrugged him away. " Can you hear it? A motor-boat? "

" I've heard it frequently. It never comes very close."

" Have you tried shouting to it? Using your loud-hailer, or whatever it's called? "

" Yes. It never answers."

" Who can it be? "

" I don't know." He spoke almost in a whisper.

She looked searchingly up into his face. " You sound as if you have a good idea, though."

" No."

It was a lie.

" Oh, be as mysterious as you like. But you're rather over-doing the atmosphere, don't you think? "

" Not deliberately."

She went back to the sideboard and helped herself to a Balkan Sobranie cigarette from the silver box, lighting it with a flourish at the flamingo-shaped table lighter. Puffing pettishly, she began to pace.

He watched her. He loved to see her act. She was so talented. He was glad they were marooned, for it meant he could watch her almost all the time.

" You're wonderfully selfish," he said. " I love you. I admire you."

" I love you, too, Lob, darling, but couldn't we go and love each other somewhere warmer? Couldn't we go back to one of those cities? Chicago or somewhere? Couldn't we risk the fog? "

" There's a lot of hungry people waiting on the docks for unwary yachts. I'm afraid it wouldn't be wise."

The motor-boat started up again and went away.

" If he can move, why can't we? "

" He's smaller. He's got less to lose. I mean, there's less risk for him." From the pocket of his white silk dressing gown he took a white box. He opened the box and took a pinch of white powder from it, sniffing it vigorously first into one nostril and then into the other. He put the box back and continued to stare out of the porthole.

She went to the big radiogram and picked up a record. It was her own, from last year's hit *Only You*. She put it on and listened to herself singing the blue number which came in the middle of the show, *Gonna Kill That Man*.

She smiled wistfully.

> " *Gonna kill that man, if I can.*
> *You have to be cruel to be kind.*
> *I can't get him out of my mind.*
> *He's the worst sort of guy you could possibly find*
> *To his vices, I guess, I am utterly blind.*
> *But if he should try to two-time me*
> *He'll discover that I won't sublime be.*
> *I'll take out my gun*
> *And I'll stop all his fun.*
> *I'm gonna kill that man —*
> *If he loves a she who ain't me.*"

It was not her usual sort of material, yet it had been the number they'd all liked best, especially in London. She'd used a sort of Hoagy Carmichael technique for it. But she still didn't think much of it herself. She stopped the record and turned it over to *Dancing on the Clouds* which was much more *her*: bitter-sweet but essentially gay. Yet even this reminded her of the fog outside and she turned the bakelite volume knob off with a snap, though she could still hear her voice, very, very faintly from the turntable. It was like a ghost. It made her shiver.

Her lover came towards her.

Was it all over? she wondered. The whole thing? Was she finished?

He was handsome in his white sweater, his white gown and white flannels, but he was pale. Another ghost in this foggy purgatory.

He embraced her.

" Una."

THE FLYING BOAT

They were going back.

Captain Nye steered the DoX over the choppy waters of the harbour. Behind them, Rowe Island lay in ruins, her airship masts buckled, her hotels blasted, her streets wasted, her mines and mine-workers buried under the tumbled granite of the great volcanic hill. The placid Indian Ocean, a sheet of burnished blue steel reflecting a brazen sun, remained.

" Well, that's bloody that, then," said Frank Cornelius, stripping off his coolie blouse to reveal a loud, orange pullover. He wiped the best part of the make-up from his corrupt features. "And that's Jerry down the drain, if he isn't very careful indeed."

" I hope not." Catherine stood behind the two men who had already taken their seats. She dried her face with a Rodier towel. " It's such a beautiful day, isn't it? " She wore an open-necked white shirt and white jodhpurs. Her calf-length riding boots were light tan. Her longish hair fell in two tight waves to her shoulders. She wore little make-up. She looked wonderful.

" Best weather in the world on Rowe Island," said Captain Nye. "A great pity."

Miss Brunner was absent, as was the skeleton of the child. Nothing had gone right, really.

Captain Nye switched on all the engines and opened up the throttle, roaring out to sea. The floats began to rear beneath them, the wing-flaps whistled, and up they went into the clear, blue yonder.

Catherine wandered into the ballroom which had been refitted as a spacious lounge. Nobody felt like dancing at the moment. There were violently coloured Bakst murals on the walls. She looked enviously at the rich, fantastic scenes of fairyland forests and exotic Oriental princesses and Nubian slaves. It was a world she would feel happy in at the present moment. She was exhausted. She needed a rest, but she wanted a voluptuous rest. Hashish, honey and a handsome Hindu lover.

Professor Hira appeared, climbing the steps into the lounge and yawning. " I was asleep. I hadn't realised we were taking off so soon." His round, genial face held a faintly puzzled look " How long have we been up? "

She nodded out of the nearest window. " Not long. You can still see the island. Look."

"I won't, thanks. I've seen quite enough of Rowe Island now A terrible fiasco. I feel so guilty."

" Guilty? You shouldn't feel guilty." She closed her eyes, leaning back on the Beaumont tapestry cushions. She wished he hadn't come to interrupt what had promised to be quite a thrilling reverie. He was always too talkative when he got up. She pretended to doze.

" Yes," he said soberly. " It was all my fault. The ritual was infallible, in itself, and with the right *sort* of cosmic energy, we should have succeeded. But how was I to know that the majority of the coolies had been replaced by Malays? Those Muslims, they're the next best thing to an atheist. And then there was all the trouble with the time-concept, nobody quite agreeing on that. Again, the Malays . . ."

" Well, then —" She took a deep, lazy breath and drew her legs up onto the couch. " It was their fault. It doesn't matter now. Though it's a pity about the Governor's residence. Wasn't that a charming building? "

" Did you like it? I've had to look at a spot too much of that type of thing in Calcutta, I'm afraid."

Catherine caught only the last words. "Afraid? It's a relief to know someone else is."

"Afraid? What of? I've never seen you looking better."

"The future, I suppose. And yet I hate the past. Don't you? "

" I've never quite understood the difference. I don't see it like that."

"A woman — well — I'm forced to. In some ways, at least. I know it would be better for me if I didn't."

" If time could stand still," said Hira reflectively. " I suppose we should all be as good as dead. The whole business of entropy so accurately reflects the human condition. To remain alive one must burn fuel, use up heat, squander resources, and yet that very action contributes to the end of the universe — the heat death of everything! But to become still, to use the minimum of energy — that's pointless. It is to die, effectively. What a dreadful dilemma."

Captain Nye stepped from the pilot's cabin into the lounge. " Your brother's steering. He picks things up fast, doesn't he? "

"Anything he can get." Catherine regretted her waspish tone and added: " He's very intelligent, Frank." She looked into Nye's blue-grey eyes and smiled.

" Well," he said. " I'm going to get some sleep."

" Yes," she said. " I think it's time I hit the hay. It's been a long — long . . ." She yawned.

She nodded to Hira and followed Captain Nye to the stairs, down past the cocktail bar, the cabin area and into the cabin. As he kissed her she held him tightly, saying: " I'd better warn you. I'm very tired."

" Don't worry." He unbuttoned his jacket. " So am I."

She saw him shiver slightly. "Are you cold? "

"A tiny touch of malaria, I shouldn't wonder," he said. " Nothing to worry about."

" I'll cuddle up to you and keep you warm," she said.

Professor Hira, feeling both lonely and jealous, joined Frank in the control cabin. Frank was wearing his fur-trimmed tinted flying goggles and looked a bit like a depraved lemur. He patted Hira's knee as the Indian physicist sat down. " 'Ello, 'ello, old son! How goes it? "

" Not so dusty," said Hira. "Are you sure that chap Nye's all right? "

" What? Nye? One of the best. Why? "

" Well — going with your sister . . ."

194

"He's been sweet on her for years. Cathy knows what she's doing."

"She's such a lovely girl. A generous girl."

"Yes," said Frank vaguely. "She is." He laughed. "I quite fancy her myself. Still, I'm not the only one, eh?" He nudged Hira in the ribs. Hira blushed. The plane veered and started to dive, banking to starboard with the engines screaming. Frank inexpertly righted her, but didn't seem worried by the near-miss; he continued to chat cheerfully, telling Hira a succession of bad dirty jokes (mostly about incest, bestiality and Jews) until Hira thought he would cry.

He changed the subject as soon as he could. "I wonder what the political climate's like, back there." He motioned towards the west.

"Bloody hell! Not worth thinking about. That's as good as finished, anyway, nowadays, isn't it?"

"Does it 'finish'?"

"Well, you know what I mean. We've got our plane, we've got our health, we've got the Cornelius millions — or will have soon. We've got each other. Why should we worry?" Frank moved the joy stick from his left to his right hand and stretched this hand out towards Hira.

"I was thinking of the moral question," said Professor Hira.

"Oh, fuck that!"

Frank's hand dived into Hira's lap and squeezed.

The Indian physicist shrieked and was his.

The plane flew perilously close to the water and then began to climb as Frank took it up towards a cloud.

THE RAFT

Sun-baked, salt-caked, it lay in the middle of the Arabian Sea on a waterlogged raft made of oil-drums, ropes and rush matting. The raft had no mast, held nothing but the shapeless heap of flesh and rags which might have been dead save for the spasm which occasionally ran through it when a small wave lifted the raft or swept over it, so that it sank a little further into the warm sea. One of the drums had been holed by what looked like a series of machine-gun bullets; it was this which had helped to deprive the raft of its bouyancy.

The flesh was blistered as if it had been exposed to fire; it was blackened in places. In other places bones stuck through at odd angles. There was a flake or two of dried blood. From time to time there were sounds: a grunt, a moan, a few babbled words.

The raft was drifting out to sea. The nearest land was now Bombay, 400 miles away, where a great sitar master, dying of cholera, was the only man with any notion of the raft's where-abouts. There was not much chance of rescue, even if rescue had been desired.

Jerry felt nothing. He was one with the flotsam of the great sea; almost one with the sea itself. He was content, listening absently to the odd voice; remembering the odd image. If this were dying, it was a relaxing experience, to say the least.

196

" Remember the old days? " said Miss Brunner's voice. " Or were they the new days? I forget. The usual tense trouble." She laughed gently. " Echoes."

" Nothing but," murmured Jerry.

" But echoes from where? "

" Everywhere? "

" They would be, I suppose. Lapland won't be the same. Caves. Large bodies of water. The sky. The pleasures are constant, even if the problems change."

" Yes."

"Are the simple pleasures the *only* realities? "

Jerry couldn't reply.

" Oh, what a lovely, drifting sea this is." The voice faded away. " Who are we, I wonder? "

" Resistance," said a child, " is useless."

"Absolutely," Jerry agreed.

" The schizophrenic condition finds its most glorious expression in Hinduism," remarked Professor Hira. " Whereas Christianity is an expression of the much less interesting paranoid frame of reference. Paranoia is rarely heroic, in the mythical sense, at least."

But Jerry found this argument barren. He didn't encourage a discussion. Instead, he remembered a kiss.

" Feeling seedy? I know I am." Karl Glogauer came and went. Jerry had confused him with Flash Gordon.

" Time," said the sad voice of Captain Cornelius Brunner, " ruins everything." They would not be meeting again for another thirty-five years. " So long, Jerry."

" I love you," said Jerry.

With an effort he raised himself on his wounded hands.

" I love all of you."

He looked at the sea. The sun was setting and the water was the burning colour of blood.

" Oh! "

A few tears dripped from his awful eyes. Then the head sank back. The night came and the raft dropped lower in the water until an observer might have thought that the body floated unsupported on the surface. The sun rose, pink and mighty on the western horizon, and Jerry raised his head for one swift glimpse. The sea ran through his burnt hair and made it float like weed; it washed his torn flesh and moved the rags of his black car coat; it ran into his reddened mouth and the sockets of his eyes, and Jerry, at peace, hardly noticed.

A little later, lizard-like, he crawled to the edge of the raft and slid quietly into the water, disappearing at once.

It was going to be a long century.

PROLOGUE (concluded)

. . . and in spite of their maudlin sympathy, self-interest finally dominated everything else and so I was betrayed again, left alone. I think it must have been the final straw. Certainly, I ceased to trust anyone else for several years, then when Monica came along I forgot all that. I trusted her absolutely. And, of course, she let me down. Perhaps she didn't mean to. Perhaps it was too much of a strain. She should have kept the baby. I don't know how long I stayed in the kitchen with her after I'd done it. You could say that the balance of my mind was disturbed. I mean, what's a country for? What do you pay taxes for? What do you give your patriotism to? You expect something from your own country, your parents, your relatives? And then they don't deliver. Nobody cares. Every promise society makes to you, it doesn't keep. They kill babies before they're born, after they're born, or they do it the slow way, prolonging the moment of death for scores of years.I am not pleading guilty. By pleading insane, I am pleading innocent. Surely, I'm the victim. What does it mean? But I want to die. It's the only solution. And yet I love life. I know that seems strange. I love the lakes and the forests and all that. But it seems unnatural now. We've all got to go, haven't we? I never asked to be born. I tried to enjoy it, I tried to be positive and optimistic. I'm well-educated, you know. It was mercy-killing. Any killing is, if you look at it one way. I am trying to control myself. I'm sorry I'm sorry.

MAURICE LESCOQ, Leavetaking

199

SHOT
FOUR

POLICE DIG UP MORE HUMAN REMAINS

Police digging at Leatherhead (Surrey) where a woman's hand was found on Thursday found more remains yesterday in a navy blue zip bag at a shallow depth.

Wrapped separately in polythene were two portions of thigh, a left leg and a foot with a blue slipper on it. Police said they thought other parts of the body were ' somewhere else '.

MORNING STAR, September 4 1971

OBSERVATIONS

"There's a future in chemicals, if you ask me," said Lieutenant Cornelius. He lifted binoculars to his bleak eyes and stared without interest at the Indian aircraft carrier his CA class destroyer *Cassandra* had been tracking for two days.

Overhead flew five or six small helicopters of different nationalities, including a British *Wasp*; below floated three or four of the latest nuclear submarines, among them the *Remorseless*, the *Concorde* and the *Vorster*. The Mediterranean fairly swarmed with busy bits of metal. Not too far off, a frigate of the Imperial South Russian Navy was keeping its eye on Lt. Cornelius's ship and a Chinese 'flying ironclad' — an armoured airship of obscure origin — observed the Russian.

" Chemicals and plastics," Cornelius's No. 2, Collier, agreed, leaning over the rail of the bridge and looking down at the rather dirty decks where bored seamen lounged in each other's arms. Under the barrel of the forward 4.5 gun, the deck cargo creaked in its ropes. It was a single box, marked AMMUNITION/ DANGER. " That's what I'd put my money in. If I had any."

"Buy the plants," said Frank Cornelius. " Take over. Go for the durables. Oil. Water. Steel. Air. Chemicals. Plastics. Electronics. That's survival. My brother's got the right idea — or had — or will have . . ." He frowned and changed the subject, handing the glasses to Collier. " See if you can spot any change."

Collier was happy to get a turn with the binoculars. He straightened his shoulders and peered self-importantly through the eyepieces. "Are they having a party or something on deck? "

" They've been up to that since this morning. It's disgusting. I think it's meant to distract us from whatever they don't want us to know about."

" Big girls, ain't they," said Shaky Mo.

" Hermaphrodites."

" I thought they were on our side."

Frank went down into the Operations Room and consulted his grubby charts. He could have done with something a bit more up to date. He'd inherited the charts from his father and the political boundaries shown were nothing less than ludicrous. He moved a couple of counters to cope with the recently arrived South Russians. There was hardly space on the chart for another marker. Fragment split into fragment. Was it society or himself that was breaking up?

He was getting tired of the whole thing. A bloody great Prussian dreadnought had been after them for a week, taking a particular interest in their deck cargo. That meant a leak. Frank wondered if it wouldn't be wiser to turn round and go back to their Marseilles base or, failing that, make straight for Aden. With radio silence, there was no chance of getting his orders changed until he reached a port. He wished he hadn't taken on the responsibility of the cargo, now. If he could have been somewhere suitable when word came, he might have been able to turn a profit, given a slight shift in the balance of power at home. That was why he'd volunteered. Now he realised what a stupid idea it had been. He was never any good at the big deals. At little deals, he was great. He should have stuck at what he knew he could do well. Here he was, in the middle of the bleeding Med, while his nearest customers were at the other end of the North Sea. Fuck a duck, it was just his luck. He rubbed his greasy chin, flipping through his *Boatswain's Manual* for the right order to give the coxswain and the engineers. He'd make for Hamburg and hope for the best.

Idly turning the binoculars onto his own ship and its crew, Mo Collier focussed on the big box and noticed for the first time that it seemed to be moving to a different rhythm from that of the waves. It was pulsing, like a rapid heart beat, as if, Mo Collier grinned at the thought, two people were fucking in there. Well, that was impossible. On the other hand if the contents of the box were about to go critical, he'd better warn his captain. He let the glasses fall on their string and knock against his pelvis. He took the lift down to the Operations Room. " Sir? Sir? "

Frank looked up from his manual. " What? "

" The deck cargo. It's sort of bouncing. It might be going to blow up."

" Oh, shit," Frank put the book down and followed Mo up to the deck. He took the glasses and looked. " Oh, shit. I should have shifted it right at the beginning. He who hesitates is lost, Collier."

" Fire drill, sir? "

" Bloody hell. What's the point? " They went slowly back to the Operations Room. " Let's have a look at a map," said Frank when they got there. " No. We'll make for Sardinia and dump it. Break radio silence. Tell them our deck cargo hasn't been picked up on schedule and we're abandoning it on the nearest dry land."

" Can't we just dump it in the sea, sir? "

"Are you out of your mind? We don't want more trouble than we've got already. Oh, shit." Frank slumped down in a chair. " Oh, fuck it to buggery." He was the picture of whining impotence. Feeling this made his whine louder. At a certain pitch, his whine was echoed by a sound from the deck; the sound was almost in perfect tune, but constant, where Frank's was punctuated by his need to draw breath.

Soon the two brothers were howling in unison as night fell and the destroyer steamed for Sardinia.

GUARANTEES

Major Nye had his trousers off. He sat on a canvas stool with an old towel round him. Mrs Nye spoke through clenched teeth as she stitched at the patched trouser leg. "It's not as if we could afford it," she said. "All I seem to do is *mend*. And you're so clumsy. You must have known about the barbed wire on the beach."

"Supervised its installation, I'm afraid," admitted Major Nye. "All my fault. Sorry, lovey."

It was late in the afternoon and they were outside the beach-hut where they had been billeted. After being turned down by his old regiment (now an armoured vehicle corps), Major Nye had volunteered to help with the Brighton coastal defences. Then Ironmaster House, some twelve miles inland, had been requisitioned as the headquarters of the local territorials, so he and Mrs Nye had had to move into the beach hut. Major Nye was not particularly upset by the takeover. The beach hut was not nearly so much of a burden and it was less effort tending the barbed wire than it had been looking after the market garden. Major Nye felt a bit ashamed. The war was proving something of a holiday for him. For all she would never admit it, even Mrs Nye seemed relieved. Her wind-reddened face had taken on something of a bloom, though this might have been the result of the cold. It was winter and the beach hut was heated only by a malfunctioning oil-stove. Their daughters had not joined them; both girls had volunteered for work in London. Isobel, the ex-dancer, was looking after her brother, who was still at school. Sometimes, at weekends, one or both of the girls would bring the little boy down to see his parents.

"Nearly Christmas," Mrs Nye finished the darn with a sigh. "Is it worth doing anything at all about it this year?"

"Maybe the girls will have an idea." Major Nye went into the beach hut and drew on his trousers. He folded the tattered towel and hung it neatly over the back of the deck-chair. The trousers, like his jacket, were khaki, or had been before the elements and all the patching had turned them into a garment of many indistinguishable colours. He lit the remaining third of his thin cigarette. "Tum-te-tum. God rest ye merry gentlemen, let nothing ye dismay, et cetera, et cetera, pom-pom." He put the tin kettle on top of the oil-stove, realised it was dry, and came outside to fill it at the tap which served his and two other huts. All these huts were now occupied by coastal defence volunteers. Many volunteers were older than Major Nye. With a loud, rasping sound, the kettle filled. The tap squeaked as he turned it off. Mrs Nye shivered in his greatcoat and, stamping with cold, got up, collapsing both their canvas stools and hurrying inside.

"A strong cuppa's what you need after that, m'dear," he said.

"Don't throw away the old leaves this time," she said. "They'll last for another brew."

He nodded.

They watched the kettle boil and when it was ready he flipped the lid off the mock-Georgian, mock-silver teapot and filled it half-full. "Just give that a minute or two to stew," he said. He made a corned beef sandwich for her, using thin sliced bread and even thinner slices of meat. He put the sandwich on one of their plates, taken from the tiny rack above the tiny card table on which their provisions were laid. He handed her the plate.

"Thank you very much," said his wife. She nibbled at the sandwich. It was her tea. They were going to have a full tin of pilchards for supper.

"Well, I'd better go and check the searchlights before nightfall," he said.

206

" Very well." She looked up. " See if you can get a paper."

" Rightho ! "

Whistling the half-remembered tune of *The Bore o' Bethnal Green*, he ambled down the stony beach, following the course of his barbed wire, stopping at intervals to inspect the searchlights set on small pedestals every thirty feet. The lights had originally been used to illuminate the Pavilion during the summer months.

The sky was grey and promised rain. The sea was also grey and even the beach had a greyish tinge to it. That always seemed to happen in wartime, thought Major Nye. Above, on the promenade, he noticed that the odd fish-and-chip shop and coffee-stall hadn't yet closed. The shops were illuminated by oil-lamps and candles. All electricity was being saved for the defence effort. The places looked cosy. After making sure that all his lights were in good order, he left the beach and tramped up a ramp to the pavement, crossing the street to the shops. One of the ice-cream parlours was still open. These days, in spite of the plastic sundaes and knickerbocker glories in the window, it sold only tea and soup. The parlour also sold *The Weekly Defender*, the only newspaper generally available. A new issue was in. Large piles were stacked outside the shop. The paper's circulation was not very good. Those piles would remain virtually untouched and would be taken away when the new issue arrived. Major Nye was one of the few regular customers for *The Defender*. He picked up a copy from a pile and read the headline as he ambled into the shop, his sixty-pence piece in his hand. " Evening, squire," said the shopkeeper.

" Good evening." Major Nye couldn't remember the man's name and he was embarrassed. " The paper."

" Sixty, please. Doesn't look too good, does it? "

The headlines read: *NEW GAINS FOR BRITAIN! SPIRITS RISE AS MINISTER ANNOUNCES PLANS. 'MORALE NEVER HIGHER' SAYS KING.*

Major Nye smiled shyly. " I must admit . . ."

" Still, it can't last forever."

To Major Nye it seemed it had already lasted forever, but he was, as usual, completely reconciled. You couldn't change human nature. You couldn't change the world. He smiled again. " I suppose not."

207

" Night, night, squire."

" Goodnight to you."

It was almost dark now. He decided to walk back along the promenade, rather than along the beach. The smell of fish-and-chips made his mouth water, but he resisted temptation, knowing what Mrs Nye would say if he brought back even a few chips. It was an unnecessary expense on food which was not nourishing; also it was ' not quite the thing ' to buy hot food from a shop. They had to keep their standards up. Major Nye had always been fond of fish-and-chips. When he had worked in London, he had had them once a week. Of course, the fish was terrible now, and the chips weren't proper potato at all. And that was a consolation of sorts.

He began to go down the ramp which led to their stretch of gloomy beach. He paused and looked out at the black, gleaming water. The sea was so large. Sometimes it seemed foolish, trying to defend the coast against it. He wondered what would happen if the big anti-aircraft gun on the end of the pier ever had to fire. Probably shake the whole bally thing to bits. He smiled.

He thought he saw something bobbing on the water, quite close to the shore, about twenty yards from the pier's girders. He peered hard, wondering if it were a stray mine, but the object had passed out of sight. He shrugged and stepped onto the beach. The shingle rattled and grated as he crossed it. Further out to sea a steamer's siren moaned and the moan was echoed by the rooftops of the town so that it seemed for a little while that the whole of Brighton was expressing its misery.

ESTIMATES

Una Persson made the plane just as it was about to leave Dubrovnik. She clambered up over the coffin-shaped floats and through the passenger doors. Inside, the plane was dark and crowded; people sat on the floor or, where there wasn't room to sit, clung to pieces of frayed rope fixed to the sides and roof. Refugees, like herself; though these were thin-faced civilians. She pushed through them, noticing the number of black-robed priests aboard, and found the companionways to the upper decks. There were people sitting on these, too, and she had to go up both flights of stairs on the tips of her battered boots. At last she reached the pilot's cabin. By that time they were already airborne, though two of the big wing-mounted engines were coughing on the starboard side. She wondered from what museum the plane had been resurrected. It was German, judging by its instrument panels. There was a lot of German junk around, these days. It wasn't surprising. Over the radio and heavily distorted came sounds she recognised as the Rolling Stones singing *Mother's Little Helper*.

The flying boat circled Dubrovnik once, dipping in and out of the thick, oily smoke from the burning city. "We shan't be seeing that again," said the Polish pilot. Colonel Pyat, who was seated in the co-pilot's chair, sighed. "It'll be good to get home again. We are all ideas in the mind of Mars."

Una gave him a puzzled look. " So you say, general."

" C —" Colonel Pyat mopped his heated forehead. " My dear Una, I thought you had taken the train."

" Changed my mind. Back to Blighty, after all."

" Just as well. Maybe our luck will change with you aboard." He raised an imaginary glass. " I salute Our Lady of Liberty." He was eager to please, not sardonic.

" You're tired," she said.

" Sing a song, Una dear. An old sweet song." He was drunk, but his white uniform was neat as ever. " If those lips could only speak, if those eyes could only see, if those . . ."

" The European campaigns were wholly disastrous," said the Pole, who was also a bit drunk. She could hardly hear him over the erratic roaring of the aircraft's engines.

" Why all the refugees? " she said. " Where are the troops? "

" That's what the refugees wanted to know." The Pole laughed. They weren't making much altitude as they flew out to sea. " We *are* the troops."

" C'est la vie," said Colonel Pyat. " My dear ones will have missed me." He drew a flask from his hip pocket and tipped it up. It was empty. " Thank God," he said. " You're right, Una. I am tired. I thought England would be the answer. A triumph of imagination over inspiration. Ha, ha! "

" He lost the box," explained the Pole.

" In Labroke Grove," said Pyat. " It's been around a bit since then."

Una sighed. " So I gather. Well, it was just another straw, I suppose. Something to keep the fire going."

" Feeling the draught? " said the Pole.

" I've been feeling it all century," said Una.

From beyond the door came the sound of people at prayer, led by the droning voices of the priests. Even the plane seemed to be praying. Una went to find a parachute before they reached Windermere.

APPLICATIONS

There seemed to be gratitude in Sebastian Auchinek's large brown eyes. He looked up as the security policeman entered his cell.

" Of course I understand that you have to do this job," said Auchinek. "And rest assured, Constable Wallace, I shan't make it difficult for you. Please sit down or — " he paused " — whatever you wish."

Constable Wallace was a brute.

" I don't like spies, Mr Auchinek." His skin was coarse, his eyes were stupid and there was a sense of pent-up violence about him. "And should we prove that you're one . . ."

" I'm a loyal citizen, I assure you. I love England as much as anyone, for all that I was not born here. Your countryside, your democracy, your justice . . ."

" You're a Jew."

" Yes."

" There's been a lot of Jewish spies."

" I know."

" So . . ."

" I'm not one. I'm a business man."

"A poof? "

" No . . ."

" You go abroad a great deal. Macedonia? "

211

" Macedonia, yes. And to — well, to Belgium, Holland, Assyria . . ."

" Where? "

"Abyssinia, isn't it? "

" You've got *something* to hide," said the red face, sweating.

"A poor memory." Auchinek whimpered in anticipation.

"And I'm going to get it out of you."

" Of course. Of course."

" By force, if necessary."

" I'm not a traitor."

" I hope not."

Constable Wallace had completed the necessary rough and ready warming up ritual and he grabbed Auchinek by his grey prison jacket and pulled him to his feet. He balled his red fist and punched Auchinek in the stomach. Auchinek vomited at once, all over Constable Wallace's uniform.

" Oh, you filthy little animal." Wallace left the cell.

Auchinek had had enough. He sat back on his bed, careless of the vomit on his lips, chin and clothing. He gasped and cried and wished he hadn't had his breakfast. He should have known better. Or had he planned it? He had never been clear about his identity, his own motives, at the best of times, and now he was completely at sea. For all he knew, he might be a traitor. He should have retained his military role. It was easier.

The sound of rifle fire in the passage outside. Shouts. Running, booted feet. A clang. More shots. The bolt was withdrawn outside. Auchinek cringed as the door opened.

Catherine Cornelius, looking like a young Una Persson, stood in the doorway, an M16 over the shoulder of her brown trench-coat, a green tam-o'-shanter on her golden curls.

"Are you the chap we're to rescue? " said Catherine. " Mr A?"

"Auchinek."

" Shall we release the lot? " She indicated the other cells in the corridor.

" I don't know," he said, watching out for Wallace, who was sure to appear in a minute.

" This isn't my normal job, you see," explained Catherine pleasantly as she coaxed him from the cell and into the corridor

212

of twisted iron and broken corpses. He saw Wallace. His red throat was cut by rifle bullets. He was dead. Auchinek gazed at him in wonder.

She led him past the corpse towards the outer door, which was off its hinges. " I normally get the nursing jobs, but we're short-staffed, at present."

" Who are you? "

" Catherine Cornelius."

" No — your — outfit? "

" Biba's."

" Who do you work for? "

" I work for England, Mr Auchinek, and freedom." Self-consciously, she put the M16 on automatic and rested it on her hip as they crossed the quadrangle of Brixton Prison and reached the main gate. " There's a car waiting. Perhaps you could direct me? It's been a long time since I've been in South London."

They stepped through the blasted gate and stood in a narrow street. A Delage Diane was waiting for them, its engine running.

" It's a bit of a waste of power," she said apologetically, opening a passenger door for him, " but I find the bugger rather hard to start."

" Miss Cornelius . . ."

" Mr Auchinek."

" I don't understand."

" I'm afraid I can't help you there. The ins and outs of the revolution — if it *is* a revolution — are a bit beyond me. I just work for the cause."

" But I'm not a revolutionary. I'm a businessman. I think you know more . . ."

" Honestly, no . . ."

" Perhaps I should go back? A mistake." He hesitated beside the car.

" Don't you remember Macedonia? "

" Were you there? "

" You were an idealist. A guerilla."

" I've always been in show business. All my life. Promotions. Management."

" Well, there you are, then." She opened the door of the car for him. " Nobody's going to beat you up any more."

" I'm tired."

" I know how you feel." She got into the driving seat and fiddled with the gears. The car seemed unfamiliar to her. " We've still got a long journey ahead of us." They began to move slowly forward. " Modification of species and so on. Perhaps it isn't really a revolution at all."

Auchinek saw misery in Catherine's mouth. He began to cry. She reached the main road, crashing the gears as she turned the Delage towards the Thames.

SECURITIES

" Good ole England! " said Mrs Cornelius, raising her pint of ale and saluting a picture of a bulldog painted on the glass behind the bar.

" Oh, yore 'opeless, Mrs C! " Old Sammy in the corner guffawed, opening wide the black, wet circle of his toothless mouth and shaking all over. He lifted his own pint and poured its contents into his wasted, cancerous body.

" 'Ere, come on, I mean it," she said. " There'll orlways be an England. We've 'ad our ups an' darns, but we'll pull through."

" Well, *you* might," said Old Sammy bitterly, losing his good humour as the beer in his glass disappeared.

" 'Ave anovver," she said, by way of rewarding him for the compliment.

He brought his glass over to the bar where she sat on a high, saddle-shaped stool, her massive behind spilling over, so that the dark wood was all but hidden. " 'Aven't seen too much of you, lately," he said.

" Nar," she said. " Bin away. Visitin' an 'at, in I? "

" Go somewhere nice? "

"Abroad. Went ter see me son."

" Wot, Frank? "

" Nar! Jerry. 'E's ill."

"Anything bad? "

She snorted. " Iber-bleedin'-natin' 'e corls it! Mastur-fuckin'-batin', *I* corl it! " She turned as a third customer entered *The Portobello Star*. " Oh, it's you. Yore late, incha? "

" Sorry, my dear. Delays at immigration." Colonel Pyat wore a cream-coloured suit, lavender gloves and white spats over tan shoes. He had a pale blue shirt and a regimental tie. His light grey homburg was in the same hand that carried his stick. His manner was hesitant.

" Sammy, this is ther Kernewl — my hubby."

" How do you do? " said Pyat.

" How do? Jerry's dad, eh? "

Mrs Cornelius shook with laughter again. " Well, 'e might 'ave bin once! Gar-har-har! "

Colonel Pyat smiled weakly and cleared his throat. " What will you have, sir? "

" Same agin."

Pyat signed to the wizened old bat behind the bar. " Same again in these glasses, please. And I'll have a double vodka. Nice morning."

" Nice for some," said the old bat.

Mrs Cornelius stopped laughing and patted the colonel affectionately on the shoulder. " Cheer up, lovie. Yer *do* look as if yer've bin in ther wars! " She opened her shapeless handbag. " I'll git these. Pore ole sod." She cast her eye about the gloomy bar. " Where's yer bags? "

" I left them at the hotel."

" Hotel! "

" The Venus Hotel, in Westbourne Grove. A nice little place. Very comfortable."

" Oh, well, orl right! "

" I didn't want to put you out."

" Well, you *ain't*! " She paid for the drinks and handed him his vodka. " But I woulda thort . . . First day 'ome . . . Well . . ."

" I didn't mean to upset you, my dear." He rallied himself. " I thought I'd take you out somewhere tonight. Where do you suggest? And then, later, perhaps, we could go on a family holiday. The coast or somewhere."

She was mollified. " Crystal Palace," she said. " I ain't bin there fer a donkey's."

"Excellent." He swallowed his drink and ordered another. "Welcome austerity. Farewell authority!" He saluted himself in the mirror.

She looked critically at his clothes. "'Ad a run o' luck, 'ave yer?"

"Well, yes and no."

"'E orlways wos a very smart dresser," said Mrs C to Sammy. "No matter 'ow much 'e 'ad in 'is pocket, 'e'd orlways be dressed just so."

Sammy sniffed.

Colonel Pyat blushed.

Mrs Cornelius yawned. "It's better ter go away in the autumn. If the wevver 'olds."

"Yes," said Colonel Pyat.

"I've never 'ad an 'oliday in me life," said Sammy proudly. "Never even let 'em evacuate me!"

"That's 'cause yer never worked in her life!" Mrs Cornelius nudged him. "Eh?"

Sammy bridled. But she put her fat hand round the back of his neck and kissed him on his wrinkled forehead. "Come on, don't take offence. Yer know I never mean it."

Sammy pulled away and took his glass back to his table in the corner.

Colonel Pyat climbed on to the next stool but one. His eyes kept closing and he jerked his head up from time to time as if afraid to go to sleep. He didn't seem to have the energy, these days.

"I 'ope yer brought somefink ter eat over wiv yer?" said Mrs C. "Everyfink's runnin' art 'ere. Food. Fuel. Fun." She bellowed. "Everyfink that begins wiv 'F', eh?"

"Ha, ha, ha," he said distantly.

"One more for the road an' then we'll be off," said his wife. "Yer never reely liked pubs, did yer?"

"Excellent."

"Cheer up. It can't be as bad as orl that!"

"Europe's in a mess," he said. "Everywhere is."

"Well, we're not exactly at the 'eight of our prosperity," she told him. "Still, fings blow over."

"But the squalor!"

" Ferget it! " She guzzled her light.

" I wish I could, my dear."

" I'll 'elp yer." She leant across the empty stool between them and tickled his genitals. " Tonight."

Colonel Pyat made a peculiar giggling noise. She took him by the arm and led him through the door and into the stinking streets. " Yer'll like the Crystal Palace. It's *orl* crystal. Well, glass, reely. All different sides. Made o' glass. An' there's monsters. It's a wonder o' the world, the Crystal Palace. Like me, eh? "

Mrs Cornelius roared.

REMINISCENCE (G)

Children are stoning a tortoise. Its shell is already cracking open. It moves feebly, leaving a trail of blood and entrails across a white rock.

LATE NEWS

A 17-month-old baby girl was shot dead in Belfast tonight, Army sources said, by an IRA gunman's bullet meant for an Army patrol. A seven-year-old girl who was with her escaped injury although another bullet tore through her skirt.

MORNING STAR, September 24 1971

A drug given to women during pregnancy may cause a rare type of cancer in their daughters many years later, the British Medical Journal warned yesterday. The cancer has been found among girls aged 15 to 22 in New England and has been linked to the drug stilboestrol, which was given to their mothers for threatened miscarriages . . . Treatment has proved successful so far in the majority of cases, but one girl has died.

GUARDIAN, September 10 1971

A boy aged three was knocked down and killed by an army vehicle near the Bogside district last night. As the news spread, crowds began to stone army units in the area. Several shots were fired at the troops and petrol bombs were reported to be thrown. The army did not return the fire.

GUARDIAN, September 10 1971

The Alternative Apocalypse 7

Nothing survives, said Una Persson, who was older, more battered and wiser than Jerry had ever seen her, nothing endures.

While there's lives there's hopes. Jerry finished stripping the Banning cannon and immediately began re-assembling it. The ruby had not, after all, been faulty. It was just wearing out. The gun wouldn't last much longer. Still, it wasn't needed for much longer. He was more worried about his power armour. Some of the circuits, particularly those on his chest, were looking a bit frayed. They were holed up in the basement of a deserted old people's home in Ladbroke Grove. They listened to the scuffling of the rats with intense interest, expecting an attack.

It's almost over now, isn't it? she said without regret. Civilisation's had it. The human race has had it. And we've bloody had it. Are these all you've got? She held up a cerise Sobranie cocktail cigarette with a gold tip.

He opened a drawer in the plain deal table on which his cannon was spread. Looks like it. He rummaged through a jumble of string, coins and postcards. Yes.

Oh, well.

You might as well enjoy what's left, he said. Take it easy.

It isn't easy to take. What with everything speeding up so fast. It's all burning too quickly. Like a rocket that's out of

221

control, with the fuel regulator jammed.

Could be. He slotted one piece of scratched black metal into another. He fitted the cumbersome ammunition feed and worked a couple of slides. He didn't bother to put the safety catch on as he turned the cannon on its swivel mount so that it pointed towards the barred window. I don't know. He sighted along the gun; he stroked back his long, straight hair. Times come and go. Things re-cycle. The Jesuits . . .

Did you hear something?

Yes.

She went to the corner where her Bren lay on their mattress. She picked the Bren up and drew the strap over her leather-clad shoulder. She flipped a switch at her belt. It even took her power armour a few seconds to warm up now. After the village . . she began.

You survive, Una. It wasn't something he wanted to hear about again. It disturbed him.

She looked at him suspiciously, searching his face for a sardonic meaning. There was none.

Alive or dead, he said and fired an explosive shell through the window and into the shadowy area. Magnesium blazed for a moment. Cold air came in. A shape darted away. Jerry flipped his own switch.

Beesley, Brunner, Frank and the rest, Una said, peering cautiously upwards. All the other survivors. I think some are trying to get into the house.

It had to come. In the long term there's never much safety in numbers.

I'd always believed you worked alone. A bit of a bourgeois individualist on the quiet.

Assassination's one thing, Jerry said primly. Murder's quite another. Murder involves more people and a different moral approach and that, of course, ultimately involves more murders. A reflex. People get carried away. But assassination is just the initial preparation. The ground work. Like it or not, of course, everything boils down to murder in the end. A grenade burst in the basement and the rest of the glass flew into the room, rattling against their power armour.

There's self-defense.

I've never been able to work that one out.

Jerry pulled the table nearer to the window, then angled the Banning upwards through the bars, firing a steady, tight sweep of shells. Two of the attackers flared up and fell. Karen and Mo, said Jerry. Not for the first time. They heard footsteps over their heads and then a few creaks on the cellar stairs outside their inside door. Una opened the door and, with her Bren, took two more lives. Mitzi Beesley and Frank Cornelius. Frank, as usual, made a lot of noise, but Mitzi died quietly, sitting upright with her back against the wall, her hands in her blood-stained lap, while Frank rolled and writhed and gasped and cursed.

Two more grenades came into the room and exploded, temporarily blinding them, but hardly denting their power armour.

This is almost the end, said Jerry. I think it's down to Miss Brunner and Bishop Beesley. It had better be. Energy's getting low.

Miss Brunner rushed down the stairs, her face twisted with rage, her red eyes blazing, her sharp fangs bared. She was awkward in her tight St. Laurent skirt. She tried to get her Sten to fire. Una killed her, shooting her in the forehead with a single bullet. Miss Brunner staggered back without grace.

Bishop Beesley appeared in the area outside the window. He was holding a white flag in one hand, a Twix bar in the other. Even from here Jerry could see that the chocolate was mouldy.

I give up, said the Bishop. I now admit I was ill-advised to quarrel with you, Mr Cornelius. He crammed the Twix bar into his mouth and then reached towards his breast pocket. May I? He took out a delicate box of Chinese jade and opened it. From the box he removed a couple of pinches of sugar which he snorted into his nostrils. That's better.

Okay. Jerry nodded tiredly and pulled the Banning's trigger, plugging Beesley in the mouth. The face flared in a halo of flame and then disappeared. Jerry abandoned the gun and went to Una, who was pale and exhausted. He kissed her gently on the cheek. It's all over, at last.

They switched off their armour and lay down on the damp mattress, fucking as if their lives depended on it.

223

The Alternative Apocalypse 8

The ruins were pretty now that the fronds and lichen covered them. Birds sang. Jerry and Catherine Cornelius walked hand in hand to their favourite spot and sat down on a slab, looking out over the fused obsidian that had been the Thames. It was spring. The world was at peace.

Moments like these, said Catherine tenderly, make you feel glad to be alive.

Well, he smiled, you are, aren't you?

She stroked his knee as she lay stretched beside him, supported by one of his strong arms. It's so relaxing to be with you.

Well, familiarity, I suppose, is a lot to do with it. He, in turn, stroked her golden hair. I love you, Cathy.

You're good, Jerry, I love you, too.

They watched a spider cross the broken concrete and disappear into a black crack. They stared out over miles and miles of sun-drenched ruins.

London looks at her best on a day like this, Cathy said. I'm glad the winter's over. Now the whole world is ours. The whole new century, for that matter! She laughed. Isn't it paradise?

If it isn't, it'll do.

A light wind ruffled their hair. They got up and began to wander towards Ladbroke Grove, guided by the outline of the one complete building still standing, the Hilton tower. Black and white monkeys floated from broken wall to broken wall, calling to each other as the two people approached.

Jerry reached into his pocket. He turned on his miniature stereo taper. Hawkwind was half-way through *Captain Justice*; a VC3's synthetic sounds shuddered, roared and decayed. He put his arm round her slender shoulders. Let's take a holiday, he said, and go somewhere nice. Liverpool, maybe?

Or Florence. Those twisted girders!

Why not?

Humming, they made their way home.

LATE NEWS

Five teenage pupils from Ainslie Park School, Edinburgh, and a trainee instructor of outdoor pursuits, died near Lochan Buidhe in the Cairngorms yesterday in the worst Scottish mountain accident in memory. The tragedy was heightened by the fact that the party was found within 200 yards of a climbers' hut which could have ensured their survival.

GUARDIAN, November 23 1971

A schoolboy in a party of 21 teenagers is believed to have died on a mountain in central Tasmania. A police and helicopter search is to resume at first light for the boys who are thought to be huddled together as blizzards break over the mountain.

GUARDIAN, November 24 1971

Two babies died today in a fire at a tented tinker's camp — hours after their grandfather died in a road accident. Peter Smith (2) and his ten-month-old baby sister Irene, died as fire ripped through their makeshift canvas home at Ferebridge Camp, near Barnbroe, Lanarkshire. Earlier, their grandfather, farm labourer Mr Ian Brown (54) was killed when he was involved in an accident with a car as he was walking near the camp.

SHROPSHIRE STAR, December 18 1971

226

Farm worker Alan Stewart, who had a lung transplant at Edinburgh Royal Infirmary on Thursday — his 19th birthday — died last night. Alan of Kirkaldy, drank weedkiller from a lemonade bottle a week ago.

SHROPSHIRE STAR, December 18 1971

REMINISCENCE (H)

A man wearing a papier mache mask in the form of a skull enters the doors of a pub.

A drunk screams and attacks the wearer.

Mother's eyes.

THE FOREST

"It's like a magic wood," Cathy's voice was hushed and delighted. "So many soft greens. And, look, a squirrel! A red one!"

Frank Cornelius sniffed the air. "Lush," he said. He tested the ground with his patent-leather foot. "Springy. Give me the good old English broad-leafed tree any day of the week."

"Oo, wot luverly flars!" said Mrs Cornelius, ripping some wild orchids from the moss and holding them to her face. "This is wot I *corl* a wood, Kernewl!"

Colonel Pyat gave a modest, proprietorial, smile and wiped his forehead with a large handkerchief of coarse linen. "This is the English forest at her best. The oak. The ash. The elm. And so forth." He was pleased to see her happy.

"I 'ope yer remember where we left ther motor," said Mrs C, fiddling with the controls of her little tranny and failing to find a station. She gave up. She put the radio back in her bag. She cackled. "We don't wanna be like ther fuckin' babes in ther wood!"

Mellow sunshine filtered through the leaves of the tall elms, the strong oaks, the aristocratic poplars and the languid willows, filling the flowery glades with golden beams in which butterflies, mayflies and dragonflies sauntered.

They wandered on over sweet-smelling moss and grass and

229

feathery ferns, sometimes in silence, sometimes in a babble of joy when they saw a pretty animal or a bank of beautiful flowers or a little, shining brook rushing between mossy rocks.

" Something like this restores your faith," said Frank as they paused to watch a large-eyed doe and her faun nibbling delicately at some low-hanging leaves. He took out his rolled gold cigarette case and offered it round, quoting: ' It is from the voice of created things that we discover the Voice of God never ceasing to woo our love. Gaudefroy.' It was a quotation to which he would become particularly attached in the coming years, especially over the Christmas period of 1999, shortly before he and Bishop Beesley would pay the final reckoning in the Ladbroke Grove Raid, at a time when their theological disputes would have brought them close to blows. " Time stands still. Man is at peace. God speaks."

" I orlways said you wos the one should've gorn inter ther church," said his mother sentimentally. She took a cigarette, a Sullivans, and waved it in a vague, all-encompassing gesture. "And wot would our friend Jerry make of all this, I wonder. Turn up 'is nose? Nar! Even 'e couldn't knock this."

" Jerry . . ." said Catherine defensively, and then could think of nothing more.

" Jerry's far too involved in the affairs of the world to spare time for the simple things of life," said Frank piously.

" You'd fink 'e'd write a p.c." Mrs C puffed at her fag. " Oh, look over there! "

It was a pool overhung by willows and sapling silver birches with big white boulders all around it. A tiny waterfall cascaded into the pool from high above. They all walked towards it, listening to the water. Colonel Pyat followed behind. He didn't have the energy any more. He, too, was wondering what had become of the missing member of the Cornelius family. There had been conflicting rumours. One rumour had it that he had been resurrected. Another said he had been returned to the sea. They had all relied too heavily on him, as it turned out. So much for the optimistic slogans. Messiah to the Age of Science, indeed! Now it was plainly too late for action. The opportunities had passed. It was all fragmenting. Even this silly attempt of his to keep the family together was a reaction to the real situation which he could no longer hope to control. Messiah to the Age of Science! A bloody Teddy boy, more like. But Colonel Pyat was reconciled, really. This holiday might be the last of his life and he wished to make the most of it. He only regretted that he could not go back to die in the Ukraine. The Ukraine no longer existed. With his homeland destroyed, there was little to live for, his love for England being entirely intellectual.

Frank turned back to see what had happened to Pyat. " Come on, old boy." Frank's holiday seemed to be doing him good. His face glowed with a vitality that was almost healthy. " Don't want to miss the beauty spots now we're here, do you? Where on earth did you find this little corner of England? I didn't think places like it still existed. If they ever did."

" Oh," Pyat shrugged. " You know how it is. Strangers sometimes discover things in a place where the people who've lived there all their lives have never looked."

" Well, you've turned up trumps with this one, I must say. It's like bloody fairyland. Titania's wood." Frank was in a literary as well as a religious mood today. " I'm expecting a visit from Puck at any moment. Can you lay that on, too? "

Pyat smiled. " It isn't the wood that's enchanted." But Frank hadn't heard him; he joined his mother and sister. The two women were unrolling plastic raincoats and spreading them on the rocks. Mrs Cornelius began to unload her string bag, taking out a vacuum flask and two packets of sandwiches.

" 'Ere we are. Git stuck inter these, you lot," said Mrs C.

No wasps or ants came to disturb them as they ate their picnic beside the shady pool. Catherine was fascinated by the water. It was so dark and deep, but there was nothing sinister about it. It was tranquil and seemed to offer peace to anyone who considered entering its still waters. Because she didn't much care for these cheese and pickle sandwiches anyway, she left the other picnickers and climbed down to stand on a rock beside the pool. The conversation above sounded a long way away. She stared at her reflection for some moments until she realised with a shock that it was not quite her face which looked at her. There were strong resemblances, certainly, but this was a man's face and its hair was black. It smiled. She smiled back. She turned to remark on the phenomenon to her relatives but they had disappeared out of sight on the other side of the rocks. She felt, then, that she had been standing here much longer than she had realised. She started to climb back. There was a slight afternoon chill in the air.

" Catherine! "

The voice came from above. She looked up and was surprised when she recognised the man who had called her name. He was clad in rather tattered evening dress. He stood offering his free hand to her. His other hand held a Smith and Wesson .45, rather loosely, as if he really didn't mind if he dropped it.

" What a strange coincidence." Cathy smiled as she put her palm into Prinz Lobkowitz's. " How are you? It's been an age."

" How are you, dear? " His voice was low and intense, his expression melancholy and affectionate. " I hope you are well."

" Very well. But you, my dear, you look so tired. Are you running away from someone? " She reached up and brushed his hair back from his wrinkled forehead.

He held her to him. " Oh, Catherine." He was crying. " Oh, my dearest. It is all over. This is defeat on every level."

" We must get you something to eat," she said.

" No. I haven't much time. I came here for a reason. Colonel Pyat is here? "

" Yes — and mother, and Frank."

" I'm sorry," he said, " but . . ."

" Well, look who it isn't! " Frank Cornelius emerged from around a rock, his mother and step-father in tow. " So you know about this place, too. What a sell! It's getting like Piccadilly. Perhaps this is the real heart of the Empire, eh? We went for a little walk. Hello, Prinz L."

" Good evening." Lobkowitz was embarrassed. " I'm sorry to interrupt." Birds began to sing everywhere and red-gold sunlight flooded the scene. Prinz Lobkowitz cast a startled glance over his shoulder. " I wanted a word with Colonel Pyat."

Pyat stepped forward. Then he changed his mind and began to retreat, climbing up the white boulders until he stood looking straight down at the pool.

" Wotcher doin' up there? " said Mrs Cornelius loudly. And then she fell silent.

There was a smear of dark green on the elbow of Colonel

232

Pyat's suit. Catherine was glad that Pyat himself didn't know about it. Or did he?

Colonel Pyat sighed and turned to look down at them all.

" Prinz? " he said.

Lobkowitz reluctantly raised the heavy gun with both hands, drawing in a deep breath before pulling the trigger. Pyat seemed to bow in acknowledgement, receiving the shot courteously in the heart. Then he fell backwards and dropped into the pool. The waters closed over him.

" Oh, blimey! " said Mrs Cornelius, looking with nervous disapproval at the gun. " Oh, Gawd! "

Frank stepped prudently back into the shade of an oak.

Prinz Lobkowitz looked miserably at his old sweetheart. Then he began to climb up the rock on which Pyat had stood. Catherine watched, feeling only sympathy for both the murderer and his victim. Lobkowitz reached the top, turned, raised the revolver to his lips, kissed it and tossed it to Catherine. She caught it with instinctive deftness. At long last Lobkowitz had learned a style.

He jumped into the pool. There was a splash and a silence.

Catherine tucked the Smith and Wesson into the waist band of her skirt and walked past her mother and brother. She entered the cold wood.

" Where's she off ter? " said Mrs C. " In one of her bloody moods agin, is she? "

" Let's see if we can find the motor," said Frank, frowning. " She'll turn up again when she's ready."

"And wot are we gonna do abart cash, I'd like ter know," said his mother, practically. " Talk abart ther end o' a perfict day! " She snorted. "An' I'm a bleedin' widder agin," she said, as if suddenly realising the essence of what had happened beside the pool.

She cheered up, nudging Frank in the side.

" Still, yer've got ter larf, incha? "

He looked at her in horror.

THE FARM

Sebastian Auchinek, bringing home the cows for their evening milking, heard the shot quite clearly and looked out across the fields to see where it came from. Hereabouts, people rarely hunted at this time of the year, though possibly someone was potting a rabbit or two for his dinner. Beyond the fields, where the wheat sheaves stood waiting for the next day's attention, he could see the great, green wood, almost a silhouette now in the late afternoon sun. The shot had probably come from there. Auchinek shrugged and trudged on. He flicked at the rumps of his cows with a light willow stick. " C'mon Bessy. Git a move on there, Peg." The phrases were mumbled automatically, for the cows had trodden this path more often than had he and they needed little encouragement. They plodded up the rutted track of red earth between sweet-smelling hedgerows full of briar roses and honeysuckle, towards the stone milking sheds which lay beside the farmhouse with its warm cobblestone walls and its thick, thatched roof.

When Auchinek had first gone to earth, he would not have believed that he could have taken so easily to farming. In his old corduroy trousers, his rubber boots, his pullover, leather jerkin and flat, dirty cap, a quarter of an inch of stubble on his tanned, ruddy face, he looked as if he had farmed these parts all his life; and he felt it, too. The shot didn't bother him. Poacher or gamekeeper, human or animal, what happened beyond the confines of his farm was none of his concern. He had a lot to do before dark.

It was almost dusk by the time he had milked the cows and poured the milk into his electric separator. He drove the cows back into the nearest field and returned to manhandle the milk churns onto his cart. He harnessed up Mary, his old shire horse, and started off along the track towards the railway.

When he got to the railway, he lit the oil lamp which hung on its usual post. He had to see to get his milk onto the little wooden platform. In about an hour's time the train would stop here and pick the milk up, delivering it at the local village station for the dairyman.

Night sounds had replaced the sounds of day. A few grass-hoppers chirped in the long grass of the railway embankment. An owl hooted. Some bats flapped past. Now that his work was over, Auchinek felt pleasantly tired. He sat on his cart and lit a pipe, enjoying a smoke before returning to the farm. It was a warm, clean night, with a good moon rising. Auchinek leaned back in the seat and breathed in deeply. The old shire twitched her huge flanks and flicked her tail but was content to wait until he was ready to go. She leaned down in her yoke and began to tug at the grass with her large yellow teeth.

Auchinek heard a noise in the neighbouring field and identified it as a fox. He'd have to be careful tonight if a fox was on the prowl, though he hadn't really had much trouble from predators since he'd taken over the farm. Then the rustling grew louder and more energetic. Had the fox already found its night's meat? There came a peculiar, strangled whimper — perhaps a rabbit. Auchinek peered over the hedge, but the light from the lamp cast only shadows into the field. For a moment, though, he thought he saw an animal of some kind — a savage face that might have belonged to an ape rather than to a fox. But then it was gone. He picked up the reins. He had grown eager to get home to his supper.

"All right, Mary. Come on now, girl." The country accent came naturally to him. " Come on, old girl. Gee up, there . . ."

When he had turned a corner of the track and could see the yellow warmth glowing from his own windows he felt completely at ease again. It was funny what you sometimes thought you glimpsed at night. All that was over now. He'd never be involved again. And the war couldn't touch him. The countryside was eternal. It was a good job, however, that he wasn't superstitious. He might start to have silly fantasies about his past catching up with him. He smiled. He'd boil some eggs for his supper and have them with some of that new bread, then he'd go to bed and finish Surtees' *Hillingdon Hall*. Of late, his whole reading had been devoted to 18th and 19th century novels of rustic life, as if he were subconsciously determined to steep himself in even the metaphysical aspects of country lore. He had already read *The Vicar of Wakefield, Romany Rye, The Mill on the Floss, Clara Vaughan* and *Tess of the D'Urbevilles*, as well as other, more obscure titles. He didn't seem to enjoy anything else. Sometimes he would sample a more modern work by Mary Webb or R. F. Delderfield and he found them enjoyable, too. He was going off George Eliot and Thomas Hardy, though. He didn't think he would read anything more by them.

He drove into the farmyard and got off the cart, unharnessing the mare. As he led her past the milking shed towards her stable, he heard the milk separator going, the big blades swishing and clacking. He smiled to himself; he was more tired than he had realised. As it sometimes happened when you were feeling a bit worn out, the sound seemed to form a word.

He remembered Una Persson. What ever had happened to her? It had been a dream, that period in Macedonia and Greece. A nightmare. He'd done some funny jobs in his life before finding the one which suited him.

Ch-ch-char, went the blades. *Traitor — traitor — traitor.*

He closed the stable door, stretching and yawning. The air had turned very cold. They could be deceptive, these autumn nights.

Traitor — traitor.

He went inside. It wasn't very warm in the house, even though the range had been lit in the kitchen. He flicked open the doors of the stove to let more heat out. He could still hear that damned separator going. He shivered. He'd be glad to get under the blankets tonight.

236

THE VILLAGE

The train picked up the churns and took them to the village station where they were unloaded by the dairyman who put them in his van.

The van rattled happily as it drove down the peaceful street from the station, past the cheerful windows of the two pubs, *The Jolly Englishman* and *The Green Man*, past the village hall, where music was playing, past the church, down the alley and round the back of the little bottling plant where the milk would be readied for the morning's deliveries. Thank God the monopolies didn't control the farm produce in this part of the world, thought the dairyman. There were still a few corners of old England which hadn't yet been overrun by so-called progress. The dairyman left his van in the yard and strolled back towards the village hall. There was something special on tonight — a break in an otherwise acceptable routine.

He pushed open the doors and saw with some pleasure that they had already got the parachutist to start to strip. She was quite a good-looking woman, if a bit on the slim side for his taste. A cut over her left eye didn't improve her appearance, either. Had that been necessary? He nodded to the other village men and smiled at Bert and John, his brothers, as he took his place near the front of the stage. He licked his lips as he settled back in his chair.

Una Persson had been captured two days earlier but had had to wait, a prisoner in George Greasby's barn, while the village decided how best to use her. She was the first parachutist they had ever caught and they understood the conventions involved: a captured parachutist became a sort of slave, the property of whoever could find and hold one. Nearby villages had several male parachutists working their fields, but this was the first woman.

Conscious of George Greasby in the wings with his brazier and red-hot poker, Una had already unbuttoned her long flying coat and dropped it to the floor. She didn't much care if he burned her; all she really wanted to do was take the easiest way out and get the whole business over with as soon as possible. It was their idea of dignity and individualism that was central here, not hers. Stripping to *King Creole*, the tinny single on the cheap record player, seemed the easiest thing to do. Not that she'd ever cared much for Elvis Presley. She took off her shirt, staring into the middle-distance to avoid looking at all the fat, red heads with their bristly haircuts who made up her audience. She'd had worse. She didn't waste time: off came her boots, her trousers and her pants until she stood passive and naked, showing the few yellow bruises on her left breast, her right thigh and her stomach. It was a bit chilly in the hall. There was a slight smell of damp.

"All right, now give us a song," said George Greasby in his high-pitched voice. He waved the poker, holding it in a big, asbestos mitten.

Fred Rydd settled himself at the piano, running his stubby fingers over the keys and then thumping out a series of discords with his left hand while he struck up a rousing chorus of *A Little of What You Fancy Does You Good*.

Una had played the provinces often enough before. This wasn't very much different. She tried to remember the words. Charley Greasby, the old man's son, jumped up on the stage and slapped her bottom. " Come on, lovey, let's 'ear yer! " With lewd winks at the others, he cupped her breasts in his hard hands and pinched her nipples and yelled in her ear while performing a sort of obscene Morris dance: " I never was a one to go and stint meself. If I like a thing, I like it, that's enough. But there's lots of people say, if you like a thing a lot, it'll grow on you — and all that stuff." His breath smelled of onions.

" I like my drop of stout as well as anyone," sang Una, now that he had started her off. She felt faint. All the villagers were on their feet now, laughing and stamping and clapping. " But a drop of stout's supposed to make you fat." The whole hall seemed to be shaking. More of the thickset countrymen were clambering onto the stage. Her vision was full of corduroy, leather and woollen pullovers. The piano played maniacally on. "And there's many a lah-di-dah-di madam doesn't dare to touch it, 'cause she mustn't spoil her figure, silly cat! "

They all joined in the chorus. " I always hold in having it, if you fancy it. If you fancy it, that's understood. And suppose it makes you fat — well, don't worry over that. 'Cause a little of what you fancy does you good! "

" Come on," said Tom Greasby, who was still wearing his police constable's trousers, " let's have all the verses, my pretty. I haven't heard that one in years. The old ones are the best. Haw, haw! " He put a horny finger into her vagina. She knew it was there but she didn't feel it much as she went into the next verse.

She finished the song and was half-way through *Someday I'll Find You* when they lost control of themselves and got their corduroys and flannels down, pushing her on her back as they began, in hasty turns, to rape her.

The greatest discomfort she felt was in trying to breathe beneath the weight of their heavy, sticky bodies. She had never cared for the country and now she knew why. From the distance came the sound of the record player starting up again with Cliff Richard's *Living Doll*. She realised that her eyes were still open. She closed them. She saw a pale face smiling at her. Relieved, she smiled back.

It was time to split.

As the fifteenth rural penis rammed its way home, she left them at it.

THE HILL

"There's lights on still in the village hall," said Mrs Nye, closing the bay window. "Maybe they're having a dance down there. There's music."

"I'm glad they're enjoying themselves," said Major Nye from where he lay in crisp sheets in the topless Heal's four-poster. He had gone yellow and his lips were flaking. His pale eyes shone from deep cavities and his cheeks were hollow. "Say that for the English. They know how to make the best of things." He had just recovered from an attack of malaria. He was dying.

They had had to leave Brighton when the malaria got really bad. It had been disappointing, after building everything up there. They had moved further west, to his father's old place, a large Frank Lloyd Wright style house built on the hill. On one side the house overlooked the village, on the other, the sea. From its windows it was possible to view the valley, with its farm, forest, village and streams, and the little harbour town and the beach. There were very few fishing boats in the harbour, these days. But holidaymakers still came from time to time. It was all very picturesque. "The very best of England," as Major Nye's father had often said. But for some reason Major Nye was ill at ease here.

"I wonder where the doctor could have got to," said Mrs Nye. "I sent Elizabeth in the Morgan. It was the last of the petrol, too." Her own complexion was beginning to match her

240

husband's. Many of the village women were convinced that it would not be long before she 'followed him'. Once he had gone, she would be glad to follow. She had had quite enough. He, on the other hand, was uneasy about dying in his bed. He had never imagined that he would. It seemed wrong. He felt vaguely ashamed of himself, as if, in an obscure way, he had failed to do his duty. That was why, from time to time, he would try to get up. Then Mrs Nye would have to call her daughter to help put him back in the four-poster.

A fat, jolly girl bustled into the room. "How's the patient?" demanded Elizabeth Nye. She had become very attached to her parents just lately. A month ago she had been kicked out of the girls' school where she had been teaching and it had given her the opportunity to come home and look after them. "Shall I take over now, mums?"

Her mother sighed. "What do you think?" she asked her husband. Major Nye nodded. "That would be nice. D'you feel up to reading a bit of the book, Bess?"

"Happy to oblige. Where is the damned *tome*?"

Her mother brought it from the dressing table and handed it to her. It was a large, red book called *With the Flag to Pretoria*, a contemporary account of the Boer Wars. Elizabeth settled herself in the bedside chair, found her place, cleared her throat, and began to read:

"Chapter Twenty Three. The March on Bloemfontain and opening of the railway to the south. With the capture of Cronje in the west, and the relief of Ladysmith in the east, the first stage of Lord Roberts' campaign may be said to have ended. The powerful reinforcements sent out from home, and the skilful strategy of the commander-in-chief had turned the scale."

She read for an hour before she was sure he was asleep. In a way she felt it was a pity to encourage him to sleep when he had so little time left. She wished he was just a bit stronger so that she could take him out for the day in his wheelchair, perhaps to the village, or to the seaside. There was no chance of using her car again. The trip to the doctor's had used up the last of the fuel. She no longer despised her father and had come to feel very close to him, for his weaknesses were her own in a different guise. Simple-minded loyalty was one of them.

241

And he, too, she had discovered only yesterday, had been crossed in love as a young man.

As she was putting the book back on the dressing table he opened his eyes, smiling at her. " I wasn't asleep, you know. I was thinking about the little chap and what's going to become of him. You'll make sure he stays at school? "

" If there's a school to stay at." She felt sorry for her cynicism. " Yes, of course."

"And Oxford? "

" Oxford. Yes."

" He's a bright little chap. He was a cheerful lad. I wonder why he's so melancholy, these days."

"A stage," she said.

" No. I know it's the school. But what else could I do, Bess? "

" He'll be all right."

" But not the Army, eh? It's up to him to break the chain. Get a good civilian job."

" Yes."

" Could you get me a glass of water, do you think? "

Elizabeth poured him some water from the decanter on the bedside table. The room was so unfriendly. She tried to think of ways of making the atmosphere warmer.

" I heard on the wireless the other day that they can't find the ravens," he said.

" Ravens? Where? "

" Tower of London. All flown off. When the ravens go the White Tower will fall and when the White Tower falls, my dear, England will fall."

" There'll always be an England," she said.

" The chances are good, I admit that. Even Rome lasted in a way, and Greece and Persia before her. Even Egypt, really, But Babylon and Assyria. Well, well . . . I'm rambling." He sipped the water. "And America. So short-lived. But very powerful, Bess."

" It's all been fined down, I'll grant you," she said. " The barbarians don't come from outside the walls any more, do they? "

" We breed our own cancers," he said. "And never a cure. But perhaps that's always been the case." He let her take the glass. " Merry. Hectora. Garvey. Kalu. Grog. Brorai, I think. And Jet."

" What's that? "

" The names of the ravens."

She laughed. "Aha! "

His voice was tiring. It was little more than a croak as he continued. " I've led an ill-disciplined sort of life. No moral fibre. It's something about the army. There were thousands of people in my position. Perhaps it was just the standard of living, or something. My old colonel was a drunkard, you know, before he died. And penniless. I used to stand him the odd drink. Decent old boy." His head trembled and he shut his eyes tight. "All failures. To a man. He — " His pale lips tried to speak but could not. She bent over him.

" What was that? "

He whispered, " He committed suicide. Chucked himself out of a bally window at the Army and Navy Club."

" Maybe it was for the best."

" It's all gone, Bess." His face was horribly white, like a skull. His moustache looked incongruous, like a piece of weed which had caught on the skull. " I'm sorry."

She said awkwardly: " Nothing to be sorry about, I'd have thought. You've done your best for the family. For the country, too, if it comes to that. You've put more in than most. You deserve —"

She knew that the next sound was a death-rattle, but it didn't last long.

Her mother came in.

" He's dead," said Elizabeth. " I'll go into town tomorrow and make the arrangements."

Mrs Nye looked down at the corpse as if she couldn't recognise it.

" It's all over," said Elizabeth. She patted her mother's shoulder. The action was mechanical and for a moment it seemed to both of them that Elizabeth was actually striking her mother. Elizabeth stopped and went to the window. The lights were off in the village hall. The village was silent.

Mrs Nye cleared her throat.

" Well," she said. " Well."

THE SEASIDE

Next morning, Elizabeth cycled down to the harbour town to make the necessary arrangements. While she waited in the funeral parlour, she thought she saw Catherine Cornelius go past with two other people, a thin man and a fat woman. Elizabeth knew this was less than likely. It was just her mind playing her another morbid trick. Earlier she had had the impression that her father was still alive in the house. She would never see Catherine again. Everything was over now. Her sex-life was over. Having a sex-life involved too much responsibility and now she had her mother and her little brother to think about. She looked through the dark glass of the window at the gleaming sea; she listened to the children playing on the beach. And quite suddenly she felt full of strength; suddenly she was confident that she would have sufficient moral resolve to win through against all the difficulties which faced her. She prayed that the feeling would last.

"Clotted cream and strawberry jam and loverly choccie biscuits," said Mrs C. "That's wot I feel like, kids. That bleedin' hotel thinks we're bloody budgies, if yer ask me. The size o' them meals! Fuck that!" She led them towards the beach, much relieved by her recent discovery that Colonel Pyat had left his wallet in the car and that the wallet had been stuffed with tenners. There would be no trouble about paying the bill or having a bloody good time while they were down here. They deserved it.

They stopped at the cafeteria near the beach while Mrs Cornelius had her elevenses. The cafeteria smelled strongly of candy floss. Frank and Cathy shared a knickerbocker glory, looking rather wanly at the bright, yellow sand.

" It's a tidy sort of beach," said Frank. " Not like Margate, for instance. Very middle class, wouldn't you say? "

Catherine felt too warm, even in her light summer frock. She removed her blue cardigan and put it in her gay beach bag. She noticed that both Frank and Mum were sweating, too.

" 'Urry up an' scoff that darn, you two," said their mother, who had finished three times as much in half the time. " Eat it all up. Don' wanna waste it. It's all paid for."

They crammed the rest of the tinned strawberries, the chocolate syrup, the nuts and the ice cream into their mouths and munched while their mother busied herself with her toilet, touching up her carmine lipstick, laying on a little more scarlet rouge, another coating of pink powder, and patting at her perm with a comb. Then she took each of her children by one of its hands and led the way from the cafeteria, down the asphalt slope to the beach.

" Deckchairs, Frank." She surveyed the beach, hands on hips, like Rommel planning a campaign. " The sea's lovely, innit? " Frank went to the neat stack in the little green shelter by the wall of the promenade and got three brand new candy-striped canvas chairs. " Right," she said. " This way." She led them towards a breakwater. Not far away from the breakwater were four little children, two boys and two girls, at work on an elaborate sand palace, with turrets and towers and minarets and everything. They were digging a moat round it. Elsewhere, in a rock pool, twin girls, aged about eight, with blonde page-boy haircuts, studied crabs and starfish and seaweed.

" It's like the bloody *Rainbow Annual*," said Frank with some approval. " Tiger Tim at the Seaside. It's almost too perfect." He set up the chairs and got them just so. Then he stripped off his jacket, his shirt, his vest and his flannels to reveal a pair of yellow and black silk boxer-style bathing trunks. He stretched his thin body in the chair and drew on a large pair of wrap-around mirror sunglasses. But he was still not ready. He got up again and found the Man-tan lotion in his jacket pocket. He began smearing the stuff on his pale, spotted flesh. Meanwhile Mrs C had applied all her various creams and had lifted her loud, print dress to reveal her pink satin directoire drawers and her huge, white thighs. She sat with her legs spread, as if to catch the sunbeams in her lap. Cathy was reading a copy of *The Rescue* by Joseph Conrad. " This'll do," said Frank, regarding the distant sea. " We can come here next year. Now we've discovered it." Merry laughter rippled from the throats of the children around the sand palace. They were digging a deeper and deeper trench. A few happy seabirds wheeled and screamed. A red-sailed boat drifted by on the horizon. A small black and white cat began to walk demurely along the break-water. Frank picked up a pebble and chucked it at the cat. He missed.

"Are you going in, love? " said Mrs C. " It must be loverly for swimmin'."

Frank shuddered. " I don't think so. Currents and that. Rip-tides. Undertows."

" But there's others bathing over there." Catherine pointed. " They seem to be okay. There'd be signs if it was dangerous."

" Maybe later, then," said Frank. " I might have a bit of a summer cold."

" Oh, all right."

Everything was so ideal that Frank almost expected to see a jolly face painted on the golden disc of the sun, or even on the buckets and spades. The sand might have been dyed that bright, clean yellow; the sea might have been stained that bright, clear blue. Well, there was no point in looking a gift-horse in the mouth, was there? He leaned back and began to study the pictures in his body-building magazine.

＊ " We'll go ter that pub fer lunch," said Mrs C. " The on'y complaint I got is there's no bleedin' Bingo. That's a issential part of an 'oliday, I reckon. An' bumper cars. I like 'em. An a bit o' fish-and-chips. Yum yum."

Cathy suddenly felt funny. " I just had one of those lurches," she said. " You know. Deja vu."

246

Frank's mirror shades regarded her. " Reels within reels," he said with a thin smile. " Don't worry, love. It happens to me all the time." he sniggered.

" Frank."

" Yes, mum."

" Go an' git us an ice, there's a love."

Frank got up slowly. " I'll want some cash."

She handed him a tenner. "All the jack you need," she said. " I never bin a *rich* widder before. Git one fer yerself an' Caff."

But he returned quite quickly, empty-handed. " Sold out," he said. " They say they weren't expecting a heat-wave. Personally, I don't find it that hot."

" I'm boiling," said Cathy.

" Fuck," said their mother removing the tenner from Frank's fingers. " I don't call this much of an 'oliday resort. I mean, they don't seem ter want ter cater fer visiters. An' we 'ave got money ter spend. We're not paupers. I could git through this lot in a day at Brighton." She put the money back in her large red and yellow plastic bag. " I could do wiv a cuppa," she hinted. "Anyway, I don't like 'ome made ice cream."

Frank and Cathy were pretending to be asleep. They lay stretched in their deckchairs, facing out to sea.

Mrs Cornelius shifted in her chair, wondering whether to get up or not. She looked with some admiration at the huge sandcastle the kids were building. It was going on five feet tall and was elaborately detailed. She could almost have believed it was a real castle if she'd seen it in the distance. And the moat would soon be the size of an army trench. The energy of these kids! Where did they get it all from? They were work- ing like beavers. They were moving about so fast! The sand was fairly flying from the ditch. The castle grew and grew. Turrets and galleries and towers appeared. The children laughed and shouted, carrying their buckets of sand to key points, patting down a tesselation with their little wooden spades. It must be very good sand, thought Mrs C vaguely. It must be very easy to work with. Now two of the boys were actually burrowing into the castle, hollowing it out. A Union Jack flew proudly from the highest tower. She took a deep breath of ozone. She hadn't smelled sea like that since she was a kid herself. She reached for the radio in her bag, but changed her mind. It wasn't too bad, this beach. Her hunger and thirst diminished; she stopped fidgetting. It was peaceful. She closed her eyes, listening to the sound of the surf, the cries of the gulls, the distant chatter of the happy children. Poor old Pyat. She still wondered why he'd married her. He must have been after something. It wasn't the sex, more's the pity. She hadn't done badly out of him. She'd got something out of all her husbands, really. Not to mention the others.

Frank got up and pulled on his shirt. " Don't you feel cold, Cath? "

" What? Sorry. I was miles away."

"Aren't you chilly? "

" I was thinking it was too warm."

" You must be running a temperature." He sniffed. " Or I am. Maybe we're sickening for something."

She yawned. " It would be a shame to have our holiday cut short. Still, in a way I wouldn't be sorry. I feel a bit guilty, really. Poor Colonel Pyat."

" It was a private issue. Nothing we could do. An accident as far as we were concerned. Unavoidable. I expect he died for a cause or something. Is that a boat on the horizon? A warship? "

" I'm not sure I believe in accidents, as such." She looked to where he was pointing. " Could be. Oh, dear, I feel so lazy. And yet, at the same time, I feel I should be doing something. Aah! " She stretched. " Fancy a game of cricket, eh, Frank? "

He sneered.

She glanced at the towering sandcastle. The children had found the little cat and were pushing it into the hollowed out main entrance. They didn't mean any harm and, in fact, the cat seemed to be enjoying himself as much as the children. Soon Cathy saw the amused black and white face staring at her from one of the upper windows. She smiled back at it, remembering the pool in the forest. She dug her bare feet into the sand and wiggled her toes.

A huge, reverberating snort came from the other deckchair. With a great dopey grin on her face, Mrs C was snoozing. She looked as if she were having a happy dream.

248

" Well, she's all right, anyway," said Frank. He held his arms round his body, leaning forward in the deckchair and shivering. " I'll have to split back to the hotel if this goes on. What's got into those kids? "

There was a slight note of alarm in the children's voices. Cathy rose from her chair and walked towards them. "Anything the matter, boys and girls? " But now she could see what was wrong; the roof of the castle had caved in completely. They had got too ambitious and ruined their creation. Also the moat was beginning to fill with foaming water. The tide was coming in.

" That cat's in there," said one of the little girls in panic. She twisted at her hair with her fingers. " The roof's fallen on him, miss." The other children were all in tears, shocked by what they had done. It was plain that they thought they had killed the cat. Only one boy was trying to do something about it, digging frantically into the side of the castle with his small wooden spade. Cathy picked up the largest spade she could find and started to dig from the other side, listening for any sounds which the trapped animal might be making. She was afraid it was dead already. " Block that stream," she said, indicating the channel which fed the moat. " We don't want to be flooded any sooner than we have to be." She dug and dug, getting her frock all smeared with wet sand, while the other children stood in a silent semi-circle watching her. " Come on," she cried. " Get your spades and help." Nervously, they came forward. Evidently they would much rather have gone away and forgotten the whole incident. They picked up spades or buckets and began to dig. Sand flew in all directions. Frank came up. He stood there with his hands on his hips, his mirror shades glinting. " What the hell are you doing, Cath? "

" Trying to get the cat. Can you give us a hand, Frank? "
" I would," he said. " But this cold's got worse."

She panted. Her dress, her arms, her legs, her face and hair were now all covered in sand. " Then go back to hotel and keep warm." Not for the first time she felt annoyed and let down by him.

But he just stood there, shivering and watching as they dug on. Soon the whole castle was down and there was no sign of

249

the cat.

"Could it have escaped?" Cathy spoke to the boy who had first started digging. "Before the roof collapsed?"

"I don't think so, miss. He might be in the cellar."

"What?"

"We dug a cellar — underneath."

Catherine wiped her hot forehead. Her arms and back were aching terribly. She summoned more strength and began to dig below the surface of the beach. She was quite surprised how strong she was, considering how much energy she had already expended.

By the time they had dug a hole some six feet deep, it had become difficult to work, for water kept dripping in and sand would fall back into the pit. Cathy looked for Frank but he had retreated. Her dress and hair were soaked and gritty. She must look a mess. Then she felt her spade strike something solid; something hollow. She sank down and gasped. "Phew!" She looked up. The children were all peering over the edge at her. "Phew!" she said, "I think I've reached some sort of old breakwater. That was a waste of energy, eh? That cat *must* have run out of one of the doors or windows. What a lot of excitement for nothing." And then she heard a sound which was almost definitely a cat's mew. It came from under her feet. She scraped sand away from what she had thought was a breakwater, revealing pale, polished timber. "We've found a treasure chest," she said with a grin. The children's eyes widened. "Really and truly, miss?" said one.

"I'm not sure." She dug away more wet sand and then felt a spasm of anxiety as she exposed the whole of the box's surface, including the blank, brass plate. "You kids had better find your mums and dads," she said. She ran her hand over the surface of the coffin, wondering how it could be so warm.

"Oh, miss! Please!"

She did her best to smile. "Go on," she said, "I'll let you know if it's a treasure chest. Don't worry."

Miserably, reluctantly, they fell back from the edge of the pit.

Catherine wondered if the coffin were really an unexploded bomb? A booby trap? She'd heard of such things. And it *was* warm and there was a regular, slow ticking sound coming from

250

inside it.

"Frank," she called. "Mum?" But neither answered. A gull squawked. Or had the sound come from inside the box? She had the impression that the beach above was now deserted. She looked at the sides of the pit. "Oh, God!" Water was seeping down. The sand under her feet had the consistency of a quagmire. She was sinking into it. "Frank? Mum?" Gulls replied. They were miles away. How had she got into this situation? It was ridiculous.

There was nothing for it, she decided, but to free the box completely. If it floated, she might be able to climb on it and drift to the surface as the pit filled. If not, she could put it on its side and perhaps climb up over it. She dug as fast as she could, but wet sand kept falling back into the holes. At last she was able to grab one of the brass handles and heave it, with a disgusting, sucking sound, upwards. Something heavy bumped about inside. The ticking stopped. A muffled screech replaced it. A bird? Could the cat have got inside somehow? She looked at the four bolts securing the lid and she had an idea. The Smith and Wesson .45 was still in her waistband. She took it out and screwed up her eyes, aiming for the first bolt. She pulled the trigger. The bullet hit the bolt and knocked it out. She aimed and fired three more times and by what seemed sheer luck managed to shoot all the bolts free.

She put the gun down and then, on second thoughts, picked it up again.

She pulled away the lid of the coffin.

A dreadful stink of brine and human excrement flooded from the box. She covered her mouth, staring at the creature she had revealed. Its eyes glowed, its lips curled back from its stained teeth, its fingers were curved like claws as it wrenched at the bonds securing its wrists to the sides of the coffin. First one hand came free. Then the other. And Cathy, recognising her poor, mad brother, fainted.

"Cathy?"

She opened her eyes. She was lying on the edge of the pit. She could only have been insensible for a few seconds. She looked down and saw that the pit was full of bits of weed and

251

pebbles and shells, as well as splintered pieces of wood which had comprised the coffin.

" Cathy? "

He was standing over her, on the other side. But he had changed completely. He was dressed in a white pierrot suit with big red bobbles on the front. He had a blue conical clown's hat on his head, a triumphant grin on his face. He looked down at his costume and brushed a speck or two of sand off the front. He was once again her favourite brother. "Gosh," he said, glancing up at the sun, " is that the time? I must have been dreaming. Hello, Cathy."

She was still a bit nervous.

" Sorry about the first sight," he said. " I didn't want to alarm you. But I had to have your help, you see."

Her alarm faded. She was suddenly delighted. She might have guessed he'd do something like this. " What a wonderful surprise! " She stood on tiptoe and kissed him warmly on his lips. " You are a one, Jerry."

" Mum and Frank about? "

She looked for them. " Somewhere. Frank got cold."

Her brother grinned. " I thought it was Frank. I had to get the fuel from somewhere. And Mum? "

Cathy laughed and clung to his arm. He was the best big brother in the world. " Look," she said, pointing. " There they are. Poor old Frank! "

Frank was virtually under their feet, but in a little dip in the sand and so out of sight. He was curled into a tight ball and his flesh was all blue. His mirror sunglasses stared sightlessly from the top of his head. Cathy couldn't help smiling. " It's time Frank had a turn," she said. " I shouldn't laugh, really."

Mrs Cornelius was still sprawled in her deckchair, her legs wide, her arms folded under her breasts, her chins shaking with each mighty snore. " She's having one of her happy dreams," said Jerry. " Do you think the tide will come in this far? "

" Just," said Cathy, pointing at a mark on the breakwater. " It'll wet her feet. Nothing more. Let's leave her there to enjoy herself."

" It does seem a shame to disturb her," said Jerry. He looked up at the sky. The gulls were still circling cheerfully overhead and the sea still sparkled, but the air was darkening a bit, though there wasn't a cloud to be seen. "We could be in for some rain."

"Leave her anyway," said Cathy.

"All right." He peered towards the horizon. "If you think it's a good idea." He frowned.

"There's that boat Frank saw," said Cathy. "It's getting closer."

"Ah, well, she'll have to take her chances," said Jerry. "Yes, I noticed that. It's a destroyer." He spoke absently, looking tenderly down at her. "Do you want to go for a sail, Cathy?"

"Lovely," she said. "Or a swim?"

"I think I'll hold off swimming for a while. I'm still a bit stiff." He brushed the sand from his costume and, with long, easy strides, led her up the asphalt ramp to the promenade. "This way," he said. "It's in the harbour."

It wasn't far to walk to the old stone harbour. There was only one ship moored there and Cathy recognised the white schooner at once.

"It's the good old *Teddy Bear*!" she cried. She was delighted. All its brasswork shone and bright bunting danced in the rigging. "Oh, how wonderful!" They raced along the jetty and up the gangplank. The engines were already running. A small crowd of children stood on the quay, staring at the ship with mute curiosity. They cheered as Jerry picked Cathy up and carried her the last few paces onto the deck.

Almost as soon as they were aboard, the ship upped anchor, moved away from the jetty and out of the harbour, heading for the open sea. The children waved their pocket handkerchiefs and cheered again.

In her deckchair Mrs Cornelius stirred. The tide had begun to lap at her toes. It had already covered Frank. Behind her, the shops were beginning to close up for the day and the main street was deserted, save for Elizabeth Nye, pedalling slowly up the hill towards her home. A woman, wrapped in an old sack, turned the corner and signalled to her, but Elizabeth Nye was intent on her cycling. She didn't notice Una Persson. Una looked out to sea and recognised the destroyer. She sat down on the pavement and waited.

On the sun-deck of the yacht, Jerry found a ukelele. He collapsed into a steel and canvas Bauhaus chair and began to strum the uke while Cathy swayed peacefully in a hammock under an awning and sipped her lemonade. The coast sank slowly behind them as the *Teddy Bear* steered a course for Normandy.

" I'm not stuck up or proud. I'm just one of the crowd. A good turn I'll do when I can! " Jerry sang his favourite George Formby medley. It had been a long time. " The local doctor one night needed something put right and he wanted a handy man . . ." Cathy winked at him and tapped her feet to the rhythm. Jerry rolled his eyes at her and wagged his clown's hat as he went into a fast ukelele break. She laughed and clapped.

A few moments later they were interrupted by a dull roar from behind them. " Sounds like thunder," said Cathy. " I hope we're not in for a storm."

Jerry put down the uke and pushed back the wide cuffs from both wrists, checking his watches. " No," he said. " We're all right." He yawned. " It's been a bloody long haul, all in all. You don't mind if I get half an hour's kip in, do you? Clausius summed it up in 1865. ' The entropy of the universe tends to a maximum'. I suppose that's when it all started. Did anyone celebrate his centenary? One idea leads to another. Ho hum." His feet up on a canvas footstool, his hands folded in his lap, his healthy face at peace, the light wind tugging at the ruffles, folds, pleats and pom poms of his red, white and blue pierrot suit, Jerry Cornelius fell asleep.

Catherine Cornelius got out of her hammock. She kissed her fingertips and put them on his smooth forehead. " Dear Jerry." She went to the rail and looked back towards the vanished coast. " Goodbye, England." The sound of thunder was fainter now. Perhaps the storm was moving away.

Dropping anchor a short distance offshore from the razed and smoking resort, the destroyer fired a few last rounds over the hill and got a direct hit on the village on the other side. A 4.5″ shell took out the house. Four Sunstrike missiles turned the forest into an inferno. The farm, however, had been burning since the previous night.